Abandoned

Vicky Ball

A CIP catalogue record for this book is
available from the British Library
ISBN: 9781739367510
Typeset in **Garamond**

*This book is a work of fiction. Names, characters,
businesses, organizations, places and events are the
product of the author's imagination. Any resemblance to
actual persons, living or dead, events or locales is entirely
coincidental.*

www.BurtonMayersBooks.com

For David, Hannah and Megan

ACKNOWLEDGEMENTS

A big thank you to Clare who willingly shared her experiences to help me make the character of Ella more realistic.

To Chris Malone for her fabulous professional proofreading.

To my beta readers - Louise Tollick, Clarence Bean, Martyn Whitehead and Kerrick Newstead. It has been amazing to have you as my beta readers. Your help is much appreciated.

To my writing group, Mid Week Writers - Dee, Gemma, Berenice and Alec. I love that we can still meet and share our work together. You are all superstars.

To my wonderful readers, I am so honoured and grateful for all your lovely words and support.

To Richard at Burton Mayers Books, for continuing to support me in my writing dream.

To my parents, Martyn and Gillian, for always being enthusiastic about what I do and telling everyone about my book.

And finally to David, Hannah and Megan who keep me sane in the craziness of life, who love me and support me through everything.

ABANDONED

PART 1:
MADDIE

CHAPTER ONE

Ever feel like there's something missing from your life? That's how I've always felt. I long for someone to care about me, I mean really care. There must be someone out there who will.

'Hey, what you up for?' a quiet mousy girl next to me asks. I've never even looked at her let alone spoken to her. She seems nice enough.

'I'm getting the English award,' I answer, as I twiddle my thumbs and twist my hair round and round; anything to keep the nerves at bay.

'That's great.' She stares back at me and I realise this is the moment when I am supposed to return the question.

'What about you?'

'French, Art, kindness…' she continues to rattle off the list. Okay, now I hate her and am totally regretting asking. This is why I have few friends; people are so annoying.

I glance at the door. She'll come soon, won't she? But the negative voice in my head tells me how ridiculous I am. She promised, I argue back. When did that ever make a difference?

The trumpet sounds, signalling we all quieten down. Seriously, that's what happens at our school, pretentious nonsense. The space where my mother should sit is still painfully empty.

I don't listen as the principal drones on in his monotonal voice. I stopped listening to him years ago. My eyes start to feel heavy and suddenly it seems an effort to stay awake. The girl next to me gives me a nudge.

'It's English next,' she whispers. I try to smile but fear it comes out as more of a grimace. I look over again at Mum's seat, but still nothing. I hate that I am hopeful.

When my name is called, I reluctantly stand up, tuck my shirt in, try desperately to flatten my wild hair, and walk slowly towards the front of the hall, trying to ignore the stares from around me. *Don't fall up the steps*, I tell myself as I approach the stage. I still remember last year when Johnny did just that. The whole school erupted into laughter and no matter how many shushes the teachers did, it kept going for at least five minutes. He is still teased about it. I am not going to be that person. Thankfully I am on the stage without a hitch. I shake the principal's sweaty hand and wonder whether he would think me rude if I wipe it on my skirt afterwards. I return to my seat, my award done. Nothing more to stay awake for.

The rest of the ceremony, if you could call it that, passes like a blur until we are forced to stand up and sing the school song. The orchestra starts.

I cannot get out of there fast enough until I spot the gorgeous blonde sitting by the door, casually scrolling through her phone. Who is she? And why have I never seen her before? She is gone. No chance to gaze at her further.

I know you shouldn't compare yourself to others but in comparison to her I am a mess, straggly brown hair that literally has no style, not short, not tall. In fact there's nothing special about me at all.

'That was a waste of time,' I mutter to no one in particular as we exit the hall. I am desperate to get home and have it out with Mum.

Our house is a short walk from school through the narrow streets lined with terraced houses. The road is full of cars as usual. It would be a problem if we had a car, but Mum can't afford one. I reckon she could, if she gave up some of her 'essential' items.

We live in the middle, sandwiched between all the

other houses that look just like ours. The paint is peeling on the front door and has needed a refresh ever since I can remember.

She is lying on the sofa when I enter the lounge, her normally pristine hair all messed up and sticking out all over the place. Marvin is hovering by the kitchen, meowing insistently at me.

'You promised you'd come.'

She lifts her head from the cushion. Her glazed eyes tell me exactly why she didn't come. 'Don't be like that,' she slurs.

'It was important to me.'

'I know babe but... I couldn't. I meant to but then I had a drink and found I couldn't walk.' She giggles. 'I only had one.'

'Of course, you did,' I hiss, walking away. 'It's only ever one drink with you, isn't it?'

She waves her hand at me and lies back down. The conversation is over.

Marvin walks over, brushes up against me, and meows. Who can resist those beautiful eyes?

'Come on Marv, let's get you some food.'

I don't know why I bother. She doesn't care. I've spent far too many days trying to hide her drinking problem and hoping that she'll change, but she never does. I guess I should think myself lucky that she didn't turn up drunk at the prize-giving. I definitely would never live that one down.

'Can you pop to the shop and buy me some more gin?'

I want to tell her to get it herself, but the truth is I'm glad to get out of the house, and besides, I can buy myself something too. I put Marvin's food bowl down forcefully and grab some notes from her wallet, slamming the door behind me. Mum is already asleep before I've left the room.

As I said before, I don't have too many friends. They got put off in primary school by my over-exuberant mother and the fact that I could never invite them back to my house. No one else knows about her problem, with the exception of Mum's sisters. We hardly see them anymore.

It's only a short walk to the shop, past all the old derelict hospital buildings. I used to think if anyone found out about Mum, they'd put me in there.

'Hi Maddie,' the shopkeeper greets me, cheerfully.

'Hi Frank.'

'How's it going today?'

'Hmm,' I grunt.

'That good?'

I smile slightly. Whenever I come here, I worry that he will call social services. There is no way I want to end up in foster care with other screwed-up children and parents who may or may not care about me, or worse in a children's home. I'd rather stay put; better the devil you know, and all that.

But fortunately Frank lets me buy alcohol for Mum. I'm not sure why he does, as I'm pretty sure he could get in big trouble if anyone found out, but he knows I won't tell. He merely sighs when I plonk it on the counter.

When I get home, the phone is ringing. I rush to answer it, probably junk but you never know.

'Hi, is that Becky?'

'No, it's Madison.' The voice sounds kind of familiar but I can't work out who it is.

'Oh. Hi Madison. It's Great Aunt Margaret. Is your mum there?'

I look over at the half-conscious version of mother; there's no way she's speaking to anyone right now.

'She's asleep. Can I help?'

'Oh right... Well, maybe. I'm afraid I've got bad news.' I wait patiently, different bad scenarios running through my head. What could possibly be bad news for Mum? 'I'm sorry to say your Auntie Jane has just died.'

I don't know how to reply to that. Jane is only a name I've heard, maybe met once or twice when I was younger. I know Mum hasn't seen her older sister in years. Not sure how she will react to this news.

'I'm sorry to hear that.' That's what you say, isn't it?

'I am ringing to let her know of the funeral which is next week. I don't know if she'll want to come.'

'She will come,' I say with a sense of certainty, most unlike me. 'I'll bring her.'

'That'll be lovely.' I write down all the details. I'm kind of curious to meet these other relatives and maybe also hopeful that someone will want to help me out with Mum. Someone must have cared about Mum sometime if they are ringing her about the funeral.

'Who was that?' mutters Mum from the sofa.

'Your aunt, Margaret.'

Her face crumples up in disgust. 'Oh her. What did she want?'

'To tell you that Jane is dead.'

She sits up, suddenly sober. 'What? Jane is dead?'

'That's what she said. Her funeral is next week. I wrote down all the details. Were you close?'

'We were once,' she says slowly, a tear beginning to form in her eye as she stares out of the window. 'I can't go like this.'

'You don't have to go now.'

'No, you're right. It will be fine.' It's the first time in, I don't know how long, I've seen her looking so sober, even though she's not. It gives me a little glimmer of hope.

CHAPTER TWO

'Do I look alright?'

'Mum, you look great.' The black dress is a little baggy on her but, overall, she scrubs up well as she stands in front of her oversized mirror. Her perfectly straightened brown hair makes her look like she is going to an interview.

'You better get ready too. We're going to be late.' It's not like Mum to be so anxious.

'I will. I'll meet you downstairs.'

Since I woke up, I've spent all morning trying to decide what to wear. I hate dresses, but the only black item of clothing I have is a dress, or I could wear the white shirt and navy-blue trousers, but then I'd look like I was going to school. I decide on the dress. I'll feel horrible but at least no one will know me. They won't have a clue that it's not my style. I pull a brush through my brown hair, wishing I'd got it cut recently; the ends are starting to look bedraggled.

When I get downstairs, I find Mum swigging from a bottle in the kitchen and Marvin brushing up against her, desperate for some attention. I reach down and stroke his soft black fur.

'Mum, you promised.'

'I'm only having a little to steady my nerves. No more, I promise.' I've heard that one before but I have no choice but to take her word for it.

I struggle to keep up with Mum as she marches to the bus stop. I hope I don't see anyone from school, as they'd think I was going to some gothic convention or something. I'd never live that down either. There are a lot of things you can't live down at school. One false move and you're an embarrassment for the rest of your school life. I'm pretty sure I'm that already before I even started. The blonde girl at school immediately pops into my head.

She would totally rock a funeral dress but then again, she could make a sack look cool.

The bus is late as usual; no surprises there. I swear the drivers of this route don't bother so much in our trashy little area. I bet they concentrate their real efforts on the posh side of town where, when people complain, they have the power to make you lose your job.

Mum starts pacing the bus stop, hands shaking, and tiny drops of sweat appearing on her brow.

'Don't worry; we'll get there.' She stares at me as though I am a stranger, but then nods slowly.

When the bus arrives, it is virtually full. I want to hide in the back, but the only seat is next to an old lady at the front. I opt to stand instead. Nothing personal to the old lady but she might have some kind of old lady disease, or worse, start talking to me. Mum sits on one of the seats reserved for disabled people. I pray that no one who really needs it gets on. I can see Mum arguing with them.

The church we're going to is on the other side of town. I'm not sure why, because Aunt Jane didn't live there. It's almost as though my family are trying to pretend they're posh. It's one of those massive ones with a steeple that towers above the streets. Huge, but rarely full of people.

The bus stops right outside and I help Mum off. I'm beginning to wish I'd let her drink more. She is unsteady, shaky, and not herself. Maybe drunk Mum is more fun.

'This way,' I say, guiding her in the direction of the main entrance. A lady who looks a lot like Mum, but older and more together, stands there smiling at us. Her hair is a lot shorter than Mum's. I'm guessing it's Great Aunt Margaret.

'Becky, Madison, so good to see you.' Although she has a hint of Essex about her, the accent is far posher, or at least trying to be. Mum falls into Margaret's arms and for one horrible moment, I think she will cry. I smile shyly, not sure where I fit into all this. Great Aunt Margaret is shorter than Mum which is saying something as I thought

Mum was small.

'You found it alright then?' she asks. Stupid question, in my opinion, as it's obvious we did but I reply.

'Yes thank you.'

Inside the church, it feels freezing. A little heating would be nice. I wish I'd bought my coat.

'Beautiful, isn't it?'

I stare at Great Aunt Margaret. She doesn't know me at all if she thinks I would find this place beautiful.

'Lovely,' I lie. I guess I can see why someone would appreciate the stained-glass windows and the weird-looking statues - and the gravestones (ew gross) - if they were ninety, but I'm fifteen. I'd rather be in a dark cinema eating popcorn.

The pews are full of people I don't know. I wonder whether they are all relatives or if she was just very popular. Great Aunt Margaret finds us a seat in the second row. If it were up to me, we'd be hiding in the back row. I hope Mum behaves herself. As long as they don't have any of that wine they use for communion. She would probably swig the lot if she got a chance.

Great Aunt Margaret turns around and asks, 'You must be in your last year of secondary school?'

'Not quite. I'm in year ten.'

'I don't understand the numbers they use these days. It used to be first year, second year.'

Mum pipes up. 'Maddie's in fourth year, aren't you?' I shrug. I have no idea what this fourth-year stuff is all about. 'I think she is.'

Pointless conversation, as Great Aunt Margaret probably doesn't care at all. Merely polite small talk. Luckily the organ starts playing, although I say luckily, it's almost deafening. If I were younger, I would be putting my hands over my ears, but I don't want to seem rude.

The service goes on for an hour. I never realised there could be anything more boring than our prize-giving ceremony at school, but this tops it. I am so relieved when the vicar says it is all over. Finally, we can go home, but Great Aunt Margaret has other ideas.

'I hope you'll come back to my house for food and drinks?' Mum suddenly seems to perk up. I sigh, it's going to be a long day.

CHAPTER THREE

Most teenagers are embarrassed by their parents at some point or other but they don't know what it's like to have an alcoholic Mum, and to be *this* embarrassed. I watch her stumbling around her aunt's house and I see the looks from those around her, the shakes of heads. I want to die and pretend I have nothing to do with her. I consider going over to rescue her from any potential accidents but for once I don't want to. I escape to the garden instead.

Great Aunt Margaret's garden is average-sized but packed with different coloured flowers. The back fence is barely visible behind the long trellis adorned with beautiful purple blooms.

'Hey, it's Madison isn't it?' A tall blonde-haired boy stands before me.

'Um yes,' I stutter, wishing I had the right words to say.

'I'm James.' For a moment I think he is going to say he's my cousin, and that would be awful for so many reasons. 'I live next door to Margaret.'

Phew, we're not related. He's cute and a nice boy, the type any parents would approve of.

'How did you know my name?'

'Margaret could see I was getting bored in there listening to the old people going on about tea and the weather so she pointed me in your direction.' Good choice I'm thinking. 'Are you here alone?'

Now here is the dilemma; do I say I am alone or confess that I am here with that unstable mother over there? His blue eyes sparkle back at me while I consider the options. Before I can say anything else though, my decision is made for me.

'Maddie? There you are.' Mum bursts through the patio doors falling onto the grass in front of me. 'Was wondering where you'd got to.' Her dress has ridden up a little and I am desperate to pull it down and straighten her out.

I smile uneasily at James. 'This is my Mum,' I say, feeling

my face going red. His look of sympathy is too much.

'Pleased to meet you.' She throws her hand at James. 'I'm the mother. Who are you?' Right now I want to hide in a hole somewhere.

'I'm James.'

I'm praying that she won't say anything stupid. I catch a glimpse of Great Aunt Margaret inside. She smiles and rushes out. She must have received that psychic call of distress.

'Becky, come here. I need you for something.' I send Margaret an eternally grateful look. When they are gone, it is just me and James staring at each other.

'Sorry about her,' I say, finally.

'It's okay. My parents are pretty embarrassing too. One time my dad stood up at a party and started serenading my mum because it was her birthday.'

'That does sound cringy,' I laugh. I am thankful he is still talking to me, trying to make me feel better.

'Soo... do you go to school round here?'

'Greenacres Academy,' I answer. Perhaps the worst school in town. Such a lovely name but not a great school. 'How about you?'

'I'm at the boys' school.' A grammar-school boy. Now, I'm definitely feeling like this won't work out. There is no way a grammar school boy will want to hang out with an alcoholic's daughter, let alone date her, but I'm getting ahead of myself here. We're only chatting; who said anything about dating? Do I even want to date a boy? I picture the blonde girl in his place. I shake myself back to reality. That would never work.

'You must be pretty smart to get in there.' I instantly curse myself for saying something so obvious. His face reddens and he shrugs. Through the window, I can see Great Aunt Margaret guiding Mum, who can now barely walk, away from the kitchen.

'Do you like going to the cinema?' he asks suddenly.

'Yes, absolutely.' Wow, is he asking me on a date? I'm not sure how I feel about that.

'Great, maybe we could go sometime.'

'I'd love that.'

Any boy who is not put off by my Mum is worth having.

After our initial awkward start, the conversation starts flowing. I find out he has a much older brother, who is now married and that his favourite colour is orange.

When the party is over, we exchange numbers. I forget this is supposed to be a funeral. I had such a good time. Does that make me sick?

Margaret is cleaning up. Everyone else is gone except her brother, Great Uncle John; Mum is nowhere to be seen. I creep slowly towards the kitchen. I can hear Margaret talking.

'It's so sad that she's like this.'

'Her poor daughter,' John is saying.

'She should have got herself together, for Maddie at least. I know it was awful what happened but to be like this is not fair on her.'

What happened? What was so awful that it made Mum an alcoholic?

'She didn't need to do what she did,' John replies.

'You're right, but she was struggling.'

'But to-' He stops, then pops his head out of the kitchen. 'Hi, Maddie.' His formal suit now discarded, he is wearing just his shirt and trousers. The shirt is untucked. His hair needs a good brush.

'Hi,' I reply slowly. 'Where's Mum?' I'm desperate to ask what Mum did but not sure I know how to.

'She's having a lie down upstairs. You can hang out with us for a while.'

'Thanks.' I can feel my shoulders hunching up. I watch them fill the dishwasher, then I finally come out with it.

'What did Mum do that was so awful?'

Margaret stops, still facing away from me. John freezes while drying up the glass.

'It's not for me to say,' she answers, eventually.

'It's not like it doesn't affect me. I have to live with her.'

Margaret sighs. 'I know, it must be so hard for you, having to deal with all that.'

I want to scream out that she hasn't helped at all, virtually non-existent in my life till now.

'Then tell me.' John carries on drying the glass, polishing it until it seems like it will break.

'Tell you what?' Mum's voice from behind sends shivers down my spine.

'You're awake,' says Margaret cheerfully.

'Tell her what?' she demands angrily and I wonder what I've started. I look from one family member to the other.

CHAPTER FOUR

'The past is best left in the past,' Mum is saying as she strides ahead of me, away from Margaret's house. 'Whatever it is they think I've done, it's none of your business.'

Not if it affects me, I want to say, but I don't, because I don't like the look of thunder on her face. She is unpredictable, like an explosion waiting to happen.

I will find out. It may not be now, but I'll find a way. As Mum stormed out, Margaret apologised for upsetting her. She whispered that I could call her, if I needed to. I might just do that. It's about time she stepped up to help her great niece.

Marvin is whining when we get through the front door. Even though I left him extra food he clearly believes that isn't enough.

Sometimes I feel angry that, at fifteen, I am having to deal with all this. I should be out living my life with my mates not wondering when my volatile mother will show me up next.

'Who is my father?' Mum stands frozen to the spot, halfway through stirring the dinner, a rare moment when she is sober.

'You don't want to know.'

She turns away and carries on, pushing the meat around with the wooden spoon, the spaghetti is bubbling away next to it, getting dangerously close to boiling over. For her, the conversation is over.

'But I do want to. I'm fifteen and I have a right to know.'

She slams the spoon on the frying pan. I watch as it falls off and hits the floor with a thud, the sauce already leaving a stain on the floor. Marvin jumps up from where he was lying by the back door and runs out of the room.

'You have no idea what you're talking about.'

She marches out of the kitchen, leaving me more frustrated than ever before. As usual, it is down to me to finish the dinner. I'm used to it. As much as I want to throw the half-cooked food away in protest, I'm hungry.

Damn her and her stupid problems.

She appears ten minutes later.

'Dinner ready?'

'Yes,' I reply grumpily. I should throw it in her face.

'Don't be like that, Maddie.' The words stutter out, barely coherent. There's no point in trying to talk to her now she's started drinking.

'Forget about it,' I say as I slop out the food on the plate as though I were a dinner lady at school. Some of the spaghetti barely makes it, it's ends dangling over the worktop.

'The trouble with teenagers these days is that they have no idea what it's like in the real world.'

I put the plate down forcefully in front of her.

'And what real world would that be? The one where you have a stable home life, loving parents who aren't drunk most of the time, because you're right I do have no idea what that's like.'

For a moment I think she won't react then suddenly she stands up, grabs the plate of food, and tosses it aside like a rag doll before storming out, leaving me alone with my dinner, for not the first time.

When I find her later, she is crying uncontrollably in her bed. Marvin is curled up next to her. He is a lot more forgiving than I am.

'I'm sorry Mum. I didn't mean to upset you.'

'You don't understand what it was like,' she sobs.

'No. I don't, so tell me.'

'I don't even know who your father was. What kind of slut does that make me?' I don't argue with her. 'I was young, pregnant with twins, and-'

'Wait. What did you say?' She stops, eyes wide.

'Nothing, nothing. Ignore me.'

'No; you said pregnant with twins.'

'No, no. I didn't.'

'You did. Where is my twin?'

All the colour seems to drain from her face.

'Tell me,' I demand. Marvin looks up at me anxiously as
my voice raises.

'I can't,' she whispers, looking away.

'Did she die?' She shakes her head. 'She's still alive?'
I'm assuming my twin was a girl but for all I know I could
have had a boy twin. She nods slowly. 'Where is she?'

'I don't know.' Her words barely decipherable behind
the heart-breaking sobs. 'I had no choice. I didn't know
what else to do.'

'What do you mean?' She buries her head in her pillow,
trying to dig deeper into the soft material. I stroke her hair,
the silky conditioned locks easily threading through my
fingers. 'Whatever it is you can tell me, Mum. I won't
judge you.'

This is a lie but kind of the truth. I've already judged
her for her past and current actions. I'd be surprised if
anything else she did would shock me, and I don't think
she can ever truly redeem herself with me.

She lifts her head slowly, her tear-stained face suddenly
looks older.

'Promise?'

'I promise,' I lie, clutching her hand tightly.

'I gave her away.'

'Like had her adopted?' She shakes her head.
Horrifying thoughts are running through my head. What
could she have possibly done to her?

'I abandoned her. I left her outside the public toilets.' I
let go of her hand. I guess I was wrong if I thought
nothing else could shock me. I stand up slowly, staring at
her.

'You left her outside of a toilet?' I am aware that my
voice is going up. Mum clutches the pillow.

'I had to. I was a teenager. There was no way I could handle two babies on my own.'

I can't believe this. I absolutely can't believe this. I had a twin sister and for some reason, my Mum decided to abandon her.

'Why her? Why not me? Why not both of us?' Her pained expression almost pleads with me.

'She cried more.'

'Whoa! So, you gave away my twin sister because she cried too much.' She nods.

'You promised you wouldn't judge.'

I take a deep breath. 'Did I?' I say coldly and leave the room.

I have to leave before I say something I will regret. I keep walking until I am out of the house, ignoring her shouts out of the window, asking me where I'm going. I have no idea. I only know I have to get out there. A thousand thoughts run through my head. I can't make sense out of any of them. How do I get my head around the fact that Mum abandoned a baby, not just any baby, but my twin; the other half of me? I could run away. I could go and live with Great Aunt Margaret, but what if she rejected me as well? She hasn't exactly been keen on helping me out up till now.

My phone buzzes in my pocket. It's James:

Wanna meet up sometime?
How about now? I ask.
Sure. Where?
Mabel Park?
I'll be there.

CHAPTER FIVE

Mabel Park is only a ten-minute walk away and full of a huge array of colourful flowers all neatly arranged in patterns. It is a place I often come to, when I want to escape from Mum and her stress.

'It's good to see you again.' James smiles shyly at me. He gets up from the swing he is sitting on, his feet pushing against the bouncy floor.

'You too.'

'Are you okay? You look upset?'

I don't know where to start. He probably already thinks I'm a weirdo having a Mum who is an alcoholic but then again, he is here.

'I found out some disturbing news from Mum.'

'Oh?'

'I had a twin, well maybe still do. Mum abandoned her.'

'Why would she do that?'

I shrug. 'Single Mum; couldn't cope I guess.' He nods as though he totally understands what it's like. He has the kind of face that you could tell anything to, understanding and caring.

'What you going to do?'

'No idea. It's kind of knocked me. I walked out.'

'I think I would have too.'

He clutches my hand. I instantly pull away. I don't know why. I throw him an apologetic look. A hurt expression crosses his face but it doesn't last long.

He stops and turns to me, one hand on the frame of the swings. 'You should find her.'

'How would I do that?'

He doesn't answer but he has got me thinking. What would it be like to rediscover your long-lost twin? Would I suddenly feel like everything was right in the world? My twin, the other half of me, the one who completes me.

'I could help you.'

'That's sweet but why would you want to do that?' He blushes. I worry that it's because he likes me, likes me a lot, and I don't know if I feel the same way.

'I want to help,' he answers simply. 'A twin shouldn't be separated from her twin.'

'I agree,' I laugh. 'So we find her, just like that?'

'Yeah, why not. There must be some evidence of what happened to her.'

'You're too good to me, you know.'

He smiles a little shy smile. I am so lucky to have someone like James in my life. Damn what am I doing? James is perfect boyfriend material but I'm not sure *boy*friend is what I want. Girlfriend maybe or just the blonde girl?

...

When I get home, Mum is passed out on the sofa. Nothing new there. The sofa is looking a bit worn these days, a sign of too many spillages. I consider shaking her awake to find out the answers to the questions I have, but it will only result in a grumpy mother who will be less likely to help me out. Clearly, she wasn't that worried that I'd walked out. Anyone else's Mum would be waiting anxiously, I assume, but I have no actual experience of real life.

Frustrated, I stomp loudly up the stairs, childish I know, but sometimes I have the right to be. It doesn't matter how much noise I make, once she's out, there's no disturbing her. Marvin follows me to my bedroom, eager to play, but I'm not in the mood. I pace the bedroom, ideas on how to find my sister running through my brain at top speed. Marvin follows me like it's a game. When Mum wakes up, I am downstairs tidying the lounge. She seems surprised to see me. Maybe she'd hoped I would never come back. Maybe I'm a burden to her as well.

'Where did you abandon her?'

Her face falls. 'This again.'

'Yes, this again. It's my twin. I need to find her.' She sits up, terror-stricken.

'You can't find her.'

'Why not?'

'Because she'll hate me.' I want to tell her that I already do, but I don't, because as much as I want to hate her, I don't.

'She won't.'

'How do you know that?'

I shrug. 'It might be hard to start with but she'll get used to it. She probably wants to know where she came from. I would, and besides, finding me will be a big bonus for her.'

She lays her head back down on the cushion as though this is all too much for her.

'You could be right.'

'Where did you abandon her?'

'Outside the public toilets in Greenwick.'

'Greenwick?' She nods.

Greenwick is not a place I would choose to leave my child. A slightly scummy Essex town five miles from here.

'It had to be somewhere no one knew me and the bus went there.'

'Wait you had just given birth and then you bused it to Greenwick with both of us in a buggy?'

'Well actually I had help. A bloke I know drove me over there.'

I shake my head in despair. It's all about convenience with her.

'But surely the midwives knew there were two babies?'

'I gave birth at home.'

'On your own?'

'Aunt Margaret helped me.'

'Wow okay. Did she know you were going to abandon one of us?'

'No and she was furious when she found out.'

'I'm not surprised.'

Mum actually has the common sense to look ashamed at this point. Whether she means it or not is another matter. I want to ask about who this bloke was but there are more important questions and I can see Mum is getting close to shutting down again.

'How do you know she didn't die there?'

'There was an article in the local paper.' She hoists herself off the sofa and stumbles slowly up the stairs. When she returns, she is holding a tatty newspaper article. Marvin jumps up and bats it. I grab him to move him out of the way. There is no way he is ruining that.

Baby found in public toilets, screams the headline.

I scan through it and find the part where it tells me she was alive. *Taken in by a local nurse until they can find someone to adopt her.*

'Then what?' I demand. 'What happened next? Who adopted her?'

'I have no idea. I bought the papers for a week after but it was never mentioned again.'

I need to find that nurse. The article tells me her name is Joyce Grayson and she lived on Belmont Road, Greenwick. There can't have been that many Joyce Graysons on that road.

'Thanks, Mum,' I say as I leave the house.

'Where are you going?' she shouts.

'To find my sister.' I march straight round to James' house. He lets me in after the second knock.

'Hi. Come in.' The house is quiet. 'Mum and Dad are at Sainsbury's,' he explains.

A strange concept to me, Mum would never dream of going to Sainsbury's - *only for posh people* - she always says.

James is not keen on going to Greenwick when I tell him my plan.

'Mum would kill me.'

'It's only to this lady's house. It's not like we'd be hanging out on the streets.'

'I don't know and how do we know she still lives there? It was fifteen years ago.'

'But she might. Please. I don't want to go on my own.'

He sighs. 'Fine, but I'll have to lie.'

'Thank you,' I say, leaning over and pecking him on the cheek. He looks startled. 'Sorry.' Why did I do that?

'Don't be, it was nice.'

...

It's a short bus ride to Greenwick, through the little villages, the posh ones before the rough area. I can't keep my legs still and I keep picking at my nails, a habit I've been doing a long time. I don't know why I'm so nervous. She may not even live there or she may refuse to tell us anything. It's a chance we have to take though. No one ever got anywhere without taking risks.

James has his phone out on Google maps when we get off the bus. 'I think it's left up here.' I gaze across at him. He's amazing. We've only known each other a few weeks and already I feel like I know him so well. I can't believe he'd go to all this trouble for me, yet I feel like there is something missing between us. 'Nearly there,' he says squeezing my hand. I smile. 'Don't worry, she's a nurse. She'll be lovely.'

While I know this should be true, I think back to the time when I was in hospital getting my tonsils out. The nurse in charge was horrible, always shouting at me for getting out of bed when I should have been *resting*. Resting was so boring though. I wanted to be exploring the hospital.

'This is the street,' James announces proudly. The houses are moderately sized, slightly smaller than James', bigger than mine. Some of the houses on the other side are bungalows. It's a quiet street, no children out playing, no gangs terrorising the neighbourhood. It certainly doesn't fit my image of what Greenwick is supposed to be like. 'What number did you say it was?'

I take the carefully folded article out of my pocket, making sure not to damage it in the process.

'Number 20.'

'Okay, that's on the other side.'

Will she look old now? Will she still be a nurse? As we walk down the street, the bungalows turn into small houses and hers is the last but one before the end. *Please let her still live there*, I repeat to myself several times.

'Here it is.'

We both stand and stare at the house. I grab James' hand and squeeze it tightly.

'Don't worry, it'll be fine,' he says trying to reassure me.

'You're right.' But I don't move.

'Go on. You can do it.'

I don't feel like I can but I step forward anyway. I have to be brave. There doesn't seem to be a doorbell or even a space where one used to be, so I knock, hard. I instantly regret knocking so hard, what if it sounds aggressive? A shadow appears in the doorway, moving slowly towards the door. This might be her! A white-haired lady opens the door, a big smile on her face. This has to be Joyce. She is exactly how a nurse should look.

'Hello?'

For a moment I am dumbstruck. In my head, I had planned exactly what I was going to say but now it's as if my tongue has been cut out.

'I... er... are you Joyce Grayson?'

'I am. How can I help you?' Her eyes move to James. He has the kind of face that you know you can trust.

I get out the article and hand it to her.

'You found my sister, fifteen years ago.' Her eyes widen and she clutches the radiator next to her.

'Your sister?'

'My twin sister.'

She doesn't say a word, just stares at us, looking me up and down. I hope she's not going to have a heart attack. She lets go of the radiator and runs her hand through her grey permed hair before saying finally, 'You'd better come in.'

We follow her into her cosy house past the dated wallpaper and peeling paint. This place could do with a bit of TLC. In the lounge, she directs us to the sofa by the window.

'Can I get you a drink?'

'No,' I say quickly. James opens his mouth but shuts it without a word. I just want to get on with this. She sits down in a single armchair, perching on the edge.

'You're that baby's twin? She looks like you?'

'I guess so. I mean I'm assuming we are identical.'

'Wow.'

'You took her in?'

'I did. The poor mite was gurgling away in her baby carrier, someone had obviously taken time to wrap her up carefully and make sure she wasn't cold.' This surprises me.

'A pink bear was lying next to her.'

'Why did you decide to take her in?'

'How could I not? If I left her out there who knows what might have happened.' I nod slowly. 'I don't understand. Why did your mother keep you and not your sister?'

I throw my hands up in the air. 'Who knows what Mum was thinking? She's not right in the head.'

'Teenage mother?'

'Yep.'

'It must have been hard for her. I'm sure she wouldn't have taken that decision lightly.'

'I guess not.'

I'm dying to ask what happened to the baby after, where she went, but I'm fearful of bombarding her with too many questions at once.

'She was a very sweet baby, never crying very much.' Strange, complete opposite of what Mum said. 'She slept upstairs in my bedroom for a week until they found a young couple who would adopt her.'

'And then what happened to her?' I'm desperate to know.

'They moved somewhere else. I forget where. Sorry,

my memory isn't as good as it used to be. It was somewhere further south - Sussex, Hampshire, no Kent - that was it. It was Kent. They moved to Broadstairs in Kent. They seemed like they were very well off so I'm sure she will have had a good life.'

I've never heard of Broadstairs and have no idea how far away that is.

'Is that close to here?'

'About a two-hour drive.'

'Oh.' She can tell I'm disappointed as she stands up and reaches over to me, stroking my arm.

'You must really want to meet her.' Her kindness makes the tears fall. I push them back. I have to stay in control.

'I do.'

Joyce didn't have a forwarding address but she did tell us that Broadstairs is a pretty small place. Someone there must have heard about her or know her.

'What now?' asks James, when we are outside.

'I don't know. We can't very well go to Broadstairs.'

'Not tonight we can't, but maybe somehow we can.'

'How can we? I have a Mum who can barely stand up straight, let alone drive me to a town two hours away.'

'Maybe I could ask my parents.'

'No, no, no.'

'Why not?'

'They'll think I'm some kind of tramp. You can't tell them. Promise me you won't.'

'They would not think that.' I raise my eyebrows.

'Honestly, they wouldn't.'

'Please don't tell them, not yet anyway.'

'Okay, I promise.'

CHAPTER SIX

'What happened?' Mum practically pounces on me when I get through the front door, anyone would think she cares. In the lounge, Marvin is racing up and down through his cardboard tunnel, trying to grab hold of my shoelaces when I walk by.

'We met the nurse who took her in.'

'And?'

'She got adopted by a couple in Broadstairs.'

'Broadstairs? Where's that?'

'Kent, apparently.'

'But that's miles away.' Her face falls and I try to smile. 'I'd drive you there if I could.'

Would she? And actually, why can't she? Apart from the obvious problem of her not having a car and not being able to stay sober for more than half an hour, of course. I don't argue with her. She's never stepped up before. I don't expect her to now. I know I'm alone in this world, well I was until I found out about my twin sister. What if she rejects me as well? What if I'm a disappointment to her too?

'I'm sure you'll find her one day.'

It doesn't matter to her like it does to me. She has already given her up. I'm not about to do the same.

'What did you name her?' I ask before she disappears into the other room.

She turns, her face is the saddest I have ever seen it. 'I named her Ashleigh, but no one knows that, except you.'

I leave Mum to her drunken cleaning, or whatever she is doing, and retreat to my bedroom, my place of sanctuary, the only place I can be myself. As I lie there staring up at the ceiling, I ponder how on earth I am going to find my sister in a town miles from here. There must be a way, but seeing it is not easy right now. I don't even know her name now. Then I imagine how weird it must be for her. She doesn't know her real name, she probably doesn't even know when her actual birthday was. I can't comprehend that. Does she even know she is adopted?

'Maddie, can you do my hair?' Mum opens the door loudly, interrupting my thoughts, and making me jump. Marvin sneaks in and jumps up onto the bed, instantly digging his paws into my tummy.

'What, now?'

'Yeah. I'm going out.'

'Out where?'

'With my mates,' she says, with a face that says *isn't it obvious?*

Yet again, she expects me to doll her up for her night out, while I stay in and fend for myself. I know I'm old enough to stay at home on my own but sometimes I wish we could curl up together and watch a movie, like Mums and daughters are supposed to do.

'How do you want it done?' I sigh. Her eyes light up as I follow her into her bedroom, turfing Marvin off of me.

Over the years I've become an expert in different hairstyles for Mum, all learned from YouTube. I live off the way she proudly tells her mates that I did her hair. At least I'm good at something. *You should be a hairdresser*, they all tell me, but what if I have bigger ambitions than that? Okay, I don't, but I could have.

'Can you French braid it? You're so good at that.' I'm a sucker for her praise.

When I am finished, I stand back and delight in my handiwork. I am good. I suppose we don't look unalike Mum and I but she definitely makes more of an effort when she goes out. Her hair, brown, like mine is always straightened to perfection and super silky. I look at her with envy, wishing I looked that good but knowing I could never be that bothered when I went out.

'You're a star.' She leans over and kisses me on the cheek. 'On with my glad rags.' She leaps over to the wardrobe, a new kind of energy to her step, pulling various colourful dresses out for my approval. I choose a silky green one because it goes with her green eyes. She takes it, knowing that I have far more taste than she does.

'What would I do without you?'

I often wonder this but knowing what I do about my twin sister, I'm guessing she wasn't always like this. What was she like before she had us, before she became an alcoholic?

As she is about to go out, there is a knock on the door. Mum, assuming it is her mate, races there like a child on roller skates. I can hear the drop in her tone and it's then that I know, it's not her friends. When she reappears, it's with Great Aunt Margaret.

I don't like the condescending tone she uses with me

'Hello dear.' I nod. 'I see your mother is off out?' Completely pointless and obvious statement but I see no reason to be rude.

'Yep, I'm home alone.'

Marvin appears, sniffing Margaret curiously.

'Hello, little one. You're adorable aren't you.' She strokes him under his chin before smiling back at me. 'I only came to see how you all were. I can come back another time if you'd like.'

Suddenly I fancy the company, it's beginning to get dark outside and no matter how many times I've been alone at night I still hate it.

'You can stay. We haven't got much food though.'

'That's okay, I can order some in if you like.' She laughs at my enthusiastic response, it's not every day we get a takeaway, or even at all.

'Yes please.'

I detect a hint of jealousy from Mum as she leaves us laughing in the lounge. I want to shout at her that she chose to go out and leave me, to put her friends before me again. I try to avoid her gaze but can't resist a sneaky peek as she turns the corner, a big frown on her face. For some reason, this makes me feel happy.

'What would you like? Fish and chips? Chinese? Pizza?' Ask any teenager and they would most likely say pizza but I love Chinese food. I can count on one hand the number of times we've had a takeaway. Mum never has the money for it.

'Chinese please.' I watch as Great Aunt Margaret navigates her phone and pulls up a menu of a local Chinese takeaway. I've never seen an old person so quick on their phone. Marvin sniffs her bag. I'm hoping he won't wee on it.

'What?' she asks amused.

'You're so-'

'Good with mobile phones?'

'Yes, sorry; I didn't mean to be rude.'

'Ha! No; it's fine. I've had a lot of practice and I hate being out of touch with the world. I'm not going to let something like new technology make me a dinosaur.' She says it with such pride that I want to laugh but I don't want to risk offending her.

As we wait for the Chinese to arrive, Great Aunt Margaret begins tidying the kitchen. She says she is making room for the food but it's gone far beyond that. I hate that she feels pity for me. I don't need that. Marvin runs from one end of the kitchen to the other, not used to all this activity. Margaret very patiently steps around him every time even though he almost trips her up several times.

As she scrubs the worktop, she glances over at me.

'How are things with you both, after the funeral?'

I pull a face. What she really means is have I found out Mum's secret. 'Okay I guess. I know about my twin.'

She stops scrubbing, the flakes of food remaining in place, and looks across at me. 'Oh.'

Neither of us speak as she continues cleaning until I say:

'Great Aunt Margaret, can I ask you something?'

'Of course, ask me anything.'

'What was Mum like before she had us? Before she

29

started drinking?'

'She was the life and soul of the party, always out having fun.'

'Like she is tonight?'

'Yes, like that, but all the time. She rarely got down about anything.' Unlike now where she mopes around most of the time.

'Do you think she regrets having me?'

'She doesn't regret you. She just regrets giving your sister away.'

'She has a funny way of showing it.'

'Don't be fooled by her tough exterior. She may act like she doesn't care but inside she is hurting like hell.'

'What was my dad like?' Mum claims she doesn't know who the father is but I'm not convinced.

'No idea. She kept him a secret from all of us. We knew she had a boyfriend but we never met him. Her Mum hassled her about bringing him round for dinner but she always resisted. All I know is he was a boy from school.'

'I'd love to meet him but she won't tell me anything apart from he was a creep,' I say sadly. Great Aunt Margaret shrugs.

'It's difficult to get anything out of someone who doesn't want to tell you.'

When the food arrives, the kitchen has been transformed. Mum won't recognise it. We sit at the table and eat. I haven't seen the table this empty ever. It almost feels like we're a family. What a strange thought. I give Marvin his food, so we can eat ours in peace.

'I went to see the nurse who found her, she was lovely. Just the right person to find her but all she knew is that she got adopted by a couple in Kent.'

'What are you going to do now?'

'No clue. I want to go there and find her but even if I could get there, I don't know her name or anything. All I know is she looks like me. I can't just walk around hoping I'll bump into myself.'

Margaret laughs at this, then her face turns serious. 'I could take you.'

CHAPTER SEVEN

'This kitchen looks too bloody tidy.' I'm trying to stay out of Mum's way; post-night-out is never a fun place to be. 'Always has to interfere that woman.' I roll my eyes and turn the volume up on the TV. 'Turn that down, I've got a headache,' she yells, coming into the room.

'You wouldn't have if you hadn't got raging drunk last night.'

Marvin is nowhere to be seen amidst all the shouting.

'What? Oh, I'm sorry if I went out and had fun. You're so boring Maddie, can't let me live my life. I wish I'd never...' She stops, fear in her eyes.

'Had me? Is that what you were going to say?' I slam the remote on the floor, not caring that the battery has been thrown out. Mum doesn't say a word as I leave the house.

Halfway down the street, with no plan in mind of where to go, I realise I haven't even brushed my hair this morning. It's lucky I got dressed. At least I'm not wandering down the street in my pyjamas.

I think about going to James' house, he'd help me in a minute, but I'm too embarrassed. I look a right state and he shouldn't have to bail me out of every problem. I should be able to run my own life. I keep walking, more out of anger than anything else, until my phone starts to ring in my pocket. I pull it out in fury, ready to give Mum a mouthful but it's not her, it's Great Aunt Margaret.

'Hi,' I say, trying not to sound too angry.

'Are you okay love? Your Mum rang me, she was worried about you.' That'll be a first, Mum worrying about me.

'I'm walking out the anger.'

'Want me to join you?'

'If you'd like.'

'Where are you?'

She's there within minutes, it's like she was waiting around the corner or something. I'm not used to someone being this concerned about me.

'She didn't mean it you know.' I glance over at her in the car. 'She did want you.' I shrug. It's hard to know what to believe anymore. 'She wishes she'd had you when she was older, with a bloke that wasn't a creep and had been able to settle down properly.'

'None of that is my fault though, is it?' I shout so loudly it shocks me.

'No,' she answers quietly. 'I'm sorry you have to put up with all this.'

'Just take me home.'

She doesn't say another word on the short drive home but the awkward vibe between us makes me feel uncomfortable.

'Maddie, Maddie, I love you,' Mum gushes, the minute I walk in the door. She's back on the drink again, and in a way I'm relieved. She's easier to deal with when she's a happy drunk. 'I'm sorry Maddie. Can you ever forgive me?'

'Of course I can.' I push her off me. She's starting to smother me with her hug. 'Don't I always?' She breathes out, a breath held too long. Later on, when it is the two of us again, she leans on my shoulder. 'I did want you; you know? Do still want you.'

I roll my eyes; do we have to go through this again. She blurts out something stupid and spends days apologising for it.

Marvin tentatively peeks his head round the door. Seeing it is all calm he jumps up onto the sofa, desperate to join in with the big cuddle.

'I've said it's fine Mum. You don't need to bring it up again.'

'Sorry.' Her eyes start to droop, the previous night out and the day's events getting on top of her. 'It was very nice of Great Aunt Margaret to clean up for us.'

I know she doesn't mean it, but I appreciate the effort it is taking her to say it. She can be lovely when she wants to be.

...

James texts me when I am about to turn off my light.

You still awake?

I could ignore him but I don't.

Yeah, why?

Just thinking about you

Aw sweet

Do you wanna meet up tomorrow

Yeah maybe, I answer briefly, not wanting to get his hopes up.

Just maybe?

Ok yeah definitely then

I close my eyes with thoughts of a boy who loves me, someone who can see past all the crap in my life and still wants to travel the road with me. Yet why doesn't that excite me as much as it should?

...

'Take her up on the offer,' James says when I meet him the next morning.

'But I-'

'No buts if your aunt is offering to take you to Broadstairs then go.'

'But how will I find her?'

'I had an idea about that.'

'Oh yeah.' I love James' ideas, he's so smart.

'You know how on Facebook-' The word Facebook makes me want to throw up but I listen anyway. '-they have these local groups. Like there's one for our town.'

'There is?'

'Yeah.'

'What do they talk about?'

'Oh, I don't know dumb stuff like who's seen my cat or did you see that slightly suspicious man the other night; cue big pile on about various suspicious men they've seen.'

I chuckle.

'Don't mean to be rude but why are you on Facebook? Isn't it like for old people?'

He laughs.

'I find it interesting.' I nod but I don't get it.

'And what's that got to do with me finding my sister?'

'You could ask on there if anyone knows her.'

'But I don't know her name.'

'But she might know she's adopted or someone would. We could ask if anyone knows someone who was adopted in 2006.'

He's got a point.

'You're so wise, you know that?' He blushes and smiles a cute little grin. 'Only problem is I'm not on Facebook.'

'I am though.'

'Let do it then,' I say with more force than I'd intended.

He gets out his phone and logs on to Facebook. He searches for a local group in Broadstairs. Before he posts, we stop and we have a giggle at some of the posts.

Where can I get rid of my empty crisp packets. I want to recycle them? Looking for recommendations for the best gnomes to display in my garden. Anyone seen my keys, I lost them last night while out drinking?

As predicted the last one has provoked numerous comments judging the poor person for going on a night out.

'Some of these people need to get a life,' I say bemused by the whole thing.

'Indeed.'

I wouldn't even know where to start with composing a question for the group but James seems to know exactly how to word it.

Were you adopted in 2006 from Essex? Information wanted regarding a girl who was adopted then. She has a family member who would love to see her.

'You don't want to mention that her twin wants to see her?'

'Would you want to find out that you had a twin from Facebook?'

'No. Fair point.'

He clicks "post" and the message stares back at us, waiting for an answer.

'We should go for a walk and check it later.'

'Wise move.'

I follow him out of the door. I'm eager to get out of his house; it's so neat it unsettles me, and besides, his parents might come home. I haven't met them yet and I hate to think they might be disappointed in me, the scummy girlfriend from the rough side of town. I'll have to meet them one day but maybe when I've been to the hairdressers or just stepped out of the shower and look pristine.

James reaches out to hold my hand as we walk down the street but I move my hand slightly, hoping he won't notice. Why do I feel so uncomfortable with any physical attention from him?

'Thanks for posting that for me.'

'It was no trouble.' I love the way he sounds so posh when he talks.

We end up walking in the woods near his house, not a place I've been before. I would have turned my nose up at anything to do with trees but funnily enough, when you're with someone else, they take on a new meaning. Halfway through I suggest we check Facebook. I'm so impatient.

There are four responses, two not helpful, suggesting I try an organisation which I might have to pay for (does he think I'm made of money?), one wishing me well (thanks but unless you have something to contribute - don't bother) and a fourth one saying 'private message me please'.

'Sounds aggressive but could be useful,' I say, looking to James for his support.

'I would message him now but my service has gone. Bloody forest,' says James waving his phone around in annoyance. I laugh.

'It can wait until we get back.'

Look at me, all patient, but inside I am anything but. I can't stop thinking about what information this person could give me. Could they possibly have the answers I want? Do they know Ashleigh or whatever her name is now?

CHAPTER EIGHT

'What does it say? What does it say?' I ask frantically when we return to civilisation. His face falls and he hands me the phone.

Don't meddle in stuff like this, it never ends well.

'What the hell does that mean?' I exclaim.

'Who knows?'

'Do you think he knows something?'

'Maybe.'

James types a quick reply - *do you know something? It's really important.* Instantly we see he's typing.

No, I'm just warning you. It only ends in trouble.

'Great, four replies and all useless.' I pull a weed up in frustration from a passing garden.

'We might get some more later.'

'Yeah, maybe.' James is always optimistic, another one of his great qualities.

'Looks like Mum and Dad are home.' He points at the red flashy car in the driveway. 'Do you want to come in for a drink?'

'I should probably get home.' I plan to scarper as quick as I can but my plan is set to fail the minute the front door opens and there stands James' Mum. I can see where James got his height from, she must tower above most other women.

'Oh hi, you must be Maddie. Come in.' James throws me an apologetic look. I follow him into the house, desperately trying to think of an excuse to leave, while frantically straightening my hair and praying it doesn't look like I've been dragged through a bush.

Usually, when I've been to James' house we hang out in his bedroom; nothing happens, and we only sit and chat. This time there is an expectation that we sit in the lounge and be waited on by his mum. It's about as awkward as it gets. Just when I think it can't get any worse, his dad comes in, all smiles, and proceeds to throw more questions at me. After I have successfully dodged several questions about my family, I tell them I really do have to get home.

'I'm sorry about them,' James whispers as he shows me out.

'It's fine, at least yours care about you.'

'I'm sure your Mum does but-'

'I know, I know, she doesn't know how to show it.' I'm getting fed up with people making excuses for her. Why should I have to put up with a half-adequate Mum at my age? Why can't I long for the best?

Before I can stop him, James kisses me on the lips, full on kissing, as I step outside. 'See you soon,' he whispers.

The memory of that kiss stays with me all the way home. I wanted to feel something, I don't know electricity maybe but I didn't. What is wrong with me? All I could think of was the blonde girl.

'You look happy,' Mum comments when I walk through the door. 'When am I going to meet that boyfriend of yours?' Is never an option? I don't tell her she met him at the funeral but she was too drunk to remember.

'One day,' I answer, trying to be as vague as possible.

'I'm going out tonight.'

'Again?'

'Yes, I am allowed to go out more than once a week.' I want to argue that she goes out far more than that but I'm in too good a mood to get into an argument. Instead, I say:

'Of course you are Mum.'

. . .

Wanna come over tonight? I hadn't planned on seeing James again so soon but the thought of a night at home, by myself, is not a nice one.

Sure as long as I get to cuddle up with you.

I feel uneasy at the thought of him cuddling me but I can't say that.

. . .

I sit on Mum's bed, with Marvin on my lap slowly moving his paws up and down, and watch her get ready. I sometimes feel it should be the other way round. I'm the young cool one who should be going out on the town. I console myself with thoughts of James coming over. I don't tell Mum about it, not because she wouldn't be okay, but because I want to have some things which she doesn't know. She'd ask too many questions, and would wonder why we aren't sleeping together already. Unlike most mums she actually wants me to lose my virginity. She sees it as a badge of honour, using contraception, of course. *There's no way I want a baby in the house.* Maybe that's why I'm so adamant that I won't lose my virginity. I'm not her. I don't want to sleep with someone, not yet anyway. I want to do it in my time, in my way. This is nothing personal to James. He's amazing. He'd be horrified at the thought of doing it. He's such a nice, decent guy. For the last few weeks, I wonder how on earth I managed to get such a wonderful person for a boyfriend. Surely there's some middle-class girl he'd prefer. On top of all that, are the confusing thoughts running through my head and the possibility that I might be gay. If Mum questioned me too much, I might just blurt it out and who knows how *she* would react to that.

'What do you think?' Mum's brown hair is curled and the tight, figure-hugging purple shimmery dress looks amazing on her.

'Lovely.'

'Lovely? What does that mean? I'm not sixty.'

'Sorry. Shit hot.'

'Thank you. That's better.' I shake my head, grinning.

James is here five minutes after Mum has gone. When she took so long to get ready, I worried they would be here at the same time. I was relieved when she finally left.

'Have you eaten? I brought chips.' He holds out a bag for me as we sit down on the sofa.

Marvin is next to us in an instant, sniffing at the bag of

chips. I push him away. James smiles and pats Marvin's head.

'That's so kind. What do you wanna watch?'

He lifts his hands up. 'Whatever you want.'

We end up watching Fast and Furious 7. I love watching those kinds of movies and clearly so does James as we chuckle through it together.

'You will find her,' he says when it's over.

'You think?'

'Yeah, course. She's out there. It'll happen and there's all kinds of stuff like DNA these days to help you.' I lean into his chest, it would be so tempting to spend all night with him, cuddled up to him but he pulls away.

'I have to go.' I smile weakly. He grabs the blanket from the end of the sofa, carefully puts it over me, and tucks me in.

'Thank you,' I whisper as I watch him go.

CHAPTER NINE

'Hello.'

I stare at the half-naked man with the husky voice standing before me. Who on earth is he? Why is he in my house? He puts his hands on his hips, strutting his flat tummy at me with a creepy smile.

'Um hi.'

I quickly shuffle past him to the bathroom, hoping I don't find remnants of him in there. The giggles from Mum's bedroom are enough to make me throw up as I sneak past her room and downstairs. I need to get as far away from them as possible.

'This is Nick,' Mum announces, coming into the kitchen ten minutes later. Still in his pants, he leans against the doorway. I mutter something in his direction. I don't have the energy for this today. I'm beginning to wish I'd made James stay over too, at least then I'd have support, but he's far too polite for that. Marvin eyes Nick suspiciously, deliberately walking the long way round from his bowl to the corridor.

I continue scooping up the Coco Pops, faster now, eager to get out of here.

'Do you want a cooked breakfast?' she asks him. Milk splutters out of my mouth. Mum stares at me coldly. The thought of Mum making a cooked breakfast is laughable.

'Hey Maddie, I've heard so much about you.' What a creep. I smile weakly at him.

It's not the first boyfriend Mum's brought home but it's the first one in a long time. He is not a welcome sight now. Not only is my hair in need of a wash but I always look rubbish in the morning. That shouldn't matter to me but it does. He seems like an idiot but I care what he thinks for some stupid reason.

What has he heard about me? I wonder. I doubt it's that I'm constantly having to fend for myself when Mum is drunk or that I'm good at housework due to the fact that Mum isn't.

'I need to get going?' I push the chair out, getting up.

'So soon?' His smarmy smile is starting to get on my nerves.

'School,' I explain simply.

'Oh, I remember school. The best days of your life.' I raise my eyebrows in response, not wanting to get into an in-depth conversation with him. 'Woodwork was my favourite.' I resist the urge to tell him it's called DT now. He wouldn't understand.

'Great to meet you,' I say, rushing out of the room before he can engage me in any more mindless chatter.

'Sorry about her.' Mum's voice is unusually light and sweet. 'She's not always that grumpy.'

'It's fine. She's a teenager. That's what they're meant to do.' Cue - shrieking laughter.

Up in my room, I pull a comb through my hair and reluctantly get out of my pyjamas into my itchy school uniform. Why can't I live in America where they have no uniform? Although what would I wear? I'm hardly the height of fashion. I run down the stairs, keen to get out of the house before anyone speaks to me again. Unfortunately, Nick is standing by the front door, blocking my way.

'That uniform looks great on you.'

'Um... thank you.'

'Especially the short skirt.' Okay, this is getting weird now.

'I need to go.' He doesn't move and I wonder what will happen next. His eyes turn downwards towards my legs. I consider kicking him where it hurts but he steps aside.

'Hope to see you again.'

I run out the door, sincerely hoping I don't see him again. What a creep.

James texts me on my walk to school.

I've got an idea. I love the fact that his text messages are so perfectly punctuated.

Sounds interesting.

Meet me after school, in the park.

I'll be there.

Just got to get through five hours of lessons first. I don't have any friends at school, none I would call real friends, none I could share my darkest deepest secrets with, only Chloe. Chloe is more of an acquaintance or an annoyance. I'm not sure which. I put up with her because it's nice to have someone to talk to sometimes.

She has already saved me a seat when I get to form.

'So, how's it hanging?' she asks with a big grin on her face. I can tell that she is dying to reveal some gossip.

'Not bad,' I reply. Ignoring the fact that my Mum's new boyfriend came onto me this morning, I've had a pretty good weekend. Now that I have James, life is bearable. I know she is desperate for me to ask her what is going on.

'What's going on with you?'

'My Mum is getting married.' Her enormous grin looks ready to explode off her face.

'Who's that?' I ask, whispering towards the door. It's the blonde girl.

Chloe frowns. 'That's Lauren. She's moved into our form.' Oh really!

'Anyway, I was saying about my mum.'

'Yeah sorry. Exciting,' I say trying to muster up some enthusiasm while at the same time keeping one eye on Lauren who is literally gliding towards us.

Chloe doesn't seem to have noticed that I'm distracted and carries on. 'It is sooo exciting. And I'm going to be a bridesmaid.' I consider us too old to be a bridesmaid but I don't say that. I don't want to rain on her parade.

'Cool. Do you get to pick the dress?'

'I hope so. Mum says she's going to take me shopping. Hey, you could come too?'

For a moment I think Lauren is going to sit on our table, in the spare seat. I hold my breath as she glances around, trying to decide which seat to take.

She picks the table nearest the front and feel myself drooping in disappointment.

'Shopping; you wanna come?' Chloe repeats.

'What? Shopping?' I'm not sure how I feel about shopping with a different Mum and her daughter, too weird? 'Maybe.' I'll need to think about this.

The day goes by very slowly. Two thoughts keep me going. The first is James and his idea. He's smart. If he's thought of it, it'll be a good one. And, of course, the other thought is Lauren. It turns out she is now in several of my classes. I get to spend more than one lesson staring at the back of her beautiful head dreaming of... I don't know what. I always stop myself before I imagine that bit.

At the end of fifth lesson I can relax, I'm finally free. Let me out of this place. James is waiting at our usual meeting point, under the tree in the corner of the park. I can't remember who first came up with it. It's far enough away from the small children, less noisy, and away from the walkers who march around the edge.

He smiles with that winning smile of his and rests his arm on the tree next to him.

'Hey there,' he calls out when I am closer, his voice tender. 'Good day?'

'Hmm,' I mutter, 'Okay. You?'

'Not bad actually. We did some cool stuff in science.' He sets off on what I can only describe as a science rant. I love that he gets excited about this stuff. 'Anyway sorry,' he begins, seeing me glance around. 'We should get to business.'

'Sorry, I wasn't bored.' Well, I kind of was but I could listen to him talk on anything. It's not what he's saying it's the tone he uses and the way he looks. But something doesn't sit right. I have this amazing boyfriend but yet it isn't enough. Could it be that I can't imagine a future with him? Or that every time I picture him as a boyfriend, Lauren appears in my head.

'Well anyway, I had this idea.'

'Oh yes, the idea.'

'There's an adoption agency in Greenwick, most likely the one your sister's adoptive parents used. We should go there. They are open until six most days. We could go tomorrow night.'

'Great idea but what about your parents? They won't like you going there.'

'Don't worry about that. I'll figure it out.'

'Then yes, let's go. It's a date,' I add, grinning.

CHAPTER TEN

The adoption agency in Greenwick is a standard brick building in the midst of the roughest area of town. Despite its name, Greenwick has a distinct lack of green spaces. Nothing but high-rise flats and teenage boys in hoodies on street corners. I'm not only glad to have James here for moral support but I also feel so much safer with him by my side.

I don't consider myself middle class but I'm feeling like it compared to some of the teenagers here, who eye me suspiciously as we walk by, or maybe it's James in his posh jacket they're really staring at. I clutch his hand tightly and walk quicker than I usually would.

'This is it,' he announces excitedly.

Hands shaking, I press the buzzer marked "Holywells Adoption Agency".

'Hello?' comes the disembodied voice through the intercom.

I stare at James, frozen to the spot, words disappearing from my mouth. Fortunately, James rescues me.

'We are here to find some historical adoption records.'

'We don't normally release those records to anyone but family.'

'My girlfriend is family. Please can we come in and explain; it's a little bit complicated.' A pause follows and I wonder if she's hung up on us.

'Okay but you'll have to be quick. We close soon.'

Despite knowing it was coming, the buzzer sounds, making me jump. James pushes the door open with confidence, grabbing my hand and pulling me in. He squeezes it tight and throws me a quick reassuring smile.

The stairs in the old building smell of disinfectant, reminding me of our doctor's surgery. The hallway looks like it could do with a new paint job. The door marked "Holywells Adoption Agency" is the first door on the right.

James enters without hesitation.

A small brown-haired older lady, with the brightest red lipstick I've ever seen, sits at the desk nearest the door. Behind her, a younger less-experienced-looking woman types away furiously at her computer.

The older lady glances up, face full of intimidating questions.

'How can I help you?' Her carefully made-up lips forming the words so precisely.

I take a deep breath. I can't rely on James for everything. I need to do this.

'I'm looking for the adoption records for my twin sister.'

'Twin sister?' She raises her eyebrows, and her mouth drops open slightly.

'She was abandoned fifteen years ago in Greenwick and adopted shortly afterwards.' I hand her the news article.

'I remember this.'

'You do?'

'Yes, but I'm afraid I can't let you see the records.'

'But it's my twin sister.'

'How do I know that? Do you have proof?'

'Well… er…'

'Birth certificate?'

It is then that I realise I've never seen my birth certificate. 'It's at home,' I lie, hoping Mum didn't throw it away. That would be the sort of thing she would do.

The woman sighs heavily. 'I can't let you see them without proof.'

'But it's my sister-'

'I understand that but rules are rules. Come back with a birth certificate and maybe we can sort something out.'

Frustrated we leave, knowing there is no point in arguing with this determined woman.

'What a waste of time,' I mutter when we are outside.

'It's okay. We can come back tomorrow.'

'If I can find my birth certificate.'

'But you said-'

'I know what I said but I have no idea if Mum even has it still. What if she's lost it? Or worse threw it away?'

He can't answer this because there is no answer to this problem. He holds my hand tight on the bus home. I don't stop him, though it feels uncomfortable. We don't say a word but I know he's there for me.

Thankfully when I get home Nick has gone. The last thing I need is him getting in the way and sticking his oar in. Unbelievably Mum is hoovering when I walk through the door, not a sight you see every day or any day. She turns it off when she sees me.

'Hi love, how was your day?'

'Okay. Why are you hoovering?'

'Can't a Mum hoover now and then.'

'Sure.'

'You're late home.'

'I was with a friend.'

'That boy?' she says with a sly grin.

'Yes, that boy. His name is James.'

She is about to switch the hoover back on when I stop her.

'Mum, do you have my birth certificate?'

'Your what?'

'My birth certificate; you know, the one you get when your child is born.'

'I know what a birth certificate is. I'm not stupid. What do you need it for?' She eyes me suspiciously.

'Just wondered.'

'Is this to do with finding your sister?'

'Maybe.'

'It's probably somewhere.' Very helpful, thanks Mum. She stares up at the ceiling as though pondering where it could be. 'Ooh, I know. It's in the middle drawer next to my bed.' She seems very certain about this which surprises me. She is never certain about anything.

Before I can ask her anything else she runs upstairs. Should I go with her? Before I can decide she is sprinting down the stairs, with Marvin chasing after her like it's a new game. I am expecting good news.

'No, it wasn't there.'

'Really? Not at all.'

'Sorry. No idea where it is. If I remember I'll let you know.'

Part of me wonders if she lying. I make a note to check for myself when she is next out. I leave her to the hoovering and make my way to my bedroom. Back to square one.

When I get downstairs again Nick has arrived, full of life, wanting to know every detail about my life and standing far too close for my liking. I could run upstairs but I do want dinner. Nick orders us pizza. It feels like he is trying to butter me up, get on my good side.

After dinner is when it starts to get lively. Mum and Nick have both been drinking all through the meal. Mum switches some music on and starts to dance wildly around the lounge. I cringe but at least James isn't here to see it.

'Come on Maddie, let's dance.' She drags me by the hands to the middle of the room.

'I don't want to,' I object.

'Don't be boring.'

'Yeah. Don't be boring,' teases Nick, joining in and shouting right in my face, grabbing hold of my other hand.

I yank my hands-free and step away. 'I don't want to,' I shout.

'Oh, but Maddie,' whines Mum. She reaches for my hand again but misses and hits me right in the face, square on the nose.

I step back, fighting back the tears. Mum stops, staring at me.

'I'm so sorry, are you okay?'

'No, I'm not bloody okay.' I can't stop the tears now as I can feel a bump emerging above my eye.

'Ooh you're going to have a nasty black eye there,' comments Nick. I stare at him and run up the stairs.

When I get to my room, I slam the door shut and place my chair up against it. I ignore the bangs and shouts. They will get bored soon enough, which they do.

I cry myself to sleep, wishing I had a better life and a twin sister to take care of me.

CHAPTER ELEVEN

When I wake up, I am tempted to skip school completely. Not only do I have a black eye but my face is swollen with all the crying. It is only James' text message that gets me out of bed.

Can't wait to see you for our lunch date. I've got a few more ideas.

I'd forgotten we'd arranged to meet for a picnic in the field next to school. We're not supposed to leave our school site but it's easy to sneak out when no one is looking.

I need to get out of the house. I quickly get dressed, feed Marvin, and leave without having breakfast, before Mum wakes up.

Luckily, I had remembered to stuff some sunglasses in my bag before I left. Not sure how long I can get away with them at school for.

Mrs. Hargreaves, my form tutor, is the first to notice.

'Maddie, can you take those off. You know they're not school uniform.' I'm tempted to argue but I know there is no point with her. She is as stubborn as anything when it comes to following rules.

Reluctantly I peel them off my face. Mrs. Hargreaves has already turned away.

'Whoa, what happened to you?' says Chloe, attracting stares from neighbouring tables.

'I... er... fell into a wall.'

'A wall?' I know, I know, it's rubbish. I really should have thought up a better lie.

'In the garden.'

'Right,' she says slowly.

'I think it's kind of cool, like you've come out top in a fight.' Lauren says from in front of us. 'You know, what did the other guy look like type thing.' She laughs at her joke. Her smile lights up something inside me. I can't believe she actually spoke to me.

I see the look of shock when Mrs. Hargreaves finally turns around to face us. She doesn't say anything but I know she has seen me. She tries to hide it but her face has gone red and she is suddenly stumbling upon her words.

I try to sneak out at the end of form but the inevitable words come: 'Maddie, can I have a word?'

Mrs. Hargreaves sits down in her chair and asks me to pull up a chair next to her. I'd like nothing less than to do that but I can't tell her that. She bites her lip and begins playing with her hair, twirling round and round her finger, something I've noticed she does when she is nervous.

'How did you get that?' she asks pointing at my eye.

'I fell into a wall in the garden. I was... playing football.'

'Football?' Damn why did I say that? Everyone knows I hate sport.

'Yeah, my cousin was visiting.'

'Your cousin?' Why does everything I say sound like a lie?

'She's down for the week.'

'Maddie, you can tell me anything you know.'

'Um... yeah, of course.'

'If someone is hurting you...'

Great - now she thinks I'm being abused.

'No one is hurting me. It was an accident.' That much is true at least. I stand up. 'I have to go. I'm going to be late.'

'Okay but please feel you can talk to me whenever you need to.'

'I will,' I say rushing out of the room before she can add any more.

This is all I need. I should have stayed at home. She will probably fill in one of those forms about me now, I know how it works. In third period I am pulled out by Mrs. Drouett, who works in the pastoral office.

'Can we have a word?' she says, outside the room, with

eyes full of concern. I thought we already were having one. 'Could you just come to my office so we can talk in private?' It's a question but I don't have any choice in the matter.

What if I said no? What would they do then?

'Sure,' I answer, feeling a lot less breezy than I sound.

I follow her wordlessly down the brightly coloured corridor, filled with quotes like *Aim for the moon if you miss, you might hit a star.* They're supposed to inspire us. I'm not sure they do, not me anyway.

I've never been in Mrs. Drouett's office before. It's very neat and tidy with barely anything on her desk except a tray with one piece of paper in it and a photo frame with the photo of a blonde girl.

'Please sit down.' She gestures to the chair opposite hers. I try to avoid her gaze and instead study the numerous books on her shelf. *Safeguarding in Schools, Dealing with the Whole Child* (why would you only deal with part of a child?), and *Why They Think That Way,* among the titles.

'That's quite a black eye.'

'It's not what you think.'

'What do I think?'

'That I'm being physically abused at home.' She shifts uncomfortably in her seat. 'I'm not, by the way. It was an accident. My Mum got a little drunk last night, was dancing in the lounge, and accidentally hit me. It sounds crazy but that's the truth.' She has to believe that, surely.

'Does your Mum get drunk often?' Realising my mistake, I try to stay calm. Now it comes back to lying.

'Occasionally, you know like Mums do.' In reality, I have no idea what normal Mums do. I've not experienced one.

'Is there anything we can do to help?'

'No. Why should there be?'

'You don't have to do all this alone.' Do what alone? What is she talking about?

'Your Mum doesn't only occasionally get drunk does

she?' How does she know all this? I imagine a thick file full of notes from various teachers that they've put together as evidence waiting to convict Mum of this crime. I can't speak. I want to defend her but I can't find the words to say.

'She doesn't hurt me.'

Mrs. Drouett doesn't speak. It's clear from my face that she does, however unintentionally it is.

I try to dodge the questions the best I can, but it gets harder the more intently she stares at me. I'm lucky to get out of there alive.

...

James is waiting for me in the field behind the school as I sneak out through the gap in the fence.

'Whoa, what happened to you?' I had forgotten about the black eye.

'Mum. She got a bit carried away dancing last night.'

'Oh Maddie, I'm sorry.'

'Don't be. It's fine. It doesn't even hurt.' I sit down next to him.

'You okay? You look stressed.'

'You mean apart from the black eye? Just Mrs. Drouett being an idiot.'

'Who's Mrs. Drouett?'

'Never mind. It's not important. Tell me your idea. I need something happy to focus on?'

'We need to find your birth certificate.'

'Tell me something I don't know.'

'You can order new ones online.'

'You can?' How does he know all this?

'Yes come to mine and we'll do a search on the computer.'

'Then the adoption agency will tell us where she is?'

'Maybe. I'm not convinced it will be enough.'

'Why?'

'Hey, let's just find your birth certificate first. One step at a time.'

CHAPTER TWELVE

I've never been in James' room before. Whenever we've met before it's been in the park or downstairs in his house. Being in his room is weird and makes me feel uncomfortable. It's not just the nerdy science posters or the planets hanging from his ceiling, those are kind of cool in a smart boy way. It's that we are alone in a place where he sleeps, sitting on his Marvel duvet with his laptop.

Thankfully his parents are out. I couldn't cope with them being around.

I watch as James types away at the speed of lightening. This guy is amazing.

'How do you know how to do all this stuff?'

He just smiles and carries on typing. Clearly his school actually teaches him stuff.

I glance down at my phone, Mum is calling me.

'Get back home,' she says in a demanding way most unlike her.

'Why what's up?'

'Social services are coming round.'

'What now?'

'Yes now. You've got to help me tidy up.'

Before I can answer she has hung up. I sigh and jump up from James' bed.

'Everything okay?' he asks, looking up from the laptop.

'I have to go home. Mum is freaking out.' I really don't want to explain it all.

'Okay, well I can carry on searching.'

'Thanks you're the best.'

He stares at me as I stand next to his bed and for a moment feel like I should be pulling him into a kiss but I don't because it doesn't feel right. He's the best thing that's ever happened to me but he's not Lauren.

Mum is fuming when I get home, ready and waiting in

the lounge, pacing up and down. Hair all over the place, she doesn't look like she has slept well.

'Did you call social on me?'

'What? No, of course not.'

'Well, they called me. They wanted to arrange a visit. They think I'm an unfit mother.'

I don't argue with that but panic gnaws away inside my stomach. They can't take me away from her. I'd end up in some children's home or a foster home full of nasty kids.

'You must have said something.'

'I didn't say a word, I swear.'

'They're coming round tonight.'

I glance around the room, seeing it now from a stranger's point of view. DVDs lie out of their cases on the floor by the TV, clean clothes in a pile in the corner begging to be sorted out and cat fur sits in clumps where Marvin ran up and down this morning. The whole place needs a good tidy and hoover. The question is why hasn't Mum started yet. As always, it's down to me. I would tell her where to go but it's for my benefit that this meeting goes well.

'We had better get tidying up then,' I say decisively. Mum stands there, helpless, looking lost.

'I don't know where to start.'

'You do the kitchen. I'll do the lounge.' Her face brightens; she doesn't have to face this alone.

I hate cleaning and tidying. I don't see the point especially when no one comes round and Mum messes it up again so quickly. If she actually had a job, we could afford to get a cleaner, something I know would make us both extremely happy.

The downstairs is completely transformed when we are finished. You wouldn't believe it was the same place. Marvin, appalled by the noise of the vacuum cleaner, runs upstairs, no doubt to hide. Now he reappears, sniffing at the corners, probably wondering where all the mess is.

'As good as new,' I say when Mum has wiped the

surfaces and put away all the washing up. Her smile lights up.

Fortunately, Mum hasn't cracked open her first bottle of wine, which is pretty unusual for her. I usher her upstairs to get dressed, wondering if I can trust her to choose some decent clothes by herself. The last thing I need is her coming downstairs in one of those tiny skirts she likes to wear. It might work if it's a man but somehow, I doubt it would work with a grumpy old woman. In my experience, social workers usually are grumpy old women. I'm sure they do a great job but I'd rather they do it somewhere else.

I almost spit out the drink I'm sipping when Mum arrives back in the room wearing a long skirt and blouse. I don't think I've ever seen her looking so conservative.

'Don't look at me like that.'

'I'm not.'

'I feel like an idiot, like some stupid housewife.'

'That's what you want them to think.' She grunts. 'Don't say anything stupid.'

She raises her eyebrow but then smiles and nods. 'I'll try not to.'

We are left with half an hour before the dreaded social worker arrives. I've forbidden Mum to do anything to mess it up so she sits on the sofa playing on her phone. She taps furiously, her face set in concentration. Marvin on the other hand seems eager to mess up the lounge by dragging his toys out from the box.

'Damn it.' She chucks her phone on the sofa angrily.

'Stupid game.'

'It'll be fine Mum.' She smiles at me.

'What would I do without you?' I can think of many things she couldn't do without me but there are too many to list here. 'I love you. I'm sorry I'm such a crap Mum.'

'You're not a crap Mum.'

'Thanks. You're lying but I appreciate the gesture.'

The doorbell rings. Mum stares at me and clutches the

armrest. Marvin stops suddenly, considering whether to run away.

'It'll be fine. You answer it. You're the grown-up.'

'I can't,' she wails suddenly.

'You can Mum. Do it for us.' She breathes in and stands up sending a last look at me. I smile and nod at her. When did I become the grown-up?

I stay put on the single armchair, perching on the side of it. Marvin has let his curiosity get the better of him and is observing from the other side of the room. To my surprise, the social worker isn't a grumpy old woman but a fairly young one with the kindest smile I've ever seen.

'Hi, I'm Jackie,' she says, holding out her hand. I shake it with as much confidence as I can muster.

'Great to meet you.'

We all stand awkwardly in the lounge until she says 'Can I sit here?' pointing to the seat where Mum sat playing on her phone.

'Of course,' I answer.

'Cute cat. What's its name?'

'Marvin,' I answer, not wanting to be enticed by this woman's friendly conversation.

Mum sits at the other end of the sofa, as far away from the woman as she can be.. She folds her arms and crosses her legs away from Jackie.

'So, I'm just here to see how things are going.'

'We're all good,' Mum replies too quickly to be convincing.

'I'm sure you are,' says Jackie kindly. 'But we all struggle from time to time.' Mum looks terrified like wishes she could disappear into a hole. 'There's no shame in asking for help.'

Her voice is so hypnotising, it would be easy to tell her everything. I long for a mother like her. If only she could adopt me.

'Maddie, how did you hurt yourself?'

Before I can answer Mum jumps in with 'She fell down

the stairs.' I sigh and scrunch up my face.

'Maddie, is that what happened?' Mum's eyes are boring into me.

'Yes.' It's a bad lie.

'You told your teacher something different.' Mum looks like she is about to kill me. I feel like I'm going to cry. I can't handle this. I shouldn't have to defend Mum all the time like this.

'It was an accident.' Mum pulls at her skirt, her face tightly wound up. 'It's not a big deal.'

'You got drunk and hit her, didn't you?' she directs the question at Mum who is refusing to acknowledge her.

'She didn't mean to.'

'Becky, does this happen regularly?'

'No, I'd never hit Maddie,' she explodes, tears beginning to fall. That's when I know we're lost. 'I do drink but only a little bit and I know I'm crap at cleaning but it's not that bad really.'

Mentally I start preparing myself for that children's home. Tracey Beaker here we come.

Just when I think it can't get any worse, she adds: 'Please don't take Maddie away. I can't cope without her.' I bury my head in my hands. Now I want to hide.

'We're not going to take Maddie away.' I look up. They're not putting me in a home? 'But we are going to make some suggestions of things that you need to do.' 'Anything,' begs Mum.

'Firstly, we want you to join an AA group.' Mum sighs like a teenager and opens her mouth to object but closes it again. 'Secondly, we're going to send someone round to help you every week with housework and I'm going to visit weekly.' Mum puts her head back on the back of the sofa.

She knows she is defeated.

'How does that sound?'

'Sounds great,' I answer.

'Becky?'

'Yes, it's fine,' she says through gritted teeth.

'Great then I'll see you next week. Same time?'

'Yes,' Mum mutters.

'I'll see myself out. Lovely to meet you both.'

Neither of us speaks when she has left but I am waiting for the explosion, for it to be somehow my fault.

'I don't want to go to an AA group,' she utters quietly.

It's not what I was expecting.

'Why not?'

'It's probably full of weird old alcoholics.'

'And so what if it is, but it's probably not. I bet there are some lovely alcoholics out there.'

She laughs. 'Look at me, my new social life at AA.'

'You'll be fabulous Mum.'

CHAPTER THIRTEEN

My Saturday morning lie-in is rudely interrupted by the sounds of Taylor Swift singing loudly from my phone. It's been so long that I've forgotten what ringtone I chose. Even James only texts me. Who on earth is ringing me at this crazy hour? Who even does that any more?

I reach over and grab my phone. It's James. Why could he not just text me? Sometimes that boy is strange.

'Hi,' I answer sleepily.

'Sorry did I wake you?'

'It's fine. What's up?'

'I found your birth certificate.' I sit up.

'We can actually find her now,' I say.

'Don't get your hopes up with the agency but I do have some other ideas of how to find her. We can do this.'

When the call has ended, I lean back into my pillow, intent on getting more sleep, when Mum bursts in, letting Marvin into the room.

'Do I look okay?'

I sit up grumpily. 'For what?'

'My AA meeting. It's this morning.'

Her black skirt is a little short, but not as short as some she has, her pink top is acceptable. Not showing her cleavage and not too tight.

'Amazing.'

'Really? You're not just saying that?'

'No, I'm not. You look great.'

'Thank you. You're the best.'

'But brush your hair.'

'Was about to,' she smiles as she leaves my room. Finally, I can go back to sleep but of course, I can't. My brain is awake now and is refusing to stop and Marvin is pushing up against me, trying to headbutt me to death. I pull out my book from under the bed and start reading. I barely notice the slam of the front door as Mum goes to her meeting. Maybe seeing the social worker wasn't so bad after all. Just hope Mum is willing to change.

...

I meet James in the park in our usual spot. He waves his phone at me.

'Right here is how we order your birth certificate. Just want to check the details. When is your date of birth?'

'5th December 2006.'

'The 5th? Are you sure?' He has a puzzled look on his face.

'Yes why?'

'That's not what it says here.'

'Maybe it's someone else.'

'I don't think so.'

He passes me his phone. *Madison Phillips, date of birth 1st December 2006, mother's maiden name Phillips.*

'Wait, you're telling me that my birthday isn't 5th December?'

'It appears not.'

'But surely Mum would have known when my birthday was?'

James just stares at me.

'She's rubbish but who doesn't know your own child's birthday.' James shuffles his feet in the grass.

'I did look and see if I could find your sister's but her name could be anything now.'

I am still in shock from the revelation that for all these years I have been celebrating the wrong birthday. All those times I have been made to wait five whole days more. I am five days older than I thought.

'No one else is registered on that date.'

'When did she abandon her?' asks James. 'It must be in the news article.'

I take it out of my pocket. I really should take a picture of it in case I lose it. The date at the top of the article says the seventh of December. She kept my sister for seven whole days before she made the decision to get rid of one of us.

'But she must be registered somehow later though, right? Or she wouldn't be a legal person.'

'Oh yes, absolutely but they wouldn't have known her name or birth date so it could be completely different.'

I pace the grass, kicking a rogue dandelion.

'I'll contact the adoption agency and see what they can tell us now.'

My emotions are all over the place as I leave the park. I entered with one birthday and left with another. I don't know whether to feel upset that Mum got it wrong or angry at her but one thing I do know is I need to have it out with her.

James walks me home, through the rain, trying to avoid the many puddles that have suddenly appeared in the downpour.

'Do you want me to come in?' he inquires once when we are outside my house.

'No, it's fine. I need to speak to her alone.'

'Okay, text me later.'

'I will.' He stands there, clearly wanting to kiss me but looking so shy about it. I turn away so he doesn't but then feel bad.

'See you tomorrow.'

'James?' I say as he begins to walk home.

'Yes?'

'Thanks, for everything.'

'You're welcome.'

...

Nick is round when I get through the door. He's the last person I want to see. Seeing them snuggled up on the sofa is enough to make me sick.

'Hey babe, how's it going?' he shouts above the TV.

I respond with a fake smile.

'Where's Marvin?' No answer. 'Has anyone fed him?' I shake my head in anger and fill up his bowl in the kitchen just in case he does decide to make an appearance, though with Nick here it's unlikely.

'Mum, can I talk to you?' I say entering the room again.

'Hmm, yes,' she answers without even turning away from the TV.

'I mean in private.' She looks up, annoyed.

'But I'm in the middle of watching this.' It's an old Friends episode, probably one she has seen a thousand times, which she can pause anyway.

'Please,' I say quietly.

'Give your Mum a break. She's relaxing.' Bloody Nick.

He can stop interfering.

'Nothing to do with you.' He sits up, a big frown on his face.

'Don't speak to me like that.'

'I'm not being rude. It is nothing to do with you.'

'I don't like your tone-'

'Guys, guys,' Mum says, standing up with her arms out, sounding like one of the characters in Friends. 'Leave it. It's no big deal, Nick.' She grabs my arm and drags me into the kitchen. I throw a triumphant look at Nick but he's already watching TV again.

'What's so important that you made me get up?' she demands when we are in the kitchen. I hate the fact this house is so open plan. No doors to close. I can't even have a private conversation.

'When's my birthday?'

'What? You know when it is.'

'Do *you* know when it is though?'

'What kind of question is that? I'm your mother, I gave birth to you, of course I know when your bloody birthday is.'

'You told me it was 5th December.' She suddenly looks unsure of herself. 'Well, is it then?'

'I think so.'

'According to the records it isn't.' Her face is frozen. 'It's 1st December.'

'I was close.'

'You were close?' I don't care that my voice is so loud that Nick can probably hear. 'You were flipping close? It's my birthday and you don't even know when it is.'

'I had a lot going on then.' My eyes feel like they are going to pop out of my head.

'I don't believe you!'

'Don't shout at me.'

'I've been lied to all my life.'

'It wasn't a lie,' she says quietly. 'I really thought it was.'

'You're bloody hopeless.'

'Don't call your mother hopeless. She works hard for you.' Nick's voice is loud and clear from the lounge.

'None of your business,' I shout back.

Nick stands up and marches towards me like an army major intent on reaching his victim. He rests his hand on the cupboard behind me, trapping me in.

'It is my business.' I don't feel scared. All I see is this pathetic little man, trying to stand up for a drunk woman.

'Nick, don't,' Mum says feebly.

'She needs to know that you can't disrespect your elders.'

'You have no clue what it's like round here.' I duck under his arm and face him from the other side. 'You turn up five minutes ago and think you suddenly know it all. You don't.' His face is red. Clearly he doesn't like being told what to do by a girl. For a minute I wonder if he will hit me. His fist tightens but he punches the cupboard instead. Mum jumps and steps back, terror written all over her face.

As he walks away, Mum puts her hand on his shoulder to calm him down. Already she is choosing him over me.

CHAPTER FOURTEEN

'So the adoption agency is a no go.' James says down the phone.

'Why?'

'They went on about it not being enough. Anyway we don't need them.'

'We don't?'

'That nurse said a rich couple adopted your sister?'

'Right?'

'I've been doing some digging and there are two posh schools in Broadstairs. I vote we go down there and do some investigating. She's bound to go to one of them.'

'Go to Broadstairs?'

'Yes you up for it?'

'Of course. I can't believe it. We're going to see my sister. You're the best at ideas.'

'Don't go all gooey on me, we haven't found her yet.'

Scratching at the door and faint meowing indicate Marvin is wanting to get in. I can't resist that cute little fur ball. For him, I would climb a mountain so getting out of bed is not a hard feat. I scoop him up and get back into bed, knowing it won't last long as all he wants is food.

...

'I don't understand why we can't just go today,' I say.

'Because we have to plan this carefully and also come up with a reason why we are going away. Your mum may not care but my parents aren't just going to like me going to Kent for a few days.' He shrugs and smiles. 'Stop worrying. It'll happen.'

'You think so?'

'I know it will.'

I've said before that James is smart, super smart, and I know that, but sometimes he surprises me with his level of wisdom, like a wise old man yet not. Maybe that's what happens when you have parents who care.

To take my mind off things James treats me to the cinema, well actually his parents are paying. I wonder if they would be so keen on me if they knew the truth about Mum.

'What are we watching?' I left it all up to him.

'New Marvel film.'

'Awesome.' I don't like to admit that half the characters in Marvel are a mystery to me. Not all of us have the money to see every Marvel film out. I'm not going to be one of those annoying people who says *who's that?* every five minutes in a film.

Occasionally he grins at me as if to say *this is so good, isn't it?* I nod enthusiastically. It's great and all, but I don't have a clue.

When it's finished, I stand up ready to go.

'There's always a bonus scene at the end,' he says, still grinning.

'Oh yeah, right.' I sit down and take his hand in mine. At least if I have to sit here for longer, I might as well get closer. I lean my head on his shoulder. I could fall asleep right here, right now, dreaming of our happy life together. It would be so safe.

'That was so good, wasn't it?' He exclaims when we are outside the cinema.

'Amazing.'

'I love the bit where ...'

I am distracted by a familiar face behind him, Lauren. My heart quickens at the sight of her. She smiles while pushing her long blonde hair over her shoulder. Then she winks at me.

James turns to see her. 'Who's that?'

'Some girl from school.' Some girl I can't stop thinking about.

James walks me home, being the gentleman he is. I'm eager to get inside. He hasn't met Mum yet and I'm keen for it not to happen. Mum appears at the door as if by magic.

'Hello Maddie. And you must be James,' she slurs. Great just what I need. Drunk Mum on his real first meeting.

'Pleased to meet you Mrs Philips.' I applaud him for going along with the charade. He knows she was too drunk to remember they met at the funeral.

'Ooh you're posh aren't you.'

'I better go in,' I say, pushing Mum back in the door and throwing James a helpless sorry look.

'But we're just getting to know each other,' Mum protests.

'It's late and James has to get home.'

'I do but lovely to meet you though.' I'm grateful for his lies. Anyone else would run a mile.

'Why did you rush him off like that?' She scowls at me once the front door is shut. When I don't answer she adds: 'are you embarrassed by me?' What can I say but a blatant lie because of course I'm embarrassed by her. Who wouldn't be? Suddenly she starts crying, wailing like a child. I don't know where to look. 'I'm such an awful Mum.'

I shouldn't care but I do. I pull her to me in a hug and rub her back.

'You're not.'

It feels like I spend far too much time reassuring her.

CHAPTER FIFTEEN

Up to this point, I haven't told Mum anything about James and his ideas, but it seems like I should keep her in the loop, at least some of it anyway.

'Mum, James is going to help me find my sister..'

'Help you with what?' She is so busy reading her magazine that she barely looks up.

'He's going to help me find my sister,' I say louder so she can't avoid hearing it.

Still looking down she says, 'You still going on about that.'

Sometimes I want to shake Mum. She knows how important this is to me.

'Yes, I am. I need to find her. Anyway, he's got some good ideas.'

'Who has?'

I sigh. 'James.' She looks up, now interested.

'Like what?'

'He's found out the details of two posh schools. That nurse said a rich couple adopted her. She must be at one of those schools.'

'Have you found out her name?'

'Not yet.'

She suddenly looks all teary-eyed and seems to go into a dreamlike trance. 'Did he find out anything else?'

'Only my birth certificate but I told you about that already.'

She stands up, throwing the magazine to one side, making Marvin jump up from his bed.

'Please don't do this Maddie.'

'Why?'

'I can't cope with it all.' It's always about her. She tugs at her hair frantically.

'It'll be fine.' I want to add that she doesn't even have to be involved, that this is my search, not hers.

'I hate what I did. I can't face it.'

'Maybe it's time to do just that.' Now I'm starting to sound like some American counsellor. Who am I to advise her on what to do?

'You're so wise.' She stares at me with a new respect. Do I dare hope that this may be a turning point? 'Keep me posted.'

'Will do.' She sits back down and picks up the magazine again. 'How's the AA meetings going?'

'I didn't go yesterday. Too tired.' I try to hide the frustrated expression on my face. Maybe not a turning point quite yet.

When Nick turns up that night, unexpectedly, I am disappointed. I had hoped for a night with Mum, just the two of us.

'Hey babe,' he shouts coming into the room, already drunk. I glare up at him from my relaxed position on the sofa which suddenly feels not so comfortable. Mum rushes to the kitchen to make him some tea. I wish she'd act like that for me.

He plonks himself down on the sofa next to me, unbearably close, making me feel like I can't breathe. I shuffle to the side to give myself some distance from him but he sidles up closer. I continue to move towards the edge of the sofa but Nick isn't taking the hint until anger takes hold of me.

I leap up shouting, 'Can you not leave me alone?'

Nick's face shrinks back like no one has ever told him what they really think. 'Come on I'm only having a bit of fun.'

Mum re-enters the room, suspicion in her eyes. 'What's going on?' She directs the question at me.

I stand by the sofa, ready to make my escape. 'Why don't you ask Nick?'

Mum looks from Nick back to me. Nick sits back, knowing he has won this one.

'Never mind,' I add, walking away slowly.

'Later,' he whispers as I pass.

Hands shaking and legs like jelly I run up the stairs to the safety of my bedroom. I shut the door firmly, wishing I had a lock on it. How can I sleep now?

Finally, I manage to drift off after hours of unsuccessfully trying to distract myself with my phone. I am awoken by the sound of my door opening. Nick stands virtually naked in the doorway.

I jump up.

'Get out,' I yell, shrinking back towards the window.

'Nowhere to run now.'

'Get out,' I repeat. 'Get out, get out, get out.' Each time I am getting louder and louder. 'Leave me alone.'

I barely notice Mum sleepily enter the room. 'What's going on?'

'Sorry I got lost looking for the bathroom,' he says innocently.

'He's lying,' I yell so loudly it makes Mum clutch her head.

'He said it was a mistake.'

'Why do you always believe him over me?' I shout. Suddenly I've had enough. I push past them both and run down the stairs.

'Where are you going?' shouts Mum.

I don't answer but carry on. Mum runs after me, standing at the open front door. 'Come back Maddie. It's dark out there.'

'I don't care,' I shout. 'I'd rather get murdered on the street than spend another night in the same house as him.'

All the noise has made Doris next door twitch her curtains but I don't care. I don't think about the consequences, I just continue shouting.

'Get out of the street,' Mum hisses. 'Everyone's going to hear you.'

'I don't care,' I shout.

Frustrated, Mum shuts the door, leaving me standing in the middle of the road in my pyjamas, wondering what to do next. I hadn't thought this through properly. I could go to Great Aunt Margaret's but it's a long walk at this time of night and I don't actually want to get murdered on the street. I decide to take my chances and go back inside but this time I push my desk up against the inside of my bedroom door. There's no way he's getting in now.

Half an hour later, I hear a knock at the door. I freeze, pondering if I should answer it or let Mum get it which is probably not going to happen. The knocking gets louder and more insistent until I hear the words, 'Police, can you open the door?'

Damn it, we're in trouble now. I push the desk away from my door, pull my dressing gown on and run down the stairs. Mum peeps out of her bedroom.

'I'll deal with it,' I say, shooing her away. She gladly shuts the door again.

When I open the door, a very tall policeman is standing there with a shorter woman police officer.

'Is everyone alright ma'am? There have been reports of shouting.'

'It's all fine. Me having a moment, you know.' He doesn't smile at my little joke or even look remotely amused.

'Can we come in?' he says without a single movement.

'What now?'

'Yes, we want to check everything is okay.'

I sigh and hold the door open for them. The policeman walks purposely into the lounge, followed by the lady officer. His eyes dart around quickly. I have no idea what he's looking for but I suspect he will be disappointed if he thinks he will find anything exciting here.

'Anyone else in?'

'Only my mum. She's in bed.'

He nods his head and turns to me. 'You sure you're okay?'

'I'm fine. We were having a little argument. It's all good now.'

He hands me a card. 'Call me if you ever need anything.'

'Thank you,' I answer smiling sweetly at him.

When I shut the door after letting them out, I let out a huge sigh of relief. Another crisis averted.

CHAPTER SIXTEEN

The next morning Jackie turns up at the door. She smiles sympathetically at me. She knows.

Mum is lying on the sofa nursing a hangover. Thankfully Nick had to leave early. Mum does not look good. There is no way she can come in.

'Mum's not well.'

'Sorry to hear that,' she says but I can see she doesn't believe me. 'Can I come in and talk to you?'

'It's not a good time.'

'I won't be long.' She is insistent, I don't feel I can say no. I stand aside with the door wide open, regretting even answering it.

I could run out the door now, go live on the street or at James' house. Maybe they could adopt me if I beg them.

'What you doing here?' I hear an angry voice coming from the lounge. The beast has awoken. When I rush into the room, Mum is half sitting up, hair strewn all over the place.

'Good morning, Becky. It's good to see you.'

'It's not great to see you.'

'Perhaps you better go upstairs and let me have a chat with Maddie.'

'So you can turn her against me. No way. Nothing happened last night before you ask.' I put my hands on my head.

'Mum, it's okay.' I take her arm and pull her up. She's going up whether she likes it or not.

'Don't want to.' I drag her out of the room.

'Go lie down. You'll make things worse.' She starts crying. 'Take Marvin with you. He needs a cuddle.'

'I'm sorry Maddie. I'm a terrible Mum,' she wails, so loudly that I'm sure Jackie can hear her.

Once I've seen her into bed, with Marvin keeping an eye on her, I make the long trek back downstairs, wishing we had fewer stairs.

Jackie is sitting on the sofa with a photo album from the shelf on her lap, turning each page slowly. She looks up when she sees me and smiles.

'These are lovely photos.' It is a photo book I made one

Christmas of me and Mum. I wanted Mum to be overwhelmed with joy at the sight of it but she only said a simple word of thanks and put it to one side, focusing instead on the new phone she'd bought. I put my heart and soul into making that. 'You were a cute baby.'

'Thanks.' She places it back on the shelf, wedged in between the CDs and the few books Mum has.

'Heavy night last night?'

'Nothing I can't handle.'

'You shouldn't have to handle this though, should you?'

I take a deep breath. Tears are threatening to show themselves and embarrass me. I must hold it together.

'She doesn't mean any harm.'

'She might not be malicious but she is neglecting you.'

'I'm fifteen. I can look after myself.'

'How about you go and stay with your Great Aunt Margaret for a while?' My body feels frozen and rigid suddenly.

'Forever?'

'More like respite care.' She can dress it up with her fancy words but I don't like the sound of it at all.

'I'm fine here.'

'But you're not coping with everything.' She glances round at the mess in the lounge, Mum's underwear left by the side of the room, hoping for some magic fairy to wash them, the kitchen with its dirty crockery spilling out onto the dining room table.

'It's a bit of a mess but we've been busy that's all.'

'Maddie, it's not your job.' The tears again bubble up inside me. This time I can't stop them. The first one escapes, slides down my face like a traitor.

'I don't mind,' I mutter. 'Mum's sorting herself out. She's going to AA.'

'But she's not, is she? She went to one and then didn't go to anymore.' It wasn't only one she missed, was it? All those times she went out, saying she was going but probably went drinking.

'Can't I stay with a friend instead?'

'It's possible but that would take a bit more sorting out.' 'Why?'

'We'd have to find out if they are suitable.' Surely anywhere has to be more suitable than this? 'Will you come with me and I'll take you to your aunt's house?'

'What now? But I haven't packed.' Panic is rising within me as I try desperately to think of an excuse as to why I can't go. 'Mum needs me.'

'Believe me, it'll be better for you if you go somewhere else. She won't have to worry about you and it might spur her into changing.' I can't imagine Mum seeing it like that.

'What am I going to tell her?'

'Leave that to me.'

'Can I take Marvin with me?'

Jackie smiles. 'Of course.'

I pack up, with no notice, the things that are most precious to me, in one bag. Mum's raised voice stops me. She's told her. 'You're not taking my baby,' Mum cries at Jackie.

'It's only for a few days.'

'I've already lost one baby. I can't lose another. It'll kill me.'

I don't hear Jackie's response but she doesn't spend too long placating her. She marches out and is outside my door hurrying me on. 'We need to get going, Maddie.'

'I need to get Marvin.' He's hiding under the bed in Mum's room, his big eyes willing me not to put him in the pet carrier. 'Don't worry we're not going to the vets,' I whisper but he backs away. I move slowly towards him and grab him with one lunge and shove the scrambling creature into the carrier.

I try to block out Mum's look of devastation as I leave the room.

One last look at my bedroom and my familiar belongings. Will I ever see it again?

CHAPTER SEVENTEEN

Great Aunt Margaret's house is hotter than ours. She has her heating up way too high. I feel like I'm being suffocated. Every five minutes she's checking in, asking how I am. I want to tell her to leave me alone but I know she's trying to be kind. I've waited so long for someone to care about me but suddenly it feels too much.

Marvin is stretching out on the rug in my bedroom like he agrees with me. He's not used to this heat either. I rub his tummy, and he rolls over to one side throwing his paws in the air.

'I know you're missing her but it's for the best.' Margaret says standing in the doorway. Like that's supposed to make me feel better. She doesn't have a clue how I'm feeling. 'If you get dressed, I'll take you to school.' I could walk but it's a long way now. Not just round the corner like it used to be. Walking requires organisation that I don't have right now.

Her car is as hot as her house. I am glad when we get to school. I assume Mrs. Hargreaves has heard by the way she is smiling sympathetically at me, her eyes full of concern. This is her fault. She tries to talk to me normally but the edge on her voice is a big giveaway. I smile a small smile that doesn't mean anything except *I hate you*. Surely, she gets that?

'Mrs. Hargreaves needs to get a life,' comments Lauren, coming up from behind me. 'Don't let her bother you.' It is like she can read my mind.

'Thanks,' I answer, wanting to say more but failing to get any more words out.

'See you later,' she adds, bouncing off. I stand and watch her for a minute.

No one talks for the rest of the day. I wish I could go home, real home. During French, I manage to escape to the toilet. The teacher's usually so strict about not letting us go whatever, but clearly she's heard about my home life too. May as well use it to my advantage.

I take my phone out of my pocket and sit in the cubicle and text James.

I hate my life.

I don't expect a response straight away.

When you find your sister, it will be great.

How come you're texting at school?

Haha, could ask you the same question. I'm in bed, ill.

No! What's wrong?

Just man flu. I can hear him laughing from his house. *I'll be fine though.*

Glad to hear it. We got a trip to Broadstairs soon.

That school of yours is pretty slack letting you text in lessons.

I'm in the toilet.

Okay, no details please.

Wasn't planning to.

I love you.

What?

I said I love you. Do you? Really?

I do. I'm not sure how I'm supposed to respond. Does he expect me to say it back? *You don't have to say it back.*

Okay

He sends me a barrage of heart emojis that fill the screen.

He's so sweet but I don't think I feel the same.

I better go before they send a search party.

Come by after school.

Will your Mum let me?

Both parents are on late shifts.

The thought of seeing James keeps me going through the rest of the day.

After school I'm straight round James' house. Living at Great aunt Margaret's house actually has an advantage.

James answers the door in his Star Wars dressing gown. He looks kind of cute.

'What if we find out where your sister lives?'

James begins as we hunt around the kitchen for food.

'We go there of course.'

'But we can't just turn up.'

'Why not?'

'It will be a huge shock.'

'She's fifteen not eighty. She's hardly going to have a heart attack.'

'I think you should write her a letter.'

'A letter?' Who does he think we are? Some nineteenth century women? Who writes letters these days?

'You know it's sensible.' Ugh sensible!

'I know, I know, but I want to see her. What if she refuses to even meet me?'

'*Then* we stalk her.' He grins.

James orders pizza. I stare at him in awe as he effortlessly navigates the App. I forget to tell Great Aunt Margaret where I am. I'm so used to doing things my way. She's not happy when she rings me.

'It's common courtesy to let someone know if you're going to be late home.'

'Sorry, I forgot. I'm only next door though,' I answer grumpily.

'It's okay. Go and enjoy your pizza. I'll see you later.' James is giving me that look.

'What?' I ask.

'She cares about you.'

'Don't start.' He reaches his hand out to grab mine. I move mine out of the way. 'You're right but I hate it when you're right.'

'I know you do,' he laughs. 'You're bloody determined sometimes.'

James helps me write a letter that evening. He wants to be prepared for when we do find out her address. I have no idea where to even start. I don't want to sound like an idiot. No one wants an idiot for a twin sister. James berates me yet again for being so down on myself but I've never had anyone to big me up, not until James.

When I get back to Great Aunt Margaret's I am already dreaming of my twin sister and imagining her reaction when she sees it.

Marvin is sitting quietly in my bedroom, completely unlike him. He, too, must be missing home.

CHAPTER EIGHTEEN

Loud knocking from the front door makes me jump. Someone is impatient. I peer out of the window. Mum. What is *she* doing here? I run down the stairs, several at a time, almost tripping down the last few.

'Slow down,' Great Aunt Margaret calls as she shuffles along the hallway to get the door. 'You're going to kill yourself.'

I ignore her and rush past her to answer the door. Margaret looks confused but her expression clouds over when she sees who it is.

'Maddie,' Mum exclaims loudly, pulling me roughly into a hug. I wish she had come over sober, I can already smell her breath.

'Mum,' I answer, not knowing what else to say.

She pushes me away and stares at me. 'You've got bigger.'

'It's only been a week,' I laugh. She shrugs. She has never commented on my height before.

'What are you doing here Becky?' interjects Margaret. 'You know you're not supposed to turn up like this.'

'I wanted to see my baby. That's not a crime, is it?'

'Of course not, but there are rules.'

'Sod the rules. Rules are stupid anyway.'

I know Margaret is right but I don't like it. Part of me wants to invite Mum in, the other part of me wants her to go away because I can't handle Margaret's reaction to this.

'Let me talk to her outside for five minutes,' I say, smiling at my great aunt pleadingly.

'I'm not supposed to—'

'I know but I won't tell. Pleeease it'll be only for five minutes, I promise.' She nods as I hurry outside, pushing Mum to one side of the lawn behind the bush, where we can talk in private.

'It's so good to see you,' Mum manages through tears.

'I'm sorry-'

'That doesn't matter.' She looks hurt and like she will cry even more. 'James and I are going to Broadstairs.' She stops, clutches hold of a nearby branch as though that will stop her falling over. 'That's amazing. When are you going?'

'I don't know yet but don't tell Great Aunt Margaret,' She smiles. I know she will do anything to have one up on her aunt.

I don't tell her about the letter, I don't want her pouring cold water on the idea as well.

'Not sure yet. I want to go and see her but I have no money.'

I don't tell her about the £50 I still have stashed in my room upstairs.

She takes her tiny rucksack off her back and rustles around in it for a minute before pulling out her wallet. 'I don't have much but here take some money. Go find her. I'll come next time. I can't face it yet.'

I take the money like it is gold dust and hug it close to me. I know I shouldn't do this. It's wrong in so many ways but I have to do it. If I don't, I'll always wonder. Even if it's just a quick glimpse from afar, I have to see her. Though in reality, I know that I'll never be satisfied with a glimpse.

Mum changes the subject, rattling on about Nick and how she should dump him as he's annoying her, promising me that she has been to some AA meetings. I'm not sure I believe her anymore but I appreciate her lying to me.

Great Aunt Margaret smiles at me anxiously when I go back in, alone.

'All good,' I say, feeling the money in my pocket.

She only replies to say, 'Great.'

Why do adults do that? Say great when they mean the complete opposite. It's obvious she is completely annoyed at Mum, why not come out and say it? I can handle it. I sometimes feel like Margaret treats me too much like a kid.

She doesn't realise I've been fending for myself for so long, I barely know what it's like to be a child.

I decide to go and speak to James in person. I can't deal with his sensible replies by text.

'I want to go this weekend. I know you think it's a stupid idea but I'm going anyway. You can come with me or I'll go alone.'

I wait for the well thought out arguments to persuade me otherwise but all he says is,

'Okay.'

'Really?'

'You've clearly made up your mind so I won't try and change it and I will come with you, at the weekend.'

'You will?' He nods, grinning furiously. 'This weekend?'

'I guess. I'm sure I can make up some excuse to Mum and Dad.'

'You're the best.' I hug him without thinking. He places his hand on my back awkwardly.

'You're pretty great too,' he whispers, words that should sound like music to my ears but instead send a shiver of fear up my spine.

CHAPTER NINETEEN

The day has arrived, excuses have been thought up. We are finally going to Broadstairs to find my actual twin sister. Several times I want to pinch myself that it's not a dream. I don't know how I will react when I see her. In my head I have imagined all kinds of scenarios, some I don't like to think about too much because they are not how I would like it to go.

'You ready?' James is at the door, his rucksack full of lunch for us. I nod, trying to stop my hand from shaking.

'So nice of you to take Maddie on this weekend break with your parents.' I can't tell her the truth, not yet. Great Aunt Margaret beams at him. She loves James. He is the kind of boy anyone would be happy to have for tea. She trusts him completely. Maybe she shouldn't. An innocent face can't always be trusted.

'You will look after Marvin, won't you?'

'Of course. Don't you worry.'

I walk quickly to the train station for fear of Great Aunt Margaret finding out our little plan, paranoid I know, but I feel like I have lies written all over my face.

As if he can read my mind he says: 'Relax, no one has any clue what we're doing and Mum and Dad went to their conference last night so they'll be none the wiser.' He reaches for my hand, a reassuring touch that instantly calms my nerves. As we board the train, it's like a weight has been lifted from me, for now anyway. I lay my head back on the headrest and close my eyes. Finding twin sisters is stressful work.

A rustling from James makes me open my eyes.

'Haribo?'

I take a red heart and chew it slowly, hoping my heart is not about to be ripped out by the only family member I want to care about.

It takes about an hour to get to London and change to

another train. I'm hungry despite having breakfast less than two hours ago. I stuff a chocolate bar into my mouth as we stride across to the next platform to get our final train.

'You okay?' I love that James cares so much. Makes me feel guilty as I think he loves me more than I love him. I brush that to one side. I need him now. I'll deal with that problem later.

'I'm good, I think.' He smiles and delves into his sweet bag once more. 'Why do you stay with me? And come with me on my escapades?' Instantly I regret asking. What if he says he loves me?

'You're worth it and everyone needs a helping hand. You've been through a rough time. You deserve this.'

Sympathy, not love? Too many thoughts going through my head.

When the train arrives in Broadstairs, the compartment is suddenly starting to feel really hot. I can't think straight. What if we get lost? What if she's not home? What if she is away for the weekend? Money spent on nothing.

The fresh sea air hits me when we step outside the station.

'How about we walk to the seafront first? Get some lunch and sit on the beach with some chips?'

'Great idea.' It'll help me calm down.

It's a ten-minute walk to the seafront. I've never been to Broadstairs but I can see why it's popular with the tourists, the beach is stunning. Perfect golden sand. Would be even better if you didn't have the screaming kids on the swing boats and trampolines but you can't have it all. The jetty on the left-hand side has a kind of gloomy feel to it that I don't like.

'First stop, chips.' James drags me to the nearest fish and chip shop. About time, I'm starving. We take our chips and walk down the multiple steps to the beach and sit down in one of the few empty spots, facing the sea. There is something about the sea that is so calming. I reach for a chip but am startled by something hitting me on the hand. It's a massive great seagull and he's run off with several of my chips in his beak.

'Oi,' I shout after him, but he's already landed further along the beach and being swamped by what seems like millions of other seagulls. James is rolling about laughing. 'I wanted those chips.'

'Someone should have warned us about the bloody giant seagulls,' laughs James.

I clutch the rest of my chips preciously. They are not getting any more of them. I seal the top of the bag, leaving only enough room to get two fingers in, enough to pull out one chip at a time. James smirks at my attempts to stop further attacks.

'I'm sorry, I shouldn't laugh but it's hilarious.'

'For you maybe,' I answer grumpily but can't help laughing. 'How did they get so big?'

'Um… do you really need me to answer that. I suspect they are filling up on unsuspecting tourists' chips and sandwiches.' He points at a seagull in the air with a whole sandwich. I am so shocked that I almost drop my bag of chips, almost. They are not having them.

When we are done, James gets up.

'Ready?'

'No, but let's do this.' I am determined, I will find her.

James is meticulous with details. He has the names and addresses of both schools typed up and printed out with directions on how to get to both.

The first is a short walk from the town centre. The school is named after a very rich man who donated lots of his money to the town, so James tells me. I feel intimidated by the sight of it.

'It looks like a manor house. It's massive.'

James merely smiles.

As we get closer, there are flowers attached the iron gates and photos of a boy, a very good looking one at that. Flowers that spell out Sam lie on the ground.

'I wonder who he was,' I say out loud.

We stand by the locked gate.

'So what now?' I ask, sure that James must have a plan. Before he can express it a voice from behind says: 'Ella?'

I stare blankly at a girl about my age with her hair all in braids and shake my head.

'Sorry you must have the wrong person,' I say. She looks like she has seen a ghost.

'But-'

'You know her twin?' James pipes up suddenly and I realise this girl must think I'm her.

Her confused expression widens. 'I don't understand,' she says.

I don't even know where to start but fortunately James finds the words.

'This is Maddie. Her twin sister was adopted at birth.' I notice he doesn't mention the abandoned outside a toilet bit. 'We found out she lives here. Do you know her?'

The girl nods slowly. I desperately want to shake her and find out everything but I don't want to scare her off.

'I didn't know she was adopted. I can't believe how much you look like her apart from-'

'Apart from what?'

'Never mind. Her name is Ella.'

Ella, I let the sound of my sister's name go round my head. I know her name!

'Do you know where she lives?' James asks cautiously.

'I do but I don't know if I should give you her address?'

'It's not like we're complete strangers,' I say smiling awkwardly.

'I guess not and I'm sure she'd love to meet you.'

She pulls out a piece of paper from her bag and writes down an address.

'And who are you?' asks James, wondering why he would ask. I couldn't care less.

'My name's Kaitlyn. I'm a friend of hers.'

...

Ella's house is twenty minutes' walk from the seafront. I'm glad I had those chips to give me energy. It's a busy road, fortunately, so we can spy on her unsuspectingly. I have no intention of knocking today. I only want to see her from a distance. Maybe tomorrow, I'll be brave enough to meet her.

We position ourselves by a tree, hopefully not suspicious or weird.

'Which one is her house?' I ask, hoping I don't sound too stressed.

James points at the house diagonally opposite to where we are. The house is large, surely too big for a small family unless she had brothers and sisters. The thought fills me with dread, other siblings fighting for her attention. Maybe she loves them more than me. Before I can analyse the house anymore the front door opens. I grab James' arm, probably too hard, and stare at him. I feel like I can't breathe. He smiles to reassure me.

An older lady steps outside, blonde straight hair, looking a bit frazzled. She glances around her nervously, seeking what exactly.

'Come on everyone,' she shouts. 'We're going to be late.'

A girl in a wheelchair follows, looking fed up, she has brown hair, she looks like… me!

'It's Ella,' I gasp. 'Why's she in a wheelchair?' James shrugs, seeming as bewildered as me.

CHAPTER TWENTY

I have so many questions and I want to bombard her with them now. I have to fight the desire to run up to her and demand she tells me everything but all I can do is stare. A very tall man with a receding hairline pushes Ella out of the house. He bends down and whispers something in her ear, she gives out a little smile. Her Mum stands by the car, stone-faced.

'Darling, it'll be fine,' he says loudly in a booming voice. He has a voice that instantly commands respect.

I watch, frozen to the spot, as Ella transfers herself out of the wheelchair and into the car. She seems to wince slightly at the movement but doesn't appear to be in any pain. It is then that I realise underneath all the blankets, she has no legs.

I gasp again, feeling like I will cry.

'What happened?' I whisper to no one. James doesn't reply. What is there to say to this?

With the family all safely installed in the car, it drives away. I hide behind the tree. I don't want her to see me, not like this.

'What now?' I ask of James who is still staring at the house. 'James?'

He turns to me. 'No idea. Bloody hell, poor girl.'

'I know, imagine having no legs.' I shake my head. 'We can't sit here all day.' I am so reliant on James and his grand plans that now he's frozen in shock I don't know what to do.

'Let's go back to the beach and work it out,' he says suddenly, regaining his sense of know-how.

We wander slowly back through town, through the little knick-knacky shops selling different varieties of shell necklaces and shell ornaments, and past the cafes with the smell of fried cheese wafting out of the windows.

'Do you think she had an accident?' I blurt out, making

James stop.

'Possibly.'

'Well, she can't have been born like it.'

'Maybe that's why your mother abandoned her.' My eyes widen at the thought. 'Sorry, I shouldn't have said that. I'm sure she wouldn't do that.'

'No, you're right. She could have. I wouldn't put it past her.'

'Sorry,' he replies simply. We both know what she is capable of. James may not have known her as long as me but he has got a pretty good idea of her already.

'No, she wouldn't do that.' I don't know who I'm trying to persuade. 'The big question is what are we going to do now?'

'Do you really want to knock on her door now and go *hey there, long lost twin sister here*?'

'No, I don't.' It seemed like a good idea before but now it's the worse idea ever. She has got a lot to deal with and the last thing she needs is her messed-up twin sister. 'I think we should go home.'

'Home? Really? Just like that?' He touches my forehead. 'Are you feeling okay? Little Miss determined-to-do anything-to-meet-her?' I brush him off.

'Yes really. This is all wrong. I can't turn up now. I can't barge into her life unannounced. I don't know what I'm going to do but being here is wrong.' He is silent. He takes my hand and squeezes it.

We reach the promenade in no time. I tend to walk fast when I'm stressed. James struggles to keep up and has to jog alongside me.

'Let's walk. We don't have to rush into anything. We can still enjoy the day here in Broadstairs.' I nod, not trusting myself to say anything without crying. The last thing I want to do is blub in front of James.

We turn right and head towards the clock tower that looks like it has been here for centuries, only the painted exterior appears to have been updated. Then I see her, I grab James' arm and point.

'Look it's Ella.'

Her Dad is wheeling her along the promenade past the clock tower at a great speed. She can't see me. I stand and watch her. Her hair is shorter than mine. Suddenly I get an urge to talk to her. I start running towards her, it's reckless I know.

'What are you doing?' James calls, panic in his voice.

'I have to see her,' I call back, turning only slightly before carrying on. I run frantically like I'm competing in sports day or something. James is panting behind me, barely able to speak.

'You can't do this,' he shouts. 'Stop ... and ... think about what ... you're doing.'

I don't care anymore. I have almost reached her when she turns the corner and her dad pushes her furiously straight towards a house opposite the beach. I stop, it's too late. I can't approach her outside someone's house.

James finally catches up to me and grabs my arm. 'You can't do this.'

The threatened tears fall out of my eyes. 'I know, but I wanted to see her, to talk to her,' I sob. I can't stop them now. James cradles me in his arms like I am a baby while I cry uncontrollably.

'It'll happen. Give it time. You can still post the letter though.'

We find a post box and put my letter in it. I could have posted it through her door but I don't want her to think I was at her house.

I can't bear to stay in this pretty seaside town anymore so we head back to the train, our exciting trip over already. I lean my head on James' shoulder as we rattle out of the station and past the endless fields.

It feels like my heart is breaking.

CHAPTER TWENTY-ONE

A week passes and I try to put the events of Broadstairs out of my mind. As if I haven't been through enough, today is a supervised visit with Mum. It feels weird to see Mum with all these social workers in the room. It's awkward and I hate it. As much as I have always longed for someone to love me properly. I miss her. Great Aunt Margaret tries so hard but she's not the same, she's not Mum.

'How's it been?' she asks in an unusually caring voice. I shrug, what to say? I can't very well tell her everything that's happened, or can I? I can't come right out and ask her if she abandoned Ella because she had no legs - can I?

'I've seen Ella,' I whisper.

'What?' she says so loudly that the social workers turn, concerned expressions on their faces. 'How is she?' I study her face for clues that she knows about her disability.

There's nothing for it, but it to come out with it: 'She's disabled.'

'What?'

'In a wheelchair.'

'Nooo, she can't be. She was fine when I left her.'

'You didn't know?'

'How would I know? Wait you think I abandoned her because she was disabled.' I don't answer. 'I may be an awful mother but seriously I'm hurt you would think that.' She stands up and paces the room, clearly highly agitated. 'Sorry, I didn't know.'

'Neither did I,' she shouts.

'Everything okay?' asks Jackie.

'Fine,' answers Mum, sitting back down. 'I know I've done nothing to give you confidence in me but I swear I did not abandon her because she was disabled. You do believe me, don't you?'

'I do.'

She grabs hold of me and hugs me, crying.

'Did you speak to her?' she asks finally when she has cried it out.

'No, I couldn't, not yet. I wasn't ready but I desperately wanted to.' She nods as though she feels the same.

'Let me know if you do. I'd... like to see her.'

'I will.' I wonder if she has more chances of seeing her other daughter than she does me. What are the rules regarding that? I have no idea.

Jackie drives me back to Great Aunt Margaret's house. A huge cloud of sadness descends over me in the car. I miss my Mum. However crap she was, I still miss her. My world has been turned upside down and I need her more than ever now.

'When can I go home?' I ask quietly.

'When we're certain that your mum is going in the right direction.'

'But she's going to AA meetings, isn't that enough?'

'She's going sometimes. She needs to attend every week not only when she feels like it.' I can't argue with that. I can't defend someone who won't help themselves. 'I know you miss her but you are in a safe place now.'

'I was never in danger.'

'It may not have felt like that but this is for the best. You'll understand one day.'

I'm not sure I agree with her. How can I ever understand all this?

Neither James nor Great Aunt Margaret can get me out of this mood I'm in since we got back from Broadstairs. I'm miserable and I no longer see the point in anything anymore. Even my teachers are treating me like I'm a fragile doll, asking how I am all the time. They have no clue what it's like, no one does.

A week after we got back, Great Aunt Margaret appears in the kitchen with a letter.

'It's for you.' She hands it to me with a big grin on her face.

I take it carefully, seeing the Kent postmark. It's from Ella. I told Great Aunt Margaret what happened that day in Broadstairs. She was a bit angry but she understood why we sneaked off and promised not to tell James' Mum and Dad. She thinks I'm very mature to come home and wait for the right time. Could now be the right time? Margaret nods at me, smiling

'Open it.'

I tear it open, no longer able to wait. I pull it out being careful not to rip it:

Dear Maddie, Sorry I've taken so long to reply to you. I had to sort out my feelings. That's unfair, I know, you probably desperately want us to meet (she has no idea) *but it was a shock and I was afraid of how you would react to me. I need to tell you that I'm disabled, I have no legs. Six months ago, I had an accident and lost my legs. It's a long story, I may tell you one day, but it was horrific. I can't do all the things I used to be able to do. That makes me so sad. I'm no fun to be around. I didn't want you to meet this version of me. Sometimes I hate myself, how can I expect anyone else to like me? It's also tricky as I can't tell Mum and Dad right now, it's complicated. So, if we meet, I'll need to do it without them knowing but it's going to take a bit of planning and sneaking around, not easy to do when your parents have to do pretty much everything for you.*

Anyway, I'll understand if you don't want to meet me.
This is my phone number if you want to text me.
Ella x

Her phone number is written at the bottom in very neat handwriting, so much neater than mine.

'What does it say?' I had forgotten Margaret was standing there, staring at me this whole time, holding Marvin and tickling his tummy.

'She wants to meet up, I think. She told me she's disabled and it's complicated.'

'I can imagine but I'm sure her parents will help her.'

'That's the thing; she doesn't want them to know, so

we have to somehow do it without them.'

'Do you think that's wise?' I shrug. Who knows what is wise anymore.

'I have to go with what she wants. She knows them.'

'I'll help you all I can.'

'I don't want to tell Mum, not yet. I want to meet Ella myself first.'

'Of course, I understand.'

I text Ella the minute I'm upstairs, alone.

I'd love to meet you, Maddie

The reply comes instantly. *Great. I'll make some arrangements and let you know.*

So formal, so weird. There is much more I want to say but don't feel I can.

Later that afternoon James takes me out for a walk to the park and I fill him in.

'That's amazing that she wants to meet.'

'I'm scared. What if she hates me?'

'Why would she? You're her twin. You must have some connection.'

'You would think.'

The meeting is arranged for two weekends time. This time Margaret is going to drive me. James can't come as he has a wedding to go to but he has already done so much. Margaret promises she won't interfere. She is so kind. We are meeting in a park near her house. Her friend has agreed to help her. I wonder what excuses she has had to make to her parents. It feels weird calling them her parents, as they aren't really, not biologically.

I don't sleep the night before, the possibilities of what could happen exploding through my mind at great speed. I need to sleep, but my mind says no. I'm going to be a mess. She'll hate me. She'll never speak to me again. It'll be a complete disaster. Why am I even doing this?

CHAPTER TWENTY-TWO

With Marvin safely deposited at James' house, we set off. When I spoke to Mum she sounded upset and told me not to go, that it would open too many wounds but how can I not see my twin?

The drive down south goes smoothly despite Great Aunt Margaret's fears of lots of traffic on the M25.

'Such an awful road,' she comments. 'No end of problems there. Nearly always stuck on it.' I nod pointlessly as she can't see me. 'You excited?'

'I think. Also terrified.'

'It'll be grand. I'm sure she'll love you.'

'What if she doesn't?'

'Then she's missing out.' That possibility is not worth thinking about. I couldn't bear it if she didn't want to know me.

The familiar sights of Broadstairs soon appear before us, the beautiful beach, the bustling market stalls along the top, the ice cream parlour.

'Looks like an interesting place,' comments Great Aunt Margaret.

She continues, driving away from the seafront, eager to find the car park that she'd researched. When we get out of the car, she reaches for her phone to search for the directions to the seafront. What is it about old people and phones? It seems to take them forever. However, we make it down to the park next to the seafront in no time.

'I'll go do some shopping. You call me when you're done.' Thankfully she is understanding and knows exactly when I need her to go away.

'Thanks, and thanks for bringing me down here. I really appreciate it.'

'No problem.'

The park is empty, I am early. I sit on a bench and reach for my phone, anything to distract me. A few minutes later Ella is wheeled up. She smiles slightly. The closer she gets, the more I realise how identical we are apart from the slightly different hairstyle and her more conservative clothes.

She nods at her friend who leaves without a word.

'Hi,' she says awkwardly.

'Hi.' Suddenly I don't know what to say. Shouldn't we be hugging at this point and crying?

'How are you?' she asks. Her accent is very posh making me feel surprisingly common all of a sudden.

'I'm okay. You?'

'Good.' I suspect neither of us are actually good.

'Do you have any pets?' I ask, feeling lame. What kind of question is that?

'Yes, a hamster. You?'

'A kitten called Marvin.'

'Aw, I bet he's cute.'

'He is, so cute.'

I don't ask the questions I really want to know, such as what kind of accident or what has your life been like with adoptive parents?

She must have questions for me too.

'So, this is weird.'

'It totally is.'

'When did you find out about me?' she asks tentatively.

'Only a few months ago. I was at my aunt's funeral, sorry our aunt, and the other aunts let it slip.'

'Wow. That's crazy. There are other aunts?'

'A few.'

'Must be nice being part of a big family.' How do I explain I hardly know them, that my life is one big mess?

'Kind of. Sorry if I sprung this on you.'

'No, it's fine. I had to find out sometime, huh,' she jokes.

We chat for a little bit longer until she announces she has to get back. Panic seizes hold of me. What if this is it?

What now?

'Are you staying around in town?'

'I can do if you want me to.'

'I do want but sorry if it inconveniences you.'

'It's fine.' I have no idea if it is but I'm hoping Great Aunt Margaret will be okay with it.

'I'll call you tomorrow morning. I can get out in the afternoon.'

'Okay cool.' Within minutes her friend is back and wheeling her away.

That was it. Our happy reunion. It was not the reunion I had imagined.

CHAPTER TWENTY-THREE

'Are you sure you're okay with staying here for the night?'

'Absolutely.' Great Aunt Margaret nods. 'I didn't fancy driving all that way back tonight anyway and besides, I've always wanted to visit Broadstairs.' I look at her doubtfully.

I'm not convinced she has but I smile and nod anyway. 'Thank you.'

Ella texts me almost the minute I've got out of bed.

Come to my house. I'm telling Mum and Dad. I don't want to keep any more secrets.

When I tell Margaret the plan, her eyes double in size.

'That seems a bit soon, don't you think?'

I shrug. All I know is I want to see Ella again and get to know her more. Surely we can move on from this awkward stage.

'I can't stop you but you can always call me if it gets too much.'

'Thanks, Margaret.' We hug awkwardly. We haven't known each other long and this is the best she's getting right now.

Dressed in my smartest clothes, Great Aunt Margaret drops me off at Ella's house. Hands shaking, breathing laboured, I find I can barely walk straight. Ella must be waiting on the other side of the door, as it opens the minute I knock.

'Come in, I haven't told them yet.'

'What? Aren't they going to be-'

'Shocked yeah but it's better out in the open.' I'm not so sure.

The hallway to her house is almost as big as my whole house. Mum would be shouting about how big it all was if she were here or else be intimidated into silence. Silence! Mum! Not likely. Family photos adorn the walls right from babyhood to more recent.

'Your parents didn't have any children of their own then?'

'I guess not.' I forget she has only just found out she's adopted.

'Sorry I don't mean to be nosy.' She smiles in response. Does that mean she doesn't think I'm nosy?

Before I can ask her anything else we are entering the vast lounge with its immaculate furniture. Her Mum and Dad sit on the armchairs by the window, engrossed in their books. I am already intimidated by their smart clothes and neat hairstyles. They glance up.

'Mum, Dad, I'd like you to meet someone.' It's obvious to all who I am but her Mum looks confused. Dad has gone pale and is staring at me as though I am an illusion. 'This is my twin sister, Maddie.'

Her Mum opens her mouth but nothing comes out. Dad's eyes look like they will come out of their sockets. I shuffle from one foot to the other, wishing that the ground would swallow me up and take me out of this awkward situation.

'I… er… don't know what to say,' says Ella's Mum finally. That much is obvious. Her hands start shaking as she turns a horrible pale shade of white.

'Well, you could start with why you didn't tell me I was adopted,' Ella answers angrily. I've only known her a day but the rage that is pouring out of her all of a sudden is scaring me. 'You didn't think I deserved to know,' she yells. I step back a few paces, wondering if I should run now.

'Darling, it's not that easy.' Ella's Mum has finally found her tongue, trying desperately to maintain control. 'The circumstances were-'

'I know what the circumstances were. I was given away while she was kept.' She points at me like a spoilt child whose sister has got all the best toys. Is this about me or about some vendetta she wishes to execute against her parents?

'This can't be happening.' Dad stands up and starts pacing the room furiously.

'None of you care about me,' screams Ella.

Running has never been such a great option as now. I shuffle backwards again, intent on sneaking out. Ella turns and stares at me. 'Don't go,' she whispers sweetly.

'Darling, we meant to tell you but there never seemed a right time,' says Dad with a kindness I have never heard in a parent.

'I think I should go and let you guys sort this out,' I blurt out, eager to make my escape.

'No, stay,' Ella says firmly. 'Please sit down.' She points at the chair by the TV but sitting down is the last thing I want to do.

'I don't think-'

Before I can even get comfortable in my seat, Ella launches another attack on her Mum who is growing increasingly more stressed. Finally, she clutches her head as though in pain, running her hand through her blonde bob, and walks towards the front door.

'I need some air,' declares her Mum dramatically. Ella rolls her eyes.

'Oh go on, escape why don't you.'

Her Mum ignores her and exits the house, leaving the three of us staring awkwardly at one another.

'Maddie, would you like a drink?' Dad asks.

I nod. As he walks towards the kitchen, he stops and stares at me for a second, then looks from Ella to me.

'You're identical,' he gasps. 'I had no idea Ella had a twin.' 'Wow you're a genius,' Ella mutters sarcastically.

Ella wheels round to face the extensive garden, scowling out at it. I should text Great Aunt Margaret and get her to rescue me. Before I can get out my phone though the doorbell sounds. Could Great Aunt Margaret have psychically realised I need help? I hope so. Is Ella's Mum back, having forgotten her key?

Ella doesn't move and Dad is in the kitchen so I jump

up.

'I'll get it.'

The last person I was expecting to see is at the door.

'Mum!' Mum strides into the lounge. 'How? What?' She has a grin like a child when she sees Ella but stops when she sees Ella's Dad, who has just reappeared in the lounge, two glasses in his hand. One of the glasses slips out of his grip and falls to the floor, shattering all around him. He seems not to notice it as he clutches the mantlepiece to steady himself.

'Max? What are you doing here?'

Part Two:
Ella – Six Months Earlier

CHAPTER TWENTY-FOUR

It's so bright in here. My eyes struggle to take in what's around me. White walls, noisy machines, people talking, my parents whispering in the corner. Pain, I remember pain but I don't know why. Thank goodness it's gone.

'Ella, you're awake.' Mum's face brightens into a massive smile but I can see the anxiety behind it. Dad rushes over, trying to hide the sadness in his eyes.

'Where am I?'

'You're in hospital.'

'What happened?' Vague flashes of memory rush through my mind. Broken glass, screaming.

'You had an accident.' Dad doesn't say a word but looks at the floor.

An accident, but I survived. Mum is staring at me, eyes darting over me quickly. I hate that her eyes are full of sympathy.

'Am I okay?' Stupid question as clearly, I am. I'm alive and here but something doesn't feel right. Mum and Dad exchange a worried glance. 'Tell me,' I whisper hoarsely. I need to know, whatever it is.

Mum starts to cry, heavy thick tears falling from her eyes.

'I can't do this.' She moves away to stare out of the window, brushing away her tears, trying desperately to stop them.

'Dad?'

I've never seen Dad cry but his eyes start to water. It must be bad.

'The good news is you're alive,' he jokes, much like the

Dad I've always known.

A nurse approaches, interrupting our conversation. Dad is clearly relieved, saved from a difficult conversation. I vow to take it up with him the minute she leaves.

'Great to see that you're awake.' I try to smile but can't force one out. 'I know it's a lot to take in. It'll be better if the doctor explains the extent of your injuries.'

'Er ...' Mum struggles to get out the words but her eyes say all the nurse needs to know 'She doesn't need to know right now,' she finally manages.

The nurse opens her mouth to speak but I interrupt her.

'Will someone just tell me what's going on?' I demand loudly.

'The doctor is going to come and talk to you soon. He'll explain everything.'

'Darling,' Dad begins, sitting on the end of my bed and taking hold of my hand. I follow his eyes to the end of my bed and it is then that I realise with horror what is missing. Before anyone can stop me, I pull the covers up to look beneath. The place where my legs should be is just an empty space.

I have no legs, only bandages at the end of my body. I back out quickly.

'Where are my legs?' I shout, the pain of reality starting to sink in. No one says a word. No one can meet my eye.

Dad squeezes my hand. Openly sobbing now, he couldn't get the words out whether he wanted to or not.

'Love, I know this seems terrible now.' The nurse's voice is gentle and kind but it doesn't help. I nod violently, not allowing myself to speak for fear of saying something I'll regret. 'But it doesn't have to be the end of your life.'

'Have you ever lost your legs?' I ask quietly. The nurse shakes her head solemnly. 'Then you don't have a clue what it's like.'

'But-' I put my hand out to stop her. Damn, I wish I could storm out right now. I can't deal with everyone else's emotions. I do the next best thing and bury my head in my pillow, releasing my hand from Dad's ever-tightening grip.

Despite being buried in my pillow, I can still hear Mum's sobs and Dad's quiet sighs interrupted by tiny sobs. I want them to go away.

'Ella,' begins Dad, reaching out to touch my head.

'Leave her for now,' suggests the nurse. 'She needs time to get used to this.'

How does anyone ever get used to not having legs? Do you just wake up one day realising it's okay? At the moment that point seems far away, completely unreachable.

The rattling of trolleys around me, the forever beeping machines suddenly sound all too loud in my head. I try to bury myself even more but nothing can block out the thoughts in my head. Maybe if I start screaming, they'll inject me with some drug and I'll be released into nothingness once more. I've never understood those who want to end their own lives, now I do.

Eventually, due to being hot and the discomfort I feel, I lift my head. Mum and Dad are silent now, Mum staring out of the window and Dad looking at his phone. They both turn to me, I stare back at them, feeling devastated by this horrific situation.

Mum dares to smile a little. It's enough to make the tears fall down my face again and I reach out my arms. Dad is there like a shot, hugging me so tightly I worry he'll break me. Mum joins in uneasily from the side.

When I finally break free, I am exhausted from the crying. Mum pulls the covers over me, tucking me in like I am a little child.

'I'm so sorry,' Mum says. 'I am your mother. I should keep you safe, whatever happens.'

'I'm fifteen. You can't wrap me up in cotton wool.'

'I wish I had.'

I'm beginning to wish she had too. As a teenager, you long for those moments when you can be free of your parents, go wild, away from their rules. Live independently without any of the worries of adulthood. I had freedom that night. My parents let me go, let me have the fun I so longed for. Was it worth it?

'What happened to Sam?' I suddenly remember he was with me. Mum looks at the floor. 'No, tell me he didn't die?'

Dad nods. Mum turns away, eyes full of pain.

Just when you think you can't cry anymore.

'Wait, who's looking after Blueberry?' I say suddenly.

'Don't worry, your Mum has been feeding him.'

'And changing his bedding? He hates lying in wet sawdust.'

'That too,' smiles Dad.

Eventually, the doctor comes round. He picks up the clipboard at the end of my bed and studies it.

'Ella…?'

'Yes.' Who else did he think had sneaked in here without legs?

'I've come to talk to you about your diagnosis.' I hate that word. It sounds so clinical. 'Due to the seriousness of the accident your legs were unable to be saved. I'm afraid due to the position of the amputation you are not a good candidate for prosthetic legs.'

'What does that mean?'

'You're saying she won't be able to walk again,' asks Dad, his tone almost pleading.

The doctor nods. 'I'm afraid so.'

'I'll never be able to walk at all? Why can't I?'

'It wouldn't work in your situation.'

'Can't I at least try?' I ask as tears flow down my cheeks.

He shakes his head. 'I'm sorry. You are welcome to a second opinion of course.'

I stare shell-shocked at him and wonder if he realises how devastating his words are to me.

. . .

That night when I am lying in bed alone, I wonder what my life has become. Mum and Dad didn't want to go home but I demanded to be left alone and besides, they looked like they needed the sleep. Time to think is necessary for me now. The nurse keeps popping her head in to see me, probably making sure I haven't topped myself or anything. I smile and give her the thumbs up. I suspect she knows it's all an act.

I wonder if I were to end it all, how I would do it. Which would be the most painless way? My life feels like it is already over. My parents are the only ones that would stop me doing anything stupid.

I must have drifted off because when I wake up it's dark outside. The window next to my bed is the only bit of the world I can see. Now I am regretting making Mum and Dad go home.

CHAPTER TWENTY-FIVE

'It hurts. It hurts.'

'What does sweetheart?' Dad's soothing voice is not enough to take away the pain.

'My legs.'

Mum and Dad exchange a look that I can't quite work out.

'Make it stop. Please, Dad.' His eyes full of panic, he stands frozen to the spot.

'I'll get a nurse.' He runs from the room, leaving me to lay in agony.

The spasms disappear as quickly as they came and I lay back exhausted.

'Why is that happening when she's ...' Mum's voice tails off.

'Got no legs?' I finish for her. Her face reddens.

'It's common for amputees to experience phantom pains afterwards.'

'It makes no sense,' I say frustrated. 'There's nothing there.'

'Sorry love. I know this is hard to deal with.' She has no idea.

...

For the last few days since I woke up, I have been struggling to piece together the events of that night. Sam said we should go; it would be fun. Kaitlyn screamed with delight when I told her how we were getting there. She promised not to tell Mum and Dad. I knew they wouldn't have approved.

It all happened too fast.

...

'Your breakfast is on its way,' the nurse tells me smiling. She made Mum and Dad go to the canteen to get something for themselves. I suspect they haven't eaten much at all recently. I try to lift my head to peer round the corner, to see the trolley but my body feels like a ton of bricks. The high pitched voice confirms the food lady is almost here. She peeks her head around the room slowly, her face breaking into a huge grin.

'You're awake. Can't have you lying around here sleeping all day,' she jokes. I've just met this lady but I love her already, so full of life and the only one who treats me like a normal human being. 'We've got cereal or toast with sausages. What ya fancy?'

'Toast and sausages sound grand.'

She plonks the tray on the table next to me and swivels it round so I can reach it then stands back with her hands on her hip, her eyes lighting up in amusement as I grab the first sausage and shove it in.

'What?' I ask.

'You,' she sniggers.

'What about me?'

'The speed you're eating.'

'Being asleep is hard work,' I laugh.

'I wouldn't know. I'm always working here.'

She stays a few minutes more before leaving me to eat my breakfast. The nurse is checking the chart at the end of the bed. I thought Mum and Dad might be here when I woke up but then I have no idea what time it is right now. This place feels like a timeless void.

'I'm going to check up on Katie next door. Do you need anything?' the nurse asks.

'No, I'm all good.' Of course I'm not. What a stupid thing to say but how else can I describe my present state of mind? I'm not quite suicidal, which is good I suppose. I'm not exactly swinging-from-trees happy either. It occurs to me that I'll never be able to swing from trees again not that I did it before but it was always nice to know it was an option. Now my life is this confusing, lonely mass ahead of me. I'll never be able to do anything I want to do again. Sam's face pops into my head and I instantly feel a pang of guilt. I can do more than him. I push him away. I don't

111

want that face in my head. That beautiful happy face.

When Mum and Dad reappear, their faces are fresher and less pale.

'Hi.' I try to sound brighter than I feel.

'How are you today?' asks Dad.

I shrug. 'Okay, I guess.'

'I brought you a magazine.' It's a woman's magazine with the headline *Queen Elizabeth out of hospital* screaming from the front cover and pictures of beautiful slim women in dresses next to pictures of cakes that presumably they'll provide the recipe for. It's not the kind of magazine I'd have chosen but I take it with a smile because I don't want to be rude.

'Did Sam die instantly?' The morbid side to me needs to know.

Mum presses her lips together and nods silently. 'He won't have suffered,' she whispers.

Not like me, I think. Who is the lucky one - the one who died instantly or the one who has to survive with no legs?

How much do they know about that night? They obviously want to ask but haven't yet.

'When can I come home?'

'Probably be a few weeks yet,' Dad says.

'Weeks! I can't stay here weeks.' The sight of the place is starting to depress and bore me already.

'Sorry love but it's not up to us.' Just like Dad to put the responsibility on someone else.

'I know it's not, but you must have some say. I hate being here.'

Mum breathes in. 'I can talk to the nurse, but it's difficult.'

What is difficult? I want to scream. You're not the one who's stuck here with no legs in a room on my own.

'Can I at least get moved to a room with other people in?'

'We'll see,' says Dad in an infuriatingly patronising

tone. The accident hasn't affected my brain. I can still think properly.

I clench my hands below the covers and grit my teeth, staring out of the window

A few minutes later the nurse is at the door with two policemen behind her.

'These officers wanted to ask you some questions about the accident.'

Dad stands up. 'Is it necessary now? She's only just woken up.'

'Yes, it's not a good time,' adds Mum, standing up to join Dad. 'She's barely able to think straight.'

I want to correct Mum, to speak for myself but I can't. She's right.

'We won't be long,' says the first policeman. Dad stands back as they enter the room but Mum has taken an aggressive stance which suggests she won't tolerate anyone messing with her baby.

The first police officer is an older man with a beard that looks like it needs a good trim. He smiles kindly, while the second officer, a man barely older than me follows him in nervously.

'Ella, how are you doing?' The first one starts. I shrug. Seriously what does he expect me to say to that? 'We want to ask you a few questions about the night of the accident.'

'She is very tired,' Mum interrupts again.

The officer holds up his hand. 'Please Mrs. Webster this will only take a few minutes.'

'Could you tell us in your own words what happened?'

I close my eyes, the accident coming flooding back into my mind. We were going so fast.

I open my eyes. 'We were going to a party.' He nods, encouraging me to continue. 'But we didn't make it.' I suddenly feel silly saying all this. Of course, we didn't, that much is obvious. 'There were bright lights ahead.' Tears begin to fall from my face.

'Can't you see she's upset?' Mum says rushing over to

me. I reach for her hand.

'Someone hit us.'

'Was it a car?'

'I assume so but I can't remember.'

'Did you see any markings on it? Remember the colour of it?'

'It was so dark and the lights were so bright. All I remember is lying there and watching the car drive off.' I can feel Mum flinch next to me and hold my hand, which is now visibly shaking, tighter.

'I think that's enough for now,' Dad interjects. The officer nods.

'If you remember anything else, please call us.' He hands me a card with his name on it. I take it wordlessly and stare out towards the window.

Mum strokes my hand continuously until the officers have left.

'Sorry baby, so sorry,' she keeps repeating.

'It was too much,' Dad says loudly when they are gone. 'They can't expect someone to talk about their accident so soon after.'

I nod, trying to purge the distressing images from my head.

CHAPTER TWENTY-SIX

'Today is the day.' The nurse has a sing-songy tone to her voice.

I smile back broadly. 'I can't wait.'

'Bet you're dying to get out of here.'

'No offence but yeah.'

'None taken.'

I can't tell you how many nights I have spent thinking about this day in the last few months. I'm desperate to escape the monotony here, to return to some kind of normality.

The doctor who is discharging me is frustratingly slow in his rounds this morning so I am left twiddling my thumbs with Mum and Dad. I have my wheelchair. I have everything I need to go home. I only need someone to sign a damn bit of paper, then I'm out of here.

When he finally arrives, his serious expression fills me with dread. In my head, I'm begging him not to change his mind. He holds up my chart and stares deeply into it. Surely it doesn't take that long to read it.

'All looks good here,' he says finally and the breath I've been holding can be released. He signs the papers in a dramatic manner and his face breaks into a smile. 'Good luck Ella. I'm sure I'll see you around.'

Unfortunately, he probably will. My first appointment is already booked for a few weeks' time. There is nothing more I would like to do than never see this place again but that's not going to happen.

'Have you got everything?' Mum asks me for about the thousandth time.

'Yes, Mum. I'm ready.' I try to keep the annoyance out of my tone but feel like I am not succeeding.

Two nurses lift me into my wheelchair. This will be Dad's job now.

'Thank you for everything,' Dad says to the nurses. I

want to say the same but the words won't come out. I want to be grateful. I want to be that blessed disabled person who makes the most of her situation but I don't feel that way yet. Will I ever get to that stage?

It's weird being in a car for the first time in months. Everything is big and overwhelming in the outside world. I'm out of my cocoon and it's scary. Dad had to buy a special car, just for me. I hate that they've had to adapt their whole lives for me but I guess they can afford it.

It's about a ten-minute drive home but I request to go by the coast, totally out of the way, but I haven't seen the sea in months.

'For you, anything, darling,' Dad says, full of charm. He's so competitive that I know he will take this project to heart. I am his latest thing to obsess over.

'Here we are,' says Dad cheerfully when he pulls up by the side of the road overlooking the sea. 'Fancy a quick walk?' I see him screw up his face at his choice of words and press his lips together tightly. Mum touches him on the arm.

'Sorry I mean-'

'It's fine. I know what you meant.'

He smiles and gets out of the car. I am offloaded from the car like a piece of luggage, but with more care. The uneven pavement makes my wheelchair vibrate and the holes give me the impression of falling. Nothing like the smooth hospital floors.

The cold air hits me. It's the first time I've been out in the fresh air since before the accident. The sound of the waves crashing down against the rocks below me comforts me. Life still goes on. I have to go on.

Am I paranoid or does everyone seem to stare at me as we go by? But they look away quickly when I stare back.

'Mum, why is that girl in a wheelchair?' A little voice pipes up in front of us. A boy pulls his mother's arm demanding to know an answer. I can see her whispering something furiously to him.

'It's okay,' I say. Dad stares down at me, horror in his eyes. He wants nothing more than to protect me. 'I can explain it to him,' I say to the mother.

She smiles apologetically.

The boy steps forward as I smile at him.

'I had an accident.'

'Was it a bad one?' he asks.

'Pretty bad but I didn't die. I had to spent quite a few months in hospital and I might not be able to walk again but I can still do other things.'

The boy nods, satisfied at my answer. I catch a glimpse of Mum and Dad's smiling expressions.

I find I get cold quickly, used to the hospital where the heat was on constantly. It's like a different world there. Mum draws the blanket closer around me. I should be grateful that she cares but all I feel is resentment. I want to be running along. I never used to like running but now I would love to be able to. I wish I had appreciated that before. If I had the chance I would run as fast as I can and not stop until I was exhausted.

The lift that goes down to the beach has a small, typed sign on it 'Out of order'. You don't think about how inaccessible everything is for disabled people until you need to. But what would I do if I got down to the beach anyway?

I can hardly plough through the sand.

After a short wheel along the top, I am exhausted.

'We should get you home.' Mum, ever the perceptive one, notices any little thing. I nod. Enough outside world for one day.

...

Home doesn't feel like home. Maybe it's seeing it from a wheelchair perspective. The newly-fitted ramp by the front door screams disabled person lives here. The whole street must know what has happened. I don't know what I was expecting, but to see my bedroom downstairs is heartbreaking. It's bigger. It used to be the dining room, but already it seems colder, less friendly. I glance fearfully at the window that looks out onto the street. What if someone broke in during the middle of the night? It's a safe area, I remind myself, always full of people walking by, and besides, we have nosy neighbours. Blueberry's cage, with him in it, is sitting on the table in the corner like he's always been there.

'What do you think?' Mum asks pushing her hair back behind her ears. 'I tried to make it exactly like your old room.'

'It's great,' I lie. Nothing could be further from my old room. I appreciate the effort in putting my posters up but they're all in the wrong places.

Fortunately, our house is Victorian so has wide hallways and a toilet at the back of the house. Despite it all, it's good to be home, to be somewhere familiar and cosy rather than clinical. I am struck by how quiet it is, no noisy machines, no nurses poking their heads in constantly wanting a chat. Finally, I can have some peace.

Dad sets me up in the lounge facing the TV and hands me the remote.

'What do you want to watch?' I shrug, unable to make even the simplest of decisions. I just want to be left alone to make these decisions without having someone breathing down my neck. I sound so ungrateful but I hate this. I want my old life back. I want to be normal again.

Just as I am deciding what to watch the doorbell rings. Dad goes to answer it. A familiar voice echoes through the hallway. Kaitlyn!

'She's just got home. Now is not a good time.' But I want to see her, I have to see her.

'It's fine Dad,' I shout. 'I want to see her.'

'Don't be too long,' he says as he beckons her in.

Kaitlyn walks in, hair braided to perfection, grinning. 'Am I glad to see you,' she says reaching down to hug me.

'I thought you'd forgotten about me.'

She looks down guiltily. 'I'm sorry I wanted to come

visit. I did once when you were unconscious but I couldn't bear to see you like that.'

'You're here now. That's the main thing.'

'And I have something crazy to tell you.' Her eyes race around the room. 'Where are your parents?'

'Dad's upstairs, Mum went out. What's going on?'

'I saw someone the other day outside our school. I thought it was you. She was the spitting image of you except she wasn't in a wheelchair so I was all confused thinking how could this be.'

'I don't understand.'

'No nor did I but the guy she was with told me she is your twin sister.'

'But I don't have a twin sister.'

'Apparently you do. You were adopted as a baby and your sister has tracked you down here.'

'That's impossible. I'm not adopted. She must be mistaken.'

'But she was your double.'

Suddenly it all feels too weird. Coming home after the accident is big enough but this is huge.

'Sorry I shouldn't have blurted it out like that.'

'No it's fine. It's just a lot to deal with.'

'I should go. You look exhausted.'

I want to tell her to stay but she's right. I need sleep and to process this.

I can't possibly be adopted and have a twin sister!

CHAPTER TWENTY-SEVEN

'Hold on tight Ella, for the ride of your life.'
'Sam, I don't want to,' but he doesn't hear me above the roar of the motorbike.

Last night I lay in this bed and felt like I couldn't breathe. Was it my imagination? I kept thinking what if I stop breathing and die overnight? Who would save me? Suddenly I was longing for the safety of the hospital, where at least I was not alone. The more I tried focusing on my breathing the more it felt like it wasn't happening properly. The only thing that comforted me was hearing Blueberry moving around on his wheel.

The next thing I knew was light streaming in through the thin curtains in my new room, interrupting my deep sleep, another thing I hate about this room.

While I am wondering when someone will come and release me, memories of that night plague me. I push them away. I don't want to remember it. My mind wanders to what Kaitlyn told me.

I have so many questions. Firstly, I want to know why Mum and Dad have never told me I was adopted. I'm fifteen now, old enough to know. What right did they have to keep this from me? Why did they only adopt me? Why not her as well?

I don't even know where to start with this. I need to figure out what I want. If things had been normal, if I hadn't been stuck in this chair, I would jump at the chance of meeting her.

The other thought running through my mind, is whether she is the link I feel that has been always missing in my life? It's cheesy to say that twins have a connection that transcends understanding but maybe we do.

I can't very well ask Mum and Dad about this now. They are under enough stress dealing with me and my problems. I can't add to it. Last night I heard them arguing. They thought they were being quiet but their hissing at each other in the next room was almost worse than shouting. I couldn't make out what they were saying but the words 'guilt' and 'your fault' stood out. Mum blames Dad for that night. She wasn't keen on me going out with Sam but Dad's easy-going manner won out.

I wriggle in my bed but as I do so I fall out of bed, landing with a loud thump on the floor. I try desperately to reach my bed but even if I could what would I do? There is no way I can pull myself up. Frustrated, I pull at my duvet. It falls onto the floor.

'Help,' I yell but my shouts fall on deaf ears.

I lay my head back on the hard floor in despair.

Finally, the door opens and I hear Dad's cheerful voice 'Morning Ella.'

He looks around until he spots me on the floor. 'Ella! What happened?'

'I fell out of bed.'

'Sweetheart. How long have you been here?' I don't answer as he rushes over and lifts me onto the bed. 'So sorry.' I shrug. It's depressing, I don't even know what to say.

'Want some breakfast?' He asks kindly.

'Yes please.'

He wheels the chair over and helps me into it. They're hoping I'll be able to do all this myself, with the help of physio. It'll be hard they say. I don't want to hear it.

My first breakfast back at home. Already, I can smell bacon and sausages. That wouldn't have happened before. Don't get me wrong; I'm grateful but it makes everything abnormal. My taste buds win. I can't say no to sausages.

'We're so happy you're home,' Mum says, staring at me while I eat, with a creepy smile. Dad is busying himself with the washing up.

'Me too,' I reply. It's not a lie but I can't muster the enthusiasm she wants.

'This morning we've got a visit to school arranged.'

'My school?'

'Yes, we need to get you back in school.'

I make an aggressive hand movement towards the legs that aren't there. 'How do you expect me to go back like this?'

'No need to be rude.'

'I'm not being rude Mum but I can't move without help.' 'You will. When you start physio.'

'But-' I start to protest.

'It's just a visit Ella. You're not starting back today. We need to sort a few things first.'

Dad smiles at me sympathetically from the kitchen. I chew my bacon violently. It's not worth arguing with Mum. Once she gets it into her mind about something there's no persuading her. I wanted my first day home to be chilled out, not quite a pyjama day as I've had too many of them recently but at least take it easier. It seems like Mum has other plans. I dread the thought of all my friends seeing me like this. Their judging looks. Do they think I brought this on myself?

'Will Kaitlyn be there?'

'Don't think so. I've heard she hasn't been at school since.'

...

Mallory High School looms larger than ever in front of me as Dad wheels me in the direction of the office. We have to sign in which is a strange concept. I shouldn't have to; this is my school.

'Hi Ella,' the office lady greets me. 'How are you?' Am I imagining her patronising tone? There is nothing wrong with my brain.

'I'm fine.' I'm not but she doesn't want to hear that. I'm far from fine but she doesn't really care. I wonder if she sent me one of the dozens of bunches of flowers in our lounge. Our house is starting to look like a florist.

'She's happy to be here, aren't you Ella?' Mum looks at

me expectantly.

'Um… yes.'

The office lady smiles, probably the same smile she gives to all difficult parents, the ones she's trying to fob off.

Being back in the building is the weirdest thing when you haven't been for months. I expect the stares from other students in the corridor. I expect kind words from my teachers but I don't expect my friends to look the other way. Ashamed they didn't visit me?

We head to the special needs hub. I've not been in this section before. The SENCO, Mrs Harper, a lovely smiley lady, has never spoken to me before but is now full of gushing words. I try to answer her questions but I'm starting to tire. My eyelids begin to droop.

'I told you this would be too much for Ella,' hisses Dad at Mum when Mrs Harper has left the room. She waves her hand dismissively at him. He glares back. It is clearly not over.

'So, Ella,' Mrs Harper announces coming back into the room, 'this is your care plan. It outlines what we'll be doing for you. It's fortunate for you that our school is so wheelchair friendly.' Yeah, so lucky. I feel like the luckiest girl alive. Kill me now!

'We really appreciate how accommodating you're being,' Mum says beaming at them.

I let their words drift over my head and feel myself drifting off. I am jolted awake by the sound of Mum calling my name.

'What? Sorry.'

'She's tired.' Dad defends me.

'Just a minute.' Mum is in deep conversation with Mrs Harper who is looking increasingly worried at me.

I am relieved when we leave as I feel faint. Dad is fuming, spitting out harsh words at every opportunity.

'It was too soon Liz. It's her first full day at home and you've dragged her out for this pointless meeting.'

'It wasn't pointless. It's something that needs to be sorted out.'

'Yes of course it does but not today, not like this.'

'Guys,' I say drunkenly. Maybe I should ask them now about being adopted. Not a bad distraction.

They both turn to me and shower me with too much attention.

The first place I go to when I get home is bed. I can't believe how exhausted I am. My eyes close the minute I hit the pillow. I never used to be able to sleep during the day but now it's all I can do.

'Faster?' he yells to the back. I cling tighter to him. I wanted this yet now I don't but he won't stop.

CHAPTER TWENTY-EIGHT

I wake up to Dad handing me a letter in bed as I'm thinking about getting up.

'Not sure who this is from,' he says mysteriously.

I take it from him without saying a word. He stands watching me as I open. It becomes clear very quickly who it's from.

'Just Kaitlyn. Thought I'd like to receive a letter through the post,' I explain.

'How kind of her,' he answers. 'I'll leave you to get ready.'

After he has shut the door, I carefully take the letter out. It's from Maddie:

Dear Ella,

I didn't know where to start in writing this letter but the truth is all I can tell you. My name is Maddie and I am your twin sister. Fifteen years ago, at birth, we were separated. You were adopted. I stayed with Mum. I hope you've had a good life. I had no idea about you until a family funeral recently when I found out accidentally. I have been trying to find you ever since. I don't know how much you've been told about your past or how you were adopted but I would really like to meet up sometime; we are twins after all.

I look forward to hearing from you
Maddie

The contents of Maddie's letter goes round and round in my mind. She's expecting an answer but I can't form the words to reply. The pressure to make a decision is too much. Mum and Dad's incessant arguing makes the atmosphere at home difficult. I don't want to be the cause of their breakup. They didn't argue much before, but then again, I was out, a lot.

'First physio session today,' Mum announces cheerfully as I eat breakfast as though we're going on a trip to the cinema. I wish it was such a fun trip. I have a sneaky suspicion this is not going to be at all fun.

...

Being back at the hospital almost makes me have a panic attack. I reach back to Dad's hand and touch it for some reassurance. He stops wheeling me and comes round to face me.

'You okay?' I shrug trying to fight back the tears. 'I know this is hard honey but it'll help you get back on...' He was going to say on your feet. His red face says it all.

'I hate being here again.'

'I know. I know,' Dad says stroking my shoulder.

Mum stands to one side, hands on her hips, eager to get going again. She throws Dad a look and points to her watch. I don't see the look he returns her but I can imagine it isn't good.

'Be brave,' he adds before holding my hand tightly. I can always rely on Dad to make me feel confident.

Throughout my childhood, it's always been Dad I turn to when I need help. It's not that I hate Mum but she is distant. I can't quite put my finger on why. We get on, we laugh but I don't share with her what I do with Dad.

The first session is gruelling, like doing a marathon many times over. I want to give up so many times but the kind voice of the physiotherapist stops me from breaking down in tears. She has the sort of voice that would be good on a meditation podcast and would send you to sleep.

I am beyond exhausted when we are finished. I barely remember the journey back to the house. I think I must have slept through it all.

When I wake up later, I am in my bed and it is dark. I lay alone, feeling the low rumbling of my tummy. Thoughts of my twin sister immediately spring to my mind. I have to make a decision. She must be dying to know my reaction to the letter. I can't keep her hanging any longer.

When I wake up the next morning my mind is made up. The words I'm going to say are forming in my head. I'm going to meet her but not yet.

With shaky hands, I write her a letter. She will be disappointed in my response but it's something at least. I need more time but I hate the thought she is there waiting for my reply.

When I have finished, I hear the doorbell ring which is a surprise as we don't get many visitors. It's loud, being right next door to my new room. I hear Kaitlyn's voice.

'Lovely to see you,' Mum says to her.

Mum knocks tentatively on my door. 'Ella, you have a visitor. Can she come in?'

'Yes,' I yell, sitting up in bed the best I can.

I can't wait to tell her more about Maddie.

'Wow she actually wrote you a letter.'

'I know. I couldn't believe it either. I've been thinking about it ever since, do I tell her I'll meet her or tell her to go away?'

'Why wouldn't you meet her?'

'Because she might not want to when she sees I'm in a wheelchair.'

'Don't be silly. She's your twin. You have this psychic thing going on.'

I laugh. 'Not so psychic that I knew she existed.'

'Seriously what have you got to lose?'

'How's Blueberry?' she asks, glancing in the hamster's direction.

'He's good. Same as always.' I laugh.

'I missed you, Ella,' Kaitlyn says reaching over to hug me.

'I missed you too.'

Suddenly tears start gushing from her. 'Ella it's all my fault.'

'How is it your fault?'

'I persuaded you to go to the party.'

'I can make my own decisions.'

'But you were so unsure. I bullied you into it.' Memories of that night flash before me, Kaitlyn egging me on, telling me he wouldn't love me if I didn't go. She did bully me into it but I still could have said no.

'It doesn't matter now. What's done is done. Have you seen Sam's parents? Did you go to the funeral?'

She shakes her head. 'I couldn't face it. His Mum is distraught.'

'I think they blame me.'

'How could they? He was driving.'

'Who knows but they would have come to visit me if they didn't.'

Kaitlyn doesn't say a word but stares at me sadly. I want my old life back, the one where Kaitlyn was always laughing and dragging me to wild parties, the one where we sneaked out when we were supposed to be in bed.

'What can I do?' she asks suddenly.

'Do?'

'To help.'

'Well actually. I could use your help to post the letter to Maddie.'

'Do you want me to do it?'

'I'd quite like to myself. Can you take me there?'

She looks unsure. 'Am I allowed?'

'Of course.'

'I mean will your Mum let me?'

'It's not up to her.'

'Okay. Let's go.'

Mum isn't happy about Kaitlyn taking me out as I knew she wouldn't be. If Dad hadn't been at work, he would have taken my side, but in the battle of wills between Mum and I, I win. I guess I am the more stubborn one after all.

The post box isn't far. I press ahead, speedily, in my wheelchair. Kaitlyn is out of breath trying to keep up. I almost feel guilty but she wasn't in the accident. Does part of me wish she was?

With the letter firmly posted in the slot, I breathe a sigh of excitement at what might happen next. Doubts plague me on the way back. Maybe I should have told her about the accident but how can I explain all this in a letter? I'm not sure I'm ready to re-live it anyway.

When we get back, Mum is waiting by the door. I swear she doesn't trust Kaitlyn, maybe she's right not to.

CHAPTER TWENTY-NINE

After a few more physio sessions I am starting to feel stronger. Do I dare dream that one day I could walk with artificial legs? Despite the doctor telling me it isn't possible, I don't give up hope. I long to walk tall again in the land of the living where you don't get ignored. I've noticed most people talk to Mum when we're out like I'm not capable of any rational thought. I couldn't possibly have a discussion about anything. It's my body that's damaged not my mind, I want to scream at them.

I think about Maddie all the time. I know I have to see her. She is my twin. It's not possible to continue my existence without her. But how will she react to this? To me being not fully able?

Kaitlyn visits me once a week. I'm not sure if it's out of guilt or out of curiosity but I like her company. She's funny and it's a change from Mum looking so depressed all the time.

'So you're going to meet her?'

'Yes, I need to.' Kaitlyn doesn't understand this requirement in me to connect with my other half. 'I could use your help.'

'Of course. Anything.'

Kaitlyn agrees to take me to the park to meet Maddie and not to tell my parents. She's more than happy to deceive them. They disapprove of her and only ever give out negative vibes when she's around.

With the letter posted and my phone number given out, I anxiously await Maddie's reply, hoping that she'll still want to meet me.

The next day I get the message. She must have texted me the minute she got the letter. I can't believe we are finally going to meet up. I immediately text Kaitlyn to let her know the plan is on. She responds with a thumbs up.

...

Our big meet up is finally happening. I'm so nervous I

could almost pull out. I check my hair several times until Kaitlyn tells me to stop over thinking it.

I recognise her instantly, of course. It's like looking in a mirror except she is skinnier than me, with long hair that could do with a cut, and dresses kind of funny. Do I feel the connection straight away? I'm not sure. I'm disappointed there isn't a lightning bolt moment where we hug and break down in tears together. It's awkward. We're different.

'Hi there,' she says quietly. Her accent stands out a mile round here.

'Hi.' I don't know what to say. There is so much I want to say but don't know how to. For someone who loves to talk I'm mute.

She glances down at my wheelchair and then tells me about her kitten Marvin. I hope I can meet him one day. He sounds cute. I tell her about Blueberry. We talk a bit more then it is over, too soon.

'How was it?' asks Kaitlyn when we are headed home.

'Awkward.'

'Sorry.'

'She's like a stranger.'

'She is a stranger.'

'She's my twin sister.'

'What did you expect, cheesy music and sobbing.' How can I tell her this is exactly what I expected? She gives me a look. 'That only happens in movies.'

'Does it? Really?'

'Yes, this is real life. Give it time. You can get to know her. That is if you're going to see her again.'

'She's staying in town so hopefully.'

'But you haven't arranged anything?'

'I want to... oh I'm so stupid. I don't know what to do. I don't know how this works.'

'There's no rule book for this.'

'Kaitlyn you're so wise.'

'That'll be a first.'

When I get home, Mum questions me on my visit to the park, asks me far too many questions, pointless ones. Why do I care what flowers I saw? Why does she need to know how many people were in the park?

Since the accident, Mum has been attending to my every need, she has had to be but I'm starting to feel stifled. I'm looking forward to going back to school. It'll be hard but at least I'll have some escape from all this.

When I am finally alone in my bedroom, I make a decision. I will invite Maddie here, tomorrow. She can meet Mum and Dad. I can't wait to see their faces. I wheel over to Blueberry and poke my finger through the bars of his cage. I know I am risking a bite but I want to feel his soft fur. He hasn't been handled so much recently and has begun to hate being picked up. That makes me sad.

I text Maddie and ask her. She replies almost instantly, as though waiting for me to text.

Thank you for coming all this way, I add. *I hope we can get to know each other a lot more.*

Me too

The time she has spent getting ready is obvious when she arrives in her black jeans, t-shirt, and hair tied back. Mum and Dad are in the lounge, poised and waiting. I told them I had a visitor coming, someone they have to meet. Mum, of course, had lots of questions, when doesn't she?

But I was cagey.

'Just wait and see,' I answer slyly.

I don't know why I'm doing it this way. They are obviously going to be shocked. Maybe I want them to feel the pain I'm feeling. The sense that I have no control over my life is strong.

I show her through to the lounge. If I could have taken a picture of their faces when they saw her, I would have. Dad's jaw drops and Mum's eyes look like they will pop out.

Maddie stands there awkwardly, giving them a little wave.

They talk politely until I hit them with it.

'You didn't think it necessary to tell me I was adopted then?' Maddie shuffles from one foot to the other, looking like she wants to escape out of the door.

I hate it when people tell me things are complicated like I can't handle a bit of truth in my life. I yell at them, regretting it when I see Maddie's face. I shouldn't have done this. It was a bad idea.

Mum starts breathing heavily and I start to wonder if she will have a panic attack.

'You shouldn't have brought her here,' she manages, struggling to breathe.

'She's my twin sister. I have every right.'

'I can't deal with this.'

Distraught, she leaves the house. She never could cope when things weren't going her way. Dad stares after her, confusion taking hold of him. Then just when things couldn't get any more complicated, ten minutes later, the doorbell rings. Maddie volunteers to get it, probably eager to get away from her psycho sister, wondering what I've become. I wonder that myself sometimes, how I changed from a fun-loving girl to a bitter one.

Maddie returns with a thin, haggard-looking woman who, judging by the state of her hair, looks like she just woke up.

'This is Mum,' says Maddie. Horrified is not the way I can describe it. Before anyone can say any more, my real Mum notices Dad.

'Max, what are you doing here?'

How the hell does she know Dad?

CHAPTER THIRTY

'What are you doing here Max?' Maddie's Mum, I mean my Mum (I don't even know what I'm supposed to call her), shouts at Dad. I stare at them both in confusion, my mouth hanging open.

'Wait, you know him?' Maddie demands.

My real Mum ignores her and carries on her tirade against Dad. 'I'm confused. How come you're here?'

'You're not the only one,' mutters Dad.

'Can someone tell me what is going on?' shouts Maddie loudly.

'You adopted Ella?' The real Mum asks.

Dad nods his head slowly. 'She's our child?'

'*Our child?*' I stutter. Maddie clutches her Mum's arm, a horrified expression on her face.

'You adopted our child?' She repeats.

'I didn't know she was yours or mine.'

I can't believe what I am hearing. My eyes flit from one parent to the other. All this time Dad was actually my real dad.

'But you must have,' she argues back.

'I swear Becky. I had no idea.'

'You knew I abandoned her.'

'You abandoned me?' I turn to Maddie, who looks increasingly guilty. 'You never told me.'

'I hadn't got round to that bit yet.'

'I didn't know you abandoned her. I left you that day and moved away. I thought you had an abortion as we agreed.'

'What?' Maddie and I scream at the same time. Dad instantly looks sorry.

'I didn't mean that. I mean-'

'Save it Dad,' I retort. 'I don't need your lies. You've been lying to me all my life.'

Maddie's face screws up in anger and Dad looks afraid

while real Mum is now pacing the room, muttering to herself.

'You must have.' She stops to shout to Dad. 'It's too much of a coincidence.'

'I swear on-'

'My life?' I finish for him.

'No, of course not. I love you, Ella.' I grunt in response.

'So let me get this straight, you heard about this baby I'd abandoned in a public toilet and you decided to go and adopt it, not thinking for a second it could be your baby?' A toilet?

'How would I know?'

'You are unbelievable,' Maddie screams suddenly. 'Both of you. Just my luck that I would have two messed up parents.' She grabs hold of the back of my chair and wheels me out of the room. I don't stop her.

CHAPTER THIRTY-ONE

We listen to our parents arguing from my room, the noise penetrating easily through the thin walls.

'Why didn't you tell me I was abandoned?'

Maddie sighs.

'I didn't want to. I was going to but it's hard to know how.' I nod as though I know exactly what that's like.

'Why did she abandon me?'

'Honestly, I'm not entirely sure. She says she was a teenage Mum who couldn't cope with twins but I think there's more to it than that. She's an alcoholic if you hadn't noticed.'

I want to tell her I didn't, but how can I, when it's clear to see that our mother isn't quite right? I feel bad for Maddie but then remember she is my Mum too. I should feel bad for myself as well.

'How long has she been an alcoholic?'

'Ever since we were born. I think our birth made her one.'

'Wow. That's some serious sh-'

'I know right.'

Maddie walks over to Blueberry. 'Does he bite?'

'Probably. Sorry.'

'No worries. He's cute anyway.'

We stop and listen, as I wonder if adopted Mum knows anything about this. Did she even know Dad had an affair?

This is not going to help their marriage one bit. 'Did you know that your dad is our dad?'

'I had no idea. I'm guessing they had an affair.'

The shouting stops, followed by the quick pace of someone approaching my room.

Maddie and I stare at each other awkwardly. This is whole new territory for both of us. Real Mum peeps her head around the door.

'Maddie, do you… like… want to go?' I send Maddie a

pleading look. I don't want her to leave.

'Wait outside. I'll be there in a minute.' She leaves without a glance in my direction. 'She doesn't know how to react around you. Don't take it personally that she's basically ignored you since she got here. She has no social skills.'

'I'll try not to.'

'Look this is getting a bit complicated. I'm going to go and sort Mum out but can we meet again, maybe later?'

'Sure, I'm pretty tired anyway.' All true. I need a nap after all this excitement.

I watch her leave, trying not to feel hurt that she is abandoning me yet again. After she has gone, I wheel my way into the lounge where Dad is sitting on the single armchair, head in his hands. I've never seen him look so out of control. He glances up with a weak smile when he sees me.

'Sorry about all this,' he says. I'm not sure what exactly he's referring to. Sorry for lying to me? Sorry for wanting to abort me?

I shrug. No response seems good enough to capture my true feelings.

'I had no idea you were my real child.'

'But you knew I was adopted. Why didn't you tell me that?'

'I wanted to but Mum wouldn't let me. Said it would confuse you too much. I always intended to sneak it into conversation somehow but it never seemed the right time.'

'How long were you with Maddie's mum, I mean my mum I guess, for?'

'Only a few months. It was a fling. We met in a bar, slept with each other a few times.' I always remember what they say at school. It only takes one occasion for you to get pregnant. How right they were.

'But she must have been so much younger than you?' I try to do the calculations in my head.

'She was sixteen though I didn't realise it to start with.

She told me she was eighteen. I was twenty.'

'And you were going out with Mum at the time?'

'Yeah, but we were having some difficulties.' It makes me want to ask the question, if you were having difficulties then why get married?

'Did you not want children of your own?'

'Mum couldn't. She'd had some health problems in her early teens which meant she couldn't get pregnant. It was shortly after my affair that your mum, Liz, suggested we sign up to an adoption agency.' I almost feel sorry for her. 'When we saw the baby in the news, we had just been approved, it felt like it was meant to be. She suggested we adopt you. I had no idea you were really mine.'

'How kind of you,' I say sarcastically.

'Would you rather we have left you to a children's home?'

'No, of course not but don't act like you're the martyr in all this.' He is speechless. I don't think I've ever said a nasty word to him. Usually, we get on so well.

'I'm sorry Ella. We should have told you but it's messier than we'd realised.'

'So Mum didn't realise you were seeing Maddie's mum?' I'm not sure what to call her.

'No and I don't think she does now either but I guess I'm going to have to tell her, what with Becky being here and all.'

I shake my head at the mess he has created. 'She just needs to calm down. She'll be all good later.' I doubt she will be but I'm hoping she'll come back, if only for me.

...

When Mum returns, she is a lot calmer, smiling even, but I fear it is the calm before another storm.

'I'm sorry you had to deal with all this,' she says, gently patting my head as I sit on the sofa.

'You could have told me I was adopted.'

'I know. I know, but the truth is, I didn't want you to reject me.' Not us, *me*. 'I hated the idea that you would go off looking for your real mum and leave us behind.'

'Well, I've met her now.'

'What? When?'

'She turned up here after you left.'

'Oh. I'm sure you don't want to see her ever again,' she says disparagingly. 'Not a woman you want to call your mother.' I want to defend this real mother of mine. I don't want her attacked but I feel torn.

'She has her issues, I can see.' Despite that, I want to see her again, without all this drama going on.

Dad stands in the doorway looking like it is doomsday.

'Liz, we need to talk.' This is my cue to disappear. I don't want to hear Mum's reaction to the fact that he had an affair although, undoubtedly, I will hear it all through the wall.

How I wish I could escape upstairs like a normal teenager.

...

Later, when I am alone in my room, I text Maddie and arrange to meet her and real Mum. Maybe I should call her Mum no.2 or would she be Mum no.1 as she technically had me first? Blueberry goes round and round in his wheel. A sound I would normally find comforting but tonight I have had enough.

I am honest with Mum and Dad the next morning. I tell them I'm meeting Maddie and other Mum in a park without them. Mum is furious and demands to come along, Dad worries that I'll get upset but I tell them to drop me off and that I can cope. They don't like it but there is no arguing with me.

A few hours later and Dad helps me out of the car. He leaves me in the park, telling me he wishes I'd let him stay and that he wouldn't interfere but I am firm. No, I tell him. I need my space. The last thing I need is another slanging match between him and real Mum.

Maddie and other Mum are already there. Other Mum glances around her quickly, moving her hair from side to side. She smiles at me, desperately wanting my approval. I'm not willing to give her that.

'Hi Ella,' she begins. 'I'm so sorry about yesterday. It was… well, a big fat mess.' That's one word for it. 'I never expected to see Max, your dad.'

'I know.'

'I don't know where to start.'

'How about why you abandoned me in a public toilet?' She looks like she is about to cry.

'It was so hard. I was only sixteen. My parents were not supportive. I had twins. Then… well then, I thought maybe I could manage one.'

'Why me and not her?' I say glancing at Maddie. Real Mum shrugs.

'I don't know why. It's not like I flipped a coin but it might as well have been. You cried a bit more.'

'I cried a bit more,' I say slowly. 'You abandoned me because I cried more?'

'It sounds awful when you say it like that.' Maddie shuffles uncomfortably on the bench.

'Yeah, it does,' I agree.

'I wanted you. It destroyed me to give one of you away.' She looks at Maddie and then at me. 'And I've been a crap mum to Maddie.' Maddie doesn't deny it. 'I'll do anything to make it up to both of you.'

'Little too late for that,' I say harshly.

'She's trying,' Maddie adds. 'Give her a chance.' I stare at her coldly. This stranger, who is my twin sister, is asking me to give the mother, who abandoned me in a toilet, a second chance.

'It'll be tricky. I'm not exactly mobile.'

'We'll make it work.' Real Mum sounds like she's in some TV soap drama. 'How did you end up in a wheelchair?' she asks suddenly.

'I was in an accident with my boyfriend. Motorbike. I can't talk about it except he didn't make it.' I'm desperate to change the subject before I fall apart. I can't deal with that on top of everything else. Luckily, she doesn't push it but is soon babbling on about her new boyfriend Nick. Maddie turns her head and rolls her eyes in embarrassment. Someone to quiz her about later. Maddie and I agreed we'd meet alone for dinner in an actual restaurant. I can't remember the last time I ate in a restaurant. Finding one that is wheelchair friendly makes it trickier.

'He's so good-looking and smart,' Real Mum continues. 'Do you know he bought me some flowers the other day?' It's like talking to a self-absorbed teenager. I'm starting to realise I got the better deal compared to my twin. Must have been a nightmare growing up with this. 'And I am an alcoholic but I'm getting help now and soon Maddie will be able to come home.'

'Wait, you don't live with her?'

'There was an incident,' Maddie mutters, moving her head from side to side.

'Let's not go into that now,' Mum interrupts. 'As I said, I'm getting help.'

I wonder if she has drunk anything this morning. She is very happy, too happy. In fact, compared to last night she is hyper. Is this how it is day to day? A Mum with moods that jump from one to the other?

Finally, she stops talking and asks me about me and my childhood.

'It was good, normal I guess.' Real Mum doesn't look happy about this, probably not happy that someone else did a better job than she has with Maddie. I don't tell her that Mum is a bit controlling, no need to add ammunition to the fire.

I return home exhausted, emotionally and physically, wondering what happened to my ordinary life.

CHAPTER THIRTY-TWO
SIX MONTHS AGO

'You will never guess what?' Kaitlyn shouts, making me jump and almost drop my hair brush.

'I'm sure I can't guess.'

'Georgia is having a party.'

'Awesome,' I answer, trying to sound enthusiastic but not quite managing it. Georgia is my least favourite person. I may love parties but I'd rather not bother going to one of hers.

'It will be. You and Sam will come, won't you?'

'I suppose.'

'I know it's Georgia,' she whispers in case there is anyone in the toilet cubicles. 'But it'll be so fun.'

I'm trying to muster up some enthusiasm for a girl I hate's party but it's hard.

'We'll be there,' I say, somewhat more cheerfully. I certainly am not going to miss out on anything.

'And Sam's got his new bike.'

'Hmm yeah.'

'You don't sound so keen.' How do I tell her I'm terrified about going on the thing but I don't want to sound wussy? I'm a fun-loving party girl. I can't let my image down.

'No, it's great. I can't wait.' She eyes me up as though she doesn't believe me but turns away announcing our next class is about to start. 'Damn it, we're going to be late again.' I'd lost track of time again.

'It'll be fine.'

'Didn't you hear Mrs. Bullock *the next time you are late I'll put you on punctuality report,*' I say mimicking our very annoying geography teacher.

'She's all talk,' laughs Kaitlyn.

I only hope she's right. The last thing I need is her

ringing home. Mum will kill me and we have enough arguments as it is right now. All she does is go on at me. I'm never doing it right.

We sidle casually into geography class. Fortunately, Mrs. Bullock has her back turned and is rifling through her drawers. When she turns around, her expression is confused as though she's trying to figure out if we'd always been there or not.

. . .

After the lesson, Kaitlyn is buzzing, going on and on about the party.

'You can wear that amazing dress you bought.' I must admit the thought of wearing that short black dress makes me excited. I grin childishly at her. It hasn't taken much to sell Georgia's party to me.

'Are we invited to her party?' I ask as we begin our long walk home.

'No, not exactly. Not yet anyway. But will be.' I admire her optimism but I am not convinced. I'm sure Georgia hates me as much as I hate her.

When I say this to Kaitlyn she says, 'it's not about that though is it? You don't invite just your friends, you invite the cool people, like us, to make yourself cooler.'

I laugh. She has a point. Kaitlyn and I are in the enviable position of being popular, always being surrounded by friends. Who wouldn't want to invite us to their party?

Mum is cleaning the kitchen with all her might when I get home. I swear cleaning is all she does. Of course, she does have a job, a very important one as she keeps telling us, which is why she resents doing all this cleaning. I think she loves it really though. You can almost see the joy on her face as she scrubs the surfaces. On top of that, she's a control freak. If I try and do anything she'll complain it's not good enough, so why bother?

'Hi darling. Good day?' she asks looking from the relentless scouring.

'Not bad,' I offer. I know she'll want more but I'm not about to tell all yet.

'Any homework?' I've been home literally a minute and already she's hassling me.

'Some.'

'Make sure you get it done before dinner.'

'I will,' I answer sarcastically, turning away from her, to head upstairs.

Dad's never home at this time. Sometimes I wish he were. He understands. He's the one I need to ask about the party. There's always one among the parents who will say yes to anything and Dad's it. He's the softie who will buy me what I want.

So, I got us an invite. There is glee written all over Kaitlyn's text.

Great you're the best.

I know.

When is it? Minor detail I should have asked before.

Next Saturday can't wait.

Me neither.

I run to my wardrobe, open it and stare at the gorgeous black dress. I will look amazing. This is going to be the best night of my life. Just got to wait until Dad gets home to ask him. I'm sure he'll be fine about it.

· · ·

'Next weekend you say?' Dad has barely walked through the door when I find him in his office.

'Yeah, that's okay, isn't it?'

'Normally, but Mum's arranged for us to see Granny and Grandad that evening. It's Grandad's birthday.'

'No, really?'

'Yes. Sorry Ella. You can't miss this one.'

Damn it. I love Grandad and all, but this is the party I can't miss. I have to find a way to go.

· · ·

Sam pops round after dinner. Mum was funny about us hanging out in my room to start with but I don't know what she expected, that we were going to sit in the lounge and let her grill us. Absolutely not. Can't think of anything worse.

Now she settles with banging the bathroom door loudly next to my room. She also hates that he is nearly eighteen. Thinks he is far too old for me but she can't deny he is a gentleman. She wanted to dislike him but I could see she fell for his charm as much as I did.

'Is there no way you can get out of your grandparents?'

'I wish. I can't very well not go. Grandad would be devastated.'

'How about if you went for a bit and then you came to the party a bit later?'

'Great idea but they live in the middle of nowhere. I'd have no way to get to the party and Mum and Dad are not going to drive me.'

'I could pick you up.' His eyes light up with excitement.

He means on his bike. He is desperate to show it off.

'You could,' I reply hesitantly.

'They would be fine with it, I'm sure,' taking my hesitancy to mean I didn't want to leave Grandad's house rather than I was afraid to go on his bike. 'Come on, it'll be fun.'

'Sure, why not.' When have I ever said no to a bit of fun?

'You'll have to park round the corner though. They can't know you have a motorbike. Mum would go crazy.' 'Understood.' He salutes me, making me giggle.

With our plans underfoot I am excited. I can't wait for this party. It is going to be the best night ever.

CHAPTER THIRTY-THREE
PRESENT DAY

'You hate him, don't you?'

'Huh?' 'Nick.'

'Oh yeah. I totally do. He's a creep.' Maddie grins sadly while sipping from her lemonade. We finally made it to the restaurant, not an easy feat when you have a disabled person in tow. Our first challenge is trying to open the double doors that lead inside. Most people only have to use one, but I'm too wide now. I watch, mortified, as Maddie fiddles around with the catch, ignoring the stares from fellow diners. Don't help us or anything. Eventually one of the waiters opens it with a flick of the latch, making it look so easy.

The waiter welcomes us but I can see him calculating in his mind how much effort this will require to accommodate me. He scans the room, looking for a suitable space to fit us in, despite the fact we booked this morning. I want to shout at him angrily but shouting never solves anything apparently.

When we are finally settled down, Maddie looks exhausted with it all. I feel bad that everyone has to suffer because of me.

'Just a creep?'

'Okay, an arsehole. You know he tried to come on to me.'

'No way. I hope you told him where to go.'

'Yeah, kind of.'

'It must be hard for you. Your mum, sorry our mum, sounds like a difficult person to live with.'

'That's putting it mildly. She's a bloody nightmare at times but I miss her lots. As you gathered, I got taken away from her. I'm living with Great Aunt Margaret at the moment while Mum pretends to go to AA meetings.'

'Do you want to go back?' She shrugs.

'In some ways, yes. She loves me even if she's a rubbish mum but Great Aunt Margaret's is more comfortable. I don't have to cook my own dinner and worry about all that crap.'

I can't imagine having to fend for yourself like that. Mum always cooks dinner; won't let anyone else near the kitchen.

'I'm sorry I didn't tell you about being abandoned and all.'

'It's tricky. I can understand why.'

'No, I should have told you from the start. This has all been such a mess.'

'None of it our fault. Our messed-up parent's fault.'

'Yep, that's for sure. So, what's our dad like?' I forget that my dad is now her dad. I'm not sure I like the idea of sharing him.

'He's lovely. A big softie.' She smiles.

'Maybe I can get to know him.'

'Maybe.'

For the past few days, I've been wondering where we go from here. Real Mum is from a different county, adopted Mum is crazy mad as she's just found out Dad had an affair. Dad is my real Dad. At night it goes round and round in my head.

'We have to go home tomorrow.'

'Oh.' I want to say more but don't know how to express it. I wish she could stay but how I don't know.

'I've got school again on Tuesday. You could come and visit me.' I stare at her.

We both know the chances of me visiting her in my state are non-existent. For a start, I can't stomach long journeys now and secondly, her house probably isn't wheelchair friendly. This is more than a mess.

'I'll come again though,' she adds.

'I'd like that. We can text as well, maybe FaceTime?'

'That'd be great.'

She's probably longing to know what happened on the night of the accident. I will tell her, just not yet.

At the end of our meal, I'm aching for my bed but the service here is so slow. The waiters seem to work to their own time. Awkward silences follow as Maddie and I try to think what to say to each other. We are basically strangers, strangers with a biological connection.

When we are finally done, Maddie gives me a little hug as I manoeuvre into the car. He smiles shyly at Maddie.

'Thanks for looking after her,' he says. 'Hope to see you again.' He could be speaking to any of my friends rather than his other daughter. I guess he's just as weirded out by this as me.

'Did you have a good time?' he asks, driving carefully through the high street, away from the sea. I've noticed how he seems to take extra care now in the car, most likely worried that I'll be freaked out by speed. He's not wrong.

'It was okay. It was a bit awkward.'

'It will be, for a while, but I'm sure you'll get to know each other.' I'm not so sure. I feel like we are so different.

Can we ever get over the huge gap that separates us?

'Must be strange for you too, having another daughter.'

'Yes; very. I don't know what to say to her either. Nobody gives you a rule book on what to do if you discover you have another child who's now a teenager.'

I laugh loudly.

'Another stroppy one.'

'Haha, you're not so bad.'

CHAPTER THIRTY-FOUR
SIX MONTHS AGO

'There is no way you are leaving Grandad's house early,' yells Mum, so loud I am worried the neighbours can hear.

'It's his birthday.'

'I'll be there for most of it.'

'It's rude.'

'He'll understand.'

'How on earth are you even planning to get there? I'm certainly not driving you.'

'Sam's picking me up.'

'I didn't know he could drive.'

'He only passed recently,' I lie, although technically that is true as he got his motorbike license recently.

'Anyway, you can't go.'

'But Mum-'

'What's going on in here?' Dad sails into the room, the calm spirit among the chaos.

'Ella wants to leave Grandad's house early to go to her party.'

'Why can't she?'

'Because Max, it's Grandad's birthday.' I'm getting sick of hearing it's his birthday. We all have them. It's not even a big one.

'She can stay for the dinner and then go. I'll drive her.'

'No, it's okay Sam's picking me up.'

'Oh. Okay then.'

'No, it's not okay Max.'

'Lighten up Liz. She doesn't want to spend all her time with old people.' He winks naughtily at me.

Mum is fuming, knowing she has been beaten. I take the opportunity to bask in my victory. 'Thanks Dad you're the best.' I kiss him on the cheek as I exit the room swiftly.

Their argument continues when I've left but soon

fizzles out. I hurriedly find my dress, jewellery, and make-up. This is going to be so fun.

All good for tonight I text Sam. He responds with multiple heart emojis.

...

The time goes by slowly through dinner. I can tell Mum is still angry with me and Dad. Granny asks me lots of questions about school, my friends, and Sam. Now I know where Mum gets her questioning skills from. I am itching for the moment when I can escape.

The final piece of cake is shoved in my mouth and I make my excuses and run upstairs to get changed. Mum is at the door of the spare room.

'Be careful tonight, won't you?' I suddenly wonder if she knows that I'm going on a motorbike but she can't.

'Of course. Aren't I always.' Her eyes are full of worry but she smiles nonetheless.

The doorbell sounds. It's an old-fashioned one, just the kind you'd expect your grandparents to have. Granny is beyond excited at meeting the famous Sam.

'Come in. Come in.'

'We need to go, Gran.' I rush past her, trying not to see the disappointed look on her face. Sam glances uneasily around as the family gather to see us off. Anyone would think we were leaving to get married.

'Sorry about them,' I say once the door is shut, shivering and wishing that I had thought to bring a coat.

'Families are supposed to be embarrassing.'

When we are round the corner, he produces a leather jacket out of his rucksack.

'For you.' He hands it to me. I take in the smell of it as I carefully put it on, trying not to mess my hair up. When we reach his bike, he plonks the spare helmet on my head. I could kill him. Does he know how long it took to do my hair? I want to argue with him about wearing it but I also want to be safe. 'You up for a bit of speed?'

I nod but inside my tummy feels like jelly. I'm

beginning to wish I'd let Dad take me. He throws his leg over the seat and gestures for me to sit behind him. The reality of being on a motorbike hits me when I am seated behind him. We are really doing this.

CHAPTER THIRTY-FIVE
PRESENT DAY

I've been back at school for a week now. Everyone is being so nice and I hate it. I don't want any of their fake love. I want real friends to laugh with. Fortunately Kaitlyn is there to soften the blow. When I'm feeling my lowest I can laugh with her.

Fortunately, my school is all on one level so at least I don't have to worry about negotiating stairs or lifts. However, the classrooms are not huge. Mostly I am seated at the back where I can spread out easily. I do appreciate how hard it is for the teachers but they have no idea what it's like. I don't want to stand out, I want to fit in.

Mum was rejoicing that life was back to normal this morning. Back to school, she announced in a cheerful voice. It may be normal for her but it is far from that for me. Maddie texted me last night, telling me she missed me. I doubt that's even true. I so want there to be a connection between us but I can't find it. How can she? Does she long for me like the twin she has always missed? I can't believe that is true. But of course, I will make an effort. I want it to work, but I'm just not sure where we go from here. I can't expect her to come down here to visit me regularly. If only I were mobile enough to meet her halfway. We could do London, see the sights, like the young people we are. At the moment, though, I can imagine nothing worse. I may not have been to London since the accident but I do remember half the tube stations don't have lifts. I don't want it to be one big hassle. I hate that I am so restricted by all this. I hate that I can't just up and go where I want. I want my old life back. Why didn't I appreciate what I had when I had it? Why didn't I run when I could? Why didn't I go exploring when I had the opportunity? If only I had known I would soon be in a wheelchair. If only I hadn't got on that bike that night. If only I had stood up to Sam and told him I was scared. Was it really worth acting brave, now?

My form class are polite to me, nothing more. They offer to get me things, to open doors, to help me out but I don't want their help. I don't want their politeness. I consider shouting at them all but what would that achieve?

It's hard to shake the feelings of depression that hang over me that night as I lie in bed alone. More than anything I long to be the person I was before the accident, to be full of energy again when life wasn't so difficult. Mum keeps talking about counselling, to help me adjust but what if I don't want to adjust? What if I want to wallow in my self pity? I don't see how I can ever accept this.

I lie there reading the same page over and over again in my book and not taking any of it in, hoping that I will get sleepy. Eventually, I decide to turn the light off anyway but the darkness does nothing to make me go to sleep and it only makes Blueberry shuffle around even more.

In the next room, I hear voices that start off muffled but become louder and louder as Mum gets more and more angry.

'How could you sleep with that woman?' Mum is saying.

'Liz, it meant nothing.' But did it? Did he secretly prefer her to Mum? 'Why do we have to keep talking about this? It's late, I've said I'm sorry and it was years ago.'

'You don't get it, do you? You had a baby with someone else. I can't even look at Ella now without seeing that ugly woman's face.'

Whoa. Thanks Mum. If I could march in there I would, give her a piece of my mind. What kind of mother says such a thing?

Finally, they go quiet, exhausted themselves with all the shouting. Glad of the peace, I start to drift off.

Vicky Ball

When I wake up it is still dark. I tighten my eyes, telling myself that I can still sleep but my mind has other ideas. Sam's face pops into my head, the motorbike, that dark night. I don't want to see it again.

CHAPTER THIRTY-SIX
SIX MONTHS AGO

'Isn't this exciting?' Sam asks turning round to see my reaction.

'Great,' I answer, clutching his waist tightly and shutting my eyes.

'Hold on tight.'

He revs the engine. I could tell him now that I don't want to carry on but I don't. I don't want to look weak. At first, we are slow but then very quickly he accelerates. To begin with, it is like a roller coaster, excitement that makes you want to scream, except this is real life. I open my eyes for a brief second to see the trees around us becoming a blur. I close my eyes again, praying it will be over soon.

'Want to go faster?' I can just about hear him yelling above the noise of the engine. No, I want to shout, but I don't. He takes my silence as compliance and twists the accelerator excitedly.

I dare peek out from behind his leather jacket. The dark deserted country lanes send shivers down my spine, no one out here to save me. We twist and turn round endless corners, making me feel sick. I stare off into the distance but I can't see anything beyond the circle of light from the headlight.

Suddenly a bright light ahead blinds me. It's coming closer and closer. I squeeze Sam, he's in control. He's got this. The light looms in at great speed, I close my eyes and hope. Sam screams. I've never heard a noise like that come from a man. Sam slam on the brake as the wheels lock and the tyres struggle to grip the loose road surface.

For a second I am crushed against Sam' body and then we hit the car. Sam and the bike jerk to the side, I hold on with all my strength but it isn't enough, I am thrown off. I am flying through the air and for a second I feel nothing, then I hit the ground so hard it leaves me breathless. My bones and back shake. It feels like I've just fallen from the top of my house and hit the ground, legs first. I think I might black out as I lie there in shock, the world spinning around me. There are branches and leaves in my face, scratches on my arms and my face. My back aches. I try to wriggle my legs but they won't move.

I look around for Sam or the car but all I can hear is the sound of the car's engine as it drives away. I try to yell for help.

'Please stop.' but it barely comes out as a whisper.

I am left alone, hoarsely shouting to Sam. No reply comes in the eerie silence. I lay my head back in despair, praying someone will come and rescue us.

CHAPTER THIRTY-SEVEN
PRESENT DAY

'You know what we need?'

I stare at Kaitlyn blankly. I can think of lots of things I need but I'm not getting any of them.

'A night out.'

'Um… have you forgotten about this?' I say pointing down at my wheelchair.

'It'll be fine. Leave it all to me.'

'I also have nothing to wear.'

'So, we go shopping, later after school.'

I glance sceptically up at her. That doesn't sound as easy as it should be. I hope I will have the energy to do it.

Mum isn't happy when Kaitlyn asks her to drop us in town.

'I'll come with you,' Mum suggests. That's the last thing I need.

'No Mum, we can manage.' I'm not sure we can.

'But Ella-'

'Mum, I don't want you there,' I shout rudely, instantly feeling guilty.

'Okay,' she answers in a small voice. 'Call me if you need me though.'

'Of course.' Kaitlyn smiles awkwardly next to me in the car. I can tell she is glad though. Neither of us wanted the control freak shopping with us.

Mum drops us at the shopping centre entrance. We head straight for Primark. As we're waiting to cross the road, a motorbike zooms past. It's nowhere near us but instantly my heart rate increases and breathing suddenly becomes difficult. I can't move. People swarm past me, hurrying to get across while there's a space but I am frozen to the spot. 'You okay?' asks Kaitlyn.

Her voice breaks me out of the trance that I'm in.

'Yes I'm good,' I answer, forcing myself to cross the

road. Before we even enter the shop, I know it's a mistake. People are pouring out and the heat from the number of bodies inside is wafting out. The aisle looks way too narrow.

As Kaitlyn holds the door open for me, I glance up anxiously at her. She smiles, not at all phased by the challenges ahead.

'Come on, let's go look at the sales rack.'

I follow slowly, trying to navigate past the clothes rails and discarded items strewn randomly over the floor. No one pauses to help or even appears to notice I'm there. I have to stop several times because someone has just walked out in front of me without looking. Some smile apologetically and offer a small sorry, others ignore me completely, treating me like I'm invisible.

When I finally make it to the sales rack, Kaitlyn has already sifted through half of it.

'You can see why most of this is on sale,' she chuckles. One glance at the rack and it's easy to agree. The garish colours are enough to put anyone off. 'Ah but what about this top?'

She pulls out a bright red ribbed top. I scrunch up my face, I'm pretty sure it won't fit me.

'You hold this one while I look for some.' She practically throws it at me before continuing her search. I open my mouth to protest, that I would like to look too, but it has already been assumed that I am incapable of that. Instead, I sit there feeling like a lost soul. An older lady reaches over me for the top next to me. I throw my hands up in frustration.

'Oh, sorry didn't see you there,' she laughs. I respond with a glare.

Kaitlyn spins round from her position next to the woman. 'Didn't see her? You an idiot?'

'I… er …'

'Yeah stupid,' finishes Kaitlyn and we both start laughing. 'Who's laughing now bitch,' she calls as the woman skulks away.

'You're too funny,' I giggle.

Kaitlyn has an arm full of tops. Noticeably there are no trousers or skirts. Another assumption, that I only need one type of clothing now.

'Let's go and try them on.'

I don't argue, but follow her through the crowds of people and join the queue for the fitting room. By this point, I am needing the toilet and wondering where the nearest disabled one would be.

When we get to the front of the queue, the sales assistant says 'I'm so sorry but the disabled changing room is out of order.' She says it so lightly and so casually that she can't possibly know what that means to me.

'What now then?' I ask, feeling the anger rising within me.

She glances around, confused. 'What do you mean?'

'Where can I try them on?'

'Sorry but there is nowhere else.'

That's it. We have to leave, feeling humiliated. A couple of people in the queue shake their heads in disgust at the sales assistant, others say *sorry love* to me as we go by. I just want to curl up in a ball and disappear.

'Take me to a toilet,' I demand when we are outside. I know I sound bitchy but I am past caring. Kaitlyn seems taken aback but points in the direction of the nearest department store. I only hope that it's not out of order.

When I get home, I am exhausted and have nothing to show for it. I slump off to bed without a word, too tired for all of Mum's questions, hoping she'll get the message I don't want to talk.

Later I am awoken by the buzzing of my phone. It's Maddie FaceTiming me. Her face is red and puffy.

'What's up?'

'I was supposed to meet Mum today but she didn't bloody show.'

'Oh, Maddie I'm sorry. That's terrible.'

'Sorry I shouldn't have rung but-'

'No, it's fine. What happened?'

'We were supposed to have a supervised visit at the centre. I was all psyched up and excited to see her. She was probably drunk somewhere.'

'What did Margaret say?'

'That Mum loves me. Well, clearly not enough.'

'Sorry Maddie.' I don't know what else to say because no words can make up for our real mother being the way she is. I wish I could go there and hug her now, make up for all the pain she's suffered.

'Anyway, how was your day?'

'Hmm not great. Let's just say, me and shopping don't go.'

CHAPTER THIRTY-EIGHT

'Liz, we've been through this so many times.'

'I know, and I don't know if I can forgive you for what you've done.' Mum and Dad aren't even shouting anymore but I can still hear them. I miss my room upstairs where I felt like I had privacy, where I didn't have to listen awkwardly to every conversation that my parents had in the lounge. I get that Mum is upset that Dad had an affair sixteen years ago but that was then. A lot has happened since. Why can't she just get over it? Blueberry is out in a box on the bed. I gently touch his back but already sense his teeth ready to bite me.

'Liz, please. I love you.'

'Like you love that drunkard? What did you even see in her?'

'She wasn't like that then. She was-'

'I don't want to hear it.'

Placing Blueberry back in his cage, I return to my bed and bury my head in my pillow, reaching for my headphones on the floor, anything to block them out.

Being reunited with my twin sister was supposed to be a happy occasion but it's caused nothing but trouble ever since. A part of me would like to go back to living in ignorance, to the time when I was not adopted and my parents loved each other. The other part of me knows, though, that my parent's problems have been simmering a lot longer than Maddie's appearance. Maybe this was just one possible catalyst. If not this, then it would have been something else.

I often wonder how kids cope when their parents get divorced. I have always wondered about the idea that some relationships are better apart, surely it's best to stay together until the child is grown up but now I'm starting to think differently. The atmosphere in our house is unbearable. Maybe it would be better if one of them left.

Who would I go with? Mum spends a great deal of time looking after me and I do love her but Dad is the fun, openly caring one but would he cope with me on his own? Could either of them care for me alone? I'm not a normal teenager anymore.

For not the first time since my accident, I wonder if their lives would be better off without me. With my headphones plugged in, I don't hear Dad come in. The first I know is a tap on my shoulder. His face shows signs of worry and stress. I pull the headphones out.

'Hey honey, we've got to get you ready.'

'Where we going?'

'You've got a hospital check-up.' Mum usually takes me so I am surprised it is Dad now. 'Where's Mum?'

'She's taking a break.' A break, as in relationship break? But I don't voice my concerns.

'I wish I could take a break,' I say grumpily. Dad smiles sympathetically. 'Do I have to go to the hospital today? I'm really tired.'

'I know it's hard Ella but I'm afraid you do.'

Although we go regularly, the hospital fills me with dread. I can already feel a knot forming in my chest. I would rather face a thousand spiders than go back to that place again.

'Then when you get back, Kaitlyn's coming over.' 'Oh is she? She didn't say.' Dad merely smiles.

As we are getting in the car, a motorbike speeds down the road, I clutch the side of my wheelchair and try to think of something else, anything but that night. Dad places a calm hand on my shoulder.

'It's okay. You're safe now.'

Once I am in the car surrounded by walls, I feel more relaxed.

'You know if you ever want to talk about that night I'm here.'

'Thanks Dad. I'll let you know.'

'It might be good to talk about it. If not me, a

counsellor. Dr. Webb suggested you might like to see one.'

'I don't know if I can talk about it.'

'I understand but think about it at least.'

'I will.' Talking, even thinking about it, is like reliving the biggest fear anyone ever has. No one wants to talk about that. I can't imagine that will ever change. Most days I don't even admit that Sam is dead, hoping that would make it true.

Later when we are home from the hospital and I am settled comfortably in the lounge, Kaitlyn comes round.

'Hey you,' she says cheerfully like nothing has changed. I know she is hiding behind multiple shadows as well.

'Hi, I thought you usually texted me when you were going to come over.'

'I lost my phone.'

'Lost? actually lost it?'

'Yeah. I was out last night and must have left it somewhere. So annoying. I need my phone.'

'You were out? Wow, get you.'

She laughs. 'Ha yes I know seems strange going out these days.' She says it as though we are old and have too many responsibilities to go out. Once upon a time we would have been out every night, arguing with our parents about whether we should be out on a school night.

'Where did you go?' She seems reluctant to tell me.

'I was at Georgia's house.'

'I thought you hated her.'

'Well, I kind of did but since the party I've got to know her a bit and she's not that bad.'

'Oh.' I can't think what else to say. I feel like I've been replaced.

She stays for another half an hour but it's clear from her constant watch checking and the way her eyes glance around that she wants to leave.

'I'm kind of tired,' I say, giving her the excuse she needs to leave.

'Yes of course. I'll leave you to it. I'll see myself out.'

She hurries out before I get a chance to answer. She has left and I am alone again. Why do I feel like all my friends have abandoned me, even Kaitlyn?

'I'm about to cook dinner. Do you want a nap first?' Dad appears from the direction of the stairs.

'No, I'll just watch some TV in here. Where's Mum?'

'She's eating somewhere else.'

'Oh.'

He dives into the kitchen and I hear the familiar sounds of the chopping board and the pans being got out. Suddenly it stops and he pokes his head back round the wall.

'The truth is Mum has gone to live somewhere else for a bit. Like I say, she needs a break.'

'Right but she's coming back though?' He sighs.

'I don't know. This whole thing has been hard on her. She's finding it difficult to deal with my … er… affair.'

'But that was a long time ago.'

'I know but it still hurts. I'm sorry love.'

'Why is life so complicated?' He sends me a sad smile. He used to be the dad that knew everything but now he has no answers.

CHAPTER THIRTY-NINE

'What's up? You look deep in thought.' Dad can always tell when there is something wrong.

'A message from Maddie.'

'She okay?'

'She's moving back in with her Mum.' 'Is that a good idea?'

I shrug.

'I'm not sure it's a great one but Maddie is so excited. I find it hard to understand her enthusiasm for her.'

'I suppose she's the only family she's ever known.' Do I detect a hint of guilt in his face? 'It's only natural she'd want to be with her.'

'Even if she is an alcoholic and neglects her?'

'I'm sure social services have done their checks. They wouldn't send you back home if they thought it was unsafe.'

'I suppose you're right.'

'When am I not?' He smirks. I can't argue. Infuriatingly, most of the time he is right.

'Maddie did say she was going to her AA meetings.'

'There we go then.'

'And the house looks amazing.'

'See.'

'Yes Dad; you're right. Happy now?'

'Ecstatic,' he replies beaming.

. . .

Later, when Maddie FaceTime's me, it's clear to see she's not as happy as she should be.

'How's it being back at home?'

'It's great. It's so tidy I hardly recognised it.'

'So why do you look like it's the end of the world.'

'Nick's here.'

'Oh.'

'Yeah. That bloody man. He had to turn up on my first night back, didn't he? Went on about taking us out to dinner and when I said I didn't have a dress he offered to buy me one.'

'Creepy.'

'I know right? I wish he'd do one.'

'Does your Mum know how you feel?'

'I'm pretty sure it's obvious. I barely speak to him and avoid him at any opportunity.'

After the call, Kaitlyn texts me informing me of details of our night out in the new top that I still don't have. An overwhelming sense of gloom fills me, realising that life will never be the same again. I'm consider making excuses, telling her I can't go. I don't want to be a burden on her, I don't want to constantly be worried about being out or how I'm going to cope.

'You okay?' Dad asks, coming into my room.

I don't want to cry but I can't help it.

'Not really. I hate this,' I say gesturing to the lower half of my body. 'I hate that I can't go out and have a normal life. I hate that Kaitlyn is having to look after me on nights out. I hate that I can't do anything spontaneous anymore and most of all,' I sob in a quiet voice. 'I hate Sam not being here.'

I also hate the way Dad is looking now, completely helpless with guilt written all over him, but I don't say that to him. He rushes over to cuddle me.

'Sorry Dad. I'm just having a bad day.'

'It's okay sweetie. You're allowed to have a bad day. You've been dealt a crap hand.' 'The worst,' I agree.

'I wish I could make it all better for you.'

'I know Dad. I wish that too.'

CHAPTER FORTY

'I love being here with you.' He strokes my hair, gazing into my eyes. 'And I love you.'

'I love you too Sam.' The sun is beginning to set on Louisa Bay and all the tourists have gone. There is us, lying on the beach, alone and happy.

'I wish we could just elope to a hot country, you and me.' The thought warms me inside. I'd love nothing more than to walk barefooted on the beach in a foreign land.

'Maybe one day, hey.'

He sits up, suddenly excited. 'Guess what?'

'What?'

'I'm getting a motorbike.' His eyes light up like a little kid. I'm supposed to share this excitement but I don't. It seems reckless and stupid. Of course, I don't tell him that.

'That's great.'

'I can take you for drives in the country. We could go to Canterbury.'

'We can already do that by train.'

'But it's so expensive.' But a lot safer, I want to add. 'And imagine the speed, ooh the speed.' I look at him doubtfully. 'Come on, it'll be fun.'

I snuggle into him, muttering 'Of course, it will.' He pats my head like I am his pet. I don't mind. It's good to be wanted by someone. One day we'll be with each other all the time.

...

The house is strangely quiet since Mum left. Dad is trying to be cheerful enough for both of them, but I can see he's struggling. He not only has to deal with me, but now he has to do it alone. To those who don't know him, it would seem he is doing it all and coping well, but I can see beneath the exterior where the cracks appear.

Maddie texted me with an update on being back with real Mum. The tone of her message suggested she was buzzing about it, so happy, apart from Nick obviously. I don't understand how she can want to live with an alcoholic mother. She says she's changed, but has she? I don't believe anyone changes that much in such a short space. They're both coming to visit next weekend. I'm not sure how I feel about that. I want to see Maddie again but real Mum? Not so sure. Maybe Maddie can help me see the real her, the reason she loves her so much. I certainly can't understand what Dad saw in her but like he said it was a long time ago and things have changed a lot.

I decide to broach the subject with him while he is making me cooked breakfast, a typical Saturday tradition.

'What did you like about Mum when you first met her?'

'She was smart and determined. She had to be to get through law school.'

'No, I mean real Mum.'

'Oh, her. I guess I liked that she was fun. She was always the life and soul of the party.'

'Where did you meet?'

'At a pub. Your Mum, adopted mum that is, was out with her friends, so I popped in for a drink. She was there with her mates. We hit it off instantly as soon as our eyes met across the bar.'

'Sounds like a cheesy movie,' I say making gagging movements.

'It was really. I never intended to sleep with her. It just happened.'

'But you were getting married?' His face reddens.

'Yes, I was.'

'And then you did it again.'

'I was weak and she was very persuasive. I should have said no.'

'Why didn't you?'

'Because Liz and I were going through a rough patch. She was stressed with studying so much and I was working long hours. It's no excuse but you know.'

I'm not sure how he expects me, a fifteen-year-old, to understand but I certainly don't. It's clear-cut to me. You're engaged, you don't sleep with other people. 'I'm a terrible person, but look what came of it.' He points at me dramatically with his wooden spoon.

Yay for being alive. I didn't ask to be here. I had a great fifteen years, but then it got crap. Is the rest of my life going to be this bad?

'I know what you're thinking. You've had a tough time recently but you are still alive. You could have died that night-'

'Dad, I-'

'You could have been the one laid on that road dead.'

'DAD,' I yell. 'Stop.'

'Sorry.'

'I don't want to talk about that night.'

'I get it, sorry.' Does he get it though? I keep telling him but half the time he's trying to get me to talk about it.

The following week at school drags by slowly, the new normal at an old familiar place. School used to be a fun place where I'd hang out in the toilets and laugh over annoying teachers while trying to avoid certain kids but now, I feel like I'm the one being avoided. I'm the outcast no one wants to talk to. They don't want to hang out with a girl in a wheelchair.

I am glad when it's Friday. Dad picks me up and takes me to Pizza Hut. I love pizza but I'm tired and don't want to see anyone I know. Luckily the only space big enough for my chair is in the corner, away from everyone else.

'You excited about seeing Maddie tomorrow?'

'I guess so. Not sure about seeing real Mum though.'

'Why do you call her that?'

'Because she is. What am I supposed to call her?'

He shrugs. 'I don't know, Becky.'

'But she's not Becky to me.'

'Maybe don't mention to your other Mum on Sunday that you saw her.' I do the zip across the lips gesture.

When adopted Mum wanted to see me as well this weekend, I couldn't very well say no. Besides, I do want to see her. I miss her in a weird *missing the person who nags a lot* kind of way. The house has been a bit messy since she left. It is clearly not one of Dad's priorities.

'Do you want the buffet?' Dad asks without thinking. 'Sorry I forgot.' Forgot I can't move around very easily.

'It's fine. We can still do it. I'll just balance the plate on my lap, all good.' I do the thumbs-up sign. Dad doesn't seem convinced but stays quiet. After sorting out the minor details with the waitress he pushes me over towards the buffet bar.

Our first obstacle is a lady's bag, dumped right in the middle of the aisle like it belongs there.

'Excuse me,' says Dad politely. The lady doesn't respond but carries on with her conversation. 'Excuse me.' His voice getting louder. 'Can you move your bag please?'

She turns and stares up at Dad before moving her eyes to me. Her stern expression doesn't break into a smile, not even close. She's one step away from objecting but decides not to. Slowly she reaches over and picks up her bag, chucking it unceremoniously under the table, before turning back to her friends.

Dad huffs and mutters something I can't quite hear under his breath. I focus my eyes ahead, no point in wasting any energy on such a person.

The second obstacle is in the form of a whole pizza that has somehow ended up on the floor. Dad tries desperately to steer round it but there's not enough room. He stands, frustrated with his arms folded, glancing around for a staff member. With none seemingly to be available or at least pretending not to notice, he stoops down and picks it up himself, tosses it so hard that it hits the wall opposite the buffet.

'Dad, you can't do that,' I giggle.

'If people want to leave their pizza lying around what do they expect?'

'Erm excuse me, you can't put it there.' Dad stops and stares at the young waiter, who looks like he is only a few years older than me.

'I need to get past.'

'But you can't just throw pizza on the floor.' I'm literally waiting for the fireworks.

'It wasn't mine but it was causing an obstruction and as you can see it's difficult enough trying to negotiate this thing.'

He points down at me. I really hope he's talking about the wheelchair.

'Is there a problem?' An older, hopefully more experienced waiter, approaches. The younger one steps back nervously, eager for someone else to deal with this problem.

'There was a pizza in my way so I moved it.'

'Don't worry sir, we'll deal with it.' He stands to one side and beckons us towards the buffet bar. I can almost imagine the furious whispers that will take place now. *The customer is always right.* I guess he missed that one in training.

'Anyone else for flying pizza,' Dad jokes.

By the time we get back to our seats, it is clear that Dad is exhausted.

'Dominoes delivery next time?' I joke.

He smiles sadly. 'Shouldn't have to be though.'

. . .

The following morning, I am up awake early, ready for the day's exciting events. I am excited, about seeing Maddie anyway but I don't know what I'm going to say to real Mum. Blueberry is still fast asleep in the corner, curled up like a baby, unaware of the upcoming day.

We're meeting in the park by the sea, a lot easier and less stressful than going to a restaurant. They are there waiting for me when Dad wheels me up. Maddie stands and hugs me. Real Mum looks terrified like I'm going to shout at her.

'Hi,' I say quietly.

'Hi Ella,' Maddie shouts excitedly. Mum mutters a quiet *hi*, not daring to speak. Maddie throws her a frustrated look.

'It's great to see you guys,' I say after a moment's awkward silence. 'Thanks for … er … coming.'

'It was no trouble.'

I know they had to get the train down. It can't have been easy, navigating a big city with an incompetent mother.

'I didn't want to give you up,' Real Mum suddenly blurts out, shocking us both. I'm not sure what she wants me to say to that. 'There was stuff going on. I can't talk about it but I loved you both. I feel terrible.' I stay silent, does she want me to tell her it's all okay, that being adopted was the best thing she could ever do?

'I'm sure Ella doesn't blame you Mum,' Maddie adds, her eyes jumping from real Mum to me.

'Of course not,' I lie. I can't even begin to understand how you could leave your baby in a public toilet. 'Why a public toilet though?'

With panicked eyes, she looks away. 'It seemed like a place that would be used lots.'

It's a rubbish reason and one I suspect is a lie but I can't very well start interrogating her now. I wish now Maddie had come on her own. At least then we could have been more honest with each other.

'How's it going back at Mum's?' I ask.

'Fantastic. I'm loving being back.' Real Mum nods enthusiastically.

'You should visit sometime,' she says half-heartedly.

'Maybe.'

She wants forgiveness; she wants acceptance. Neither of which I am willing to give right now.

CHAPTER FORTY-ONE

A day at home alone, something I've not had for a long time. Dad was reluctant to leave me but I said I had plenty of people I could call. Life has settled into a new normal. I try to brush the memories of the past away. There's no point dwelling on what could have been.

I begged Kaitlyn to come over but she said she was busy. Probably at Georgia's house. I hate Georgia even more now she has stolen Kaitlyn from me. I know it's irrational. We could all be friends but I don't want to share her. I sound like an idiot but I can't go and join in their fun anyway, even if I wanted to. I can see them now, mooching around town, stopping in Primark to look at the perfumes and nail varnishes.

I entertain myself with Netflix. I probably should do the homework that is piling up but when you know you won't get in trouble there's less incentive. No one is going to give me a detention. Homework makes you smarter, the teachers all say, but does it? I get the feeling they're only saying that because they're told to.

Before I can get into the show I've chosen to watch, Maddie FaceTime's me.

'You look happy,' I venture. 'Nick is no more.'

'He's dead?'

She laughs.

'No, he dumped Mum.'

'Great news.'

'It is except I feel bad for Mum. She was so down on herself last night. *I'm not good enough. I've never been good enough for anyone* kind of thing. Poor Mum.'

I fight back the urge to say that I agree with her, she's not a good enough Mum. Maddie deserves better but instead, I say: 'I'm sure she's better off without him.'

'Oh absolutely, without a doubt. I won't miss seeing his face round here.'

When I hear a key in the door, I am surprised. Dad

isn't due home until later. I hear her solid footsteps in the hall. I know that sound anywhere.

'Maddie, I need to go,' I say hurriedly. Maddie looks about to say something but I interrupt her. 'I'll call you later.' I hang up before she can say anymore.

'You're home.' Mum has the look of someone who is trying to sneak in and out without being noticed.

'Had a training day today.'

'Right.'

Mum has barely seen us in the last few weeks since she left. I know she hates Dad for what he did but it's like she can't look at me. It makes me wonder what I've done.

'I've just come to get a few things.' She runs up the stairs. Totally unfair as I can't follow her to talk to her. Frustrated, I sit in the lounge gazing up at the stairs, waiting for her return. When she does, she looks eager to go.

'Don't go yet,' I beg, hating myself for sounding so needy. She sighs but sits down on the sofa opposite me.

'Sorry. Got a lot on. It's been crazy.'

'I miss you.'

'I'm sorry sweetheart. I'll come round more I promise. Anyway, how are you? How's school?'

'It's okay.' Not much has changed, I'm still being ignored a lot and being spoken to politely, not at all what I need. 'How's the flat?'

'It's small.' I want to tell her she has no right to complain about that when she has a gorgeous house she has left, by choice.

'I know Dad was an idiot for having an affair but it was a long time ago. Couldn't you forgive him?'

She takes a deep breath and smiles in a way that scares me. 'Ella, it's so much more complicated than that.'

'Why don't you tell me then? I'm not a child anymore.'

'You wouldn't understand.'

'Maybe I would,' I say angrily.

'I doubt it, you're fifteen and-'

'And what?'

'Never mind.' She stands up. 'I need to go.'

'Go then. It's clear you don't care about us.' 'It's not like that,' she hisses at me.

'He had an affair so what? Thousands of people do.' I can see her face getting redder and redder.

'I don't care about the bloody affair. I already knew about that.' She stops, her eyes giving away that she has said too much.

'What did you say?'

'Never mind. I've got to go.'

'Mum, you can't leave. What do you mean you knew about the affair?'

She is out of the door, muttering words I can't decipher before I can question her further. If she knew about the affair then why did she leave?

PART 3
CHAPTER FORTY-TWO
Maddie

Life goes on without Nick. Mum seems happier and goes out less, preferring to spend time with me. It took almost losing me for good to realise how important I am to her. I've also seen a lot less of James since he helped me find Ella. He constantly texts me but I feel like he's more into me than I am him. He wants to hang out but I can't be bothered. I don't know how I feel about him. Even though he has been nothing but a gentleman I sense that he wants more from me. I don't even know if I want to be with any boy. I should probably break up with him and be done with it.

Jackie is happy with Mum's progress too. I feel like a proud parent at parent's evening whenever Jackie comes round and sees how tidy it all is and how well Mum looks.

But then Nick appears out of the blue, standing at the door in his skimpy shorts and tight t-shirt.

'Your Mum in?'

'She's just popped out.' I instantly regret telling him that. I don't want him to know I'm alone.

'Can I come in and wait?' I want to say no, but what excuse could I give? Too late, I've hesitated too long.

'Um... yeah.'

He marches into the lounge and plants himself in the seat that I was sitting in. It's like he knows what will annoy me the most. I'm tempted to disappear upstairs but I don't want to risk him following me. Marvin takes one look at Nick and leaves the room, head held high in disgust. Nick reaches out to stroke him as he passes by but Marvin arches his back out of the way.

'Do you want a drink?' I ask, hoping he'll say yes, so I can escape the room.

'Nah. Just had one.'

'Okay.'

I sit in the empty chair nearest the TV and switch it on before he can try to talk to me. When I glance over, he is smiling at me, his eyes looking me all over. I am about to call him out when I hear the key in the door. Thank goodness she's home.

Mum walks into the room, with armfuls of shopping bags but stops when she sees Nick.

'Oh. Hi.' I see a glimmer of hope in her eyes and I know all is lost. 'What you doing here?'

'I had to see you.'

'I'm going to go upstairs.'

'Can you unload the bags while we chat?' Mum pleads. I reluctantly agree, wishing we didn't have an open plan house.

'Oh babe, I made a terrible mistake.' I hear Nick saying. 'I should never have let you go. I realise that now. Will you take me back?'

I hope that Mum will at least make him wait a little bit but I hear her quiet voice saying, 'Of course Nick. I love you.'

Damn Mum, have you no self-respect? Angrily I throw the food into cupboards and shove the fruit into the bowl on the side as quickly as I can. I need to get out of here before I say something I'll regret.

I stomp past them ignoring Mum.

'Nick and I are back together. Sorry I don't know what's up with her?'

Is she bloody stupid? Once again, I feel like second best.

James has texted me when I get upstairs.

Do you want to come over tonight?

I don't reply. I don't want to go over there. I hate men. They ruin everything.

Are you ok?

I should tell him what's up but he's part of the

problem. He's one of them. There is no way James is perfect. I bet he's like all the other men. Nick, letching idiot; real dad, cheating bastard. I hate them all.

Are you ignoring me?

I wonder how he can know but then realise we are on WhatsApp, so he can see when I've read his message. Still I don't respond. Let him think what he wants.

'Maddie.' Mum's voice calls up the stairs in a sing-songy way. She's too happy. 'Maddie,' she says bursting into my room dramatically.

'You've been drinking.'

'Only a teeny bit.' She puts her finger and thumb together. 'Nick and I are going out. Wanna come?'

'No.'

'Don't be like this Maddie.'

'Please stay,' I plead. 'You'll come back drunk.'

'It's one night. Don't be a spoilsport.'

'But I need you.'

'You're fifteen. You can be left alone for one night.'

'Please Mum.'

'You sound like a spoilt brat.'

Anger overtakes me as I chuck my pillow at her, wishing it was a brick.

'Ooh, who's in a bad mood?' I throw my teddy at her as well. Maybe the button eyes will scratch her face.

'GET OUT.'

'Okay. Okay.' She leaves, and I hear her shuffling around outside the door, and Nick's voice.

'Maybe it's her time of the month,' he says. I resist the urge to go out there and punch him in the face.

I clutch my remaining pillow close to my chest as I fight the tears. I won't let them out at least not until they've gone. They can't see me like this.

When I finally hear the front door shut, I let go. Big shuddering tears escape as I curl up under my duvet.

A scratching and meowing at the door makes me sit up. I get up and let Marvin in.

Abandoned

I scoop him up and let him snuggle into my top, holding him tightly. He won't let me down.

CHAPTER FORTY-THREE
ELLA

I spend the night tossing and turning, getting more and more confused. How could Mum have known about the affair for all these years?

When morning comes, I am exhausted, I have barely slept.

'What's up with you?' Dad asks as I rub my eyes.

'Didn't sleep well.'

'Anything I can help with?'

'No, it's fine. Got things on my mind.' I'm not ready to share what she said yet. I will but I need to figure it out first.

The doorbell sounds. That could be Mum now. I panic. What if she thinks I've told Dad and is ready to confront him all over again?

'I'll get it.' Dad wanders in the direction of the door.

Unfamiliar voices echo into my room.

'Mr Webster, good to see you again. Could we come in? We've got some questions for Ella.'

I'm trying to work out who it is when Dad reappears at my door.

'Hey, there's some detectives here to see you. They want to talk to you about the night of the accident.'

I clutch the edge of the bed. What if I don't want to talk about it? As if he can sense what I am feeling, Dad comes over and strokes my hair.

'I'll be right there with you.'

I nod, knowing I don't really have a choice in this. I have to face it sometime. I only wish I'd had a bit more warning.

Dad helps me get dressed and into the chair. He leaves me to wheel myself out of the room while he makes them drinks.

Two men in suits sit at opposite ends of the lounge.

They smile at me sympathetically. Instantly their eyes fall to the area where my legs should be until they quickly look away.

'Hello Ella. How are you?'

'I'm good thanks.' Not sure good is the right way to describe my state of mind but it's enough for them.

'We wanted to ask you about the accident again. I know this must be hard for you to talk about but it's important that we get it clear what happened.'

I already told them before. Why do we have to keep going over it again and again?

'Okay,' I answer quietly.

'You were on your boyfriend's motorbike, is that right?' Obviously, I want to scream at them.

'That's correct.'

Dad winces as he comes into the room with two steaming coffee cups. He must hate that I went on that thing.

'What do you remember about the car that hit you? Colour? Make?'

He's asking me, who knows nothing about cars. At best I would be able to tell you the colour but it was dark and the headlights were bright.

'Nothing. The lights blinded me.' They nod as though this is what they expected to hear.

'You didn't see it drive away?'

I wrack my brain to see if there is any memory of what happened and a soft curved edge springs to mind.

'It has a rounded end.'

'That's good. Anything else? Big car? Small car?'

'Big, I think but no idea. It could have been red.' 'Thank you, Ella. You've been most helpful.' 'Why didn't they stop?' I ask suddenly.

The police officer smiles softly before his face turns to a frown.

'Because some people are selfish bastards.' The other officer's eyes widen at the sudden use of language. 'Excuse my language.' I grin.

'Do you have any ideas who did this?'

'We are working on it, I promise. I'd like to say we're getting closer to the truth but I can't say any more than that. We're determined to bring them to justice.'

Justice would be great but it won't be justice for me until I get my legs back and that's never going to happen. Sometimes I wonder what good it will do finding out who the person was that ran us over and drove off. Probably some drunk driver or some bloke on drugs. Didn't care then and I'm sure he won't care now either.

Dad is staring at me with questioning eyes when they've gone. I guess like me he is trying to work it out.

'I'm so sorry this happened to you,' he says sadly. 'I feel responsible.'

'Why? It's not your fault.'

'I should have stopped you going on that bike.'

'You didn't know I was going on a motorbike and besides do you think I wouldn't have found a way.'

'You are pretty stubborn.'

We both laugh in a sad kind of dark humour way. I wish more than anything I had said no to Sam, stood up to him, and told him I was scared about going on his bike, that I would have thought more about staying alive than staying cool in Sam's eyes. In the end, it doesn't matter at all what I look like to Sam. He's dead, I'm alive, if you call this alive.

'I'm sure the police will figure it all out.'

I shrug. 'Doesn't matter if they do, does it? I'm going to be disabled for the rest of my life whatever.'

He looks away, unable to hold my gaze anymore.

CHAPTER FORTY-FOUR
Maddie

I heard them come in late last night. They think they're being discreet but I swear they make more noise whispering than they do talking normally. I can't believe we're back to this again. I can't wait to see Nick's smarmy face at breakfast, not! I decide to take the easy route and leave the house before they're up. I can't face a hung-over Mum and her overly cheerful boyfriend.

I walk slowly to school. It's way too early but I don't care. James is waiting around the corner for me.

'Have you been avoiding me?' He asks, making me jump.

'How did you know I was going to be out here at this time?' I eye him suspiciously.

'I didn't. I've been waiting here for ages.' He shivers and pulls his coat tighter to him. That he should wait for me in the cold should make me love him even more but I feel stifled. 'So have you?'

'Have I what?'

'Been avoiding me?'

'I've got a lot going on right now. I can't deal with this.'

'I don't understand what I've done wrong. I've only ever tried to help.'

'No, you never do anything wrong,' I mutter, making James look more confused than ever. 'Look it's not you it's me.' I feel like one of those awful girlfriends on a bad soap. 'I hate all men right now.'

James' hurt eyes are nearly enough for me to take him in my arms but I don't.

'If that's what you want.' He turns away, ready to leave. 'You know where I am.'

I should run after him, tell him I love him, that I can't live without him but I don't. He's the best thing that's ever happened to me and I'm letting him walk away.

'Sorry,' I whisper so quietly I doubt even the bird next to me can hear.

The day at school goes by far too quick for my liking. I don't want to go home. I don't want to see Mum or Nick.

Right before I am about to leave school Mrs. Hargreaves corners me in the corridor.

'Can I have a word?'

'Um… yeah,' I stutter, following her into a nearby classroom, wishing I could run the other way.

'How's it all going back at your Mum's?'

I hate that everyone knows exactly what is going on in my life. They probably don't know that Nick is back though and that Mum's drinking again. If I told them that they'd pack me straight back to Great Aunt Margaret's.

'Good,' I answer unconvincingly.

'You glad to be home?'

'Of course.' I know my acting skills are not going to win any prizes. She fixes stern eyes on me, willing me to tell her the truth but what would I say? I can't tell her any of it.

'You'd tell me if there was anything wrong, wouldn't you?'

'Absolutely.' She sighs, knowing there is not much she can do, bar torture, to get the truth out of me.

She stands up. 'I better let you go then.'

I am only too happy to escape and run out of the room before she can stop me. I don't know what she expected, that I confide in her, tell her all, knowing that she is just going to tell Mrs. Droucett anyway?

Lauren is by her locker outside our form room when I finally free myself from the persistent Mrs. Hargreaves. She turns and smiles when she sees me. I find myself panicking, worrying I will say the wrong thing if she speaks to me.

'Hi Maddie.'

'Hi,' I answer back, wishing I could think of something intelligent to say.

'You going to science now?' I nod. 'Wanna walk with me?'

Of course, I do, more than anything, but I play it cool, 'Sure.'

...

I don't walk fast on the way home, desperate to put off the inevitable. Mum and Nick are curled up on the sofa when I walk in, giggling sickeningly at each other, like little children.

'Hey Maddie,' Mum shouts far too loudly for someone in the same room. She moves closer to Nick and pats the seat next to her. 'Come join us. We're watching... what we watching?' Nick shrugs.

'No idea; not been paying attention.' They make me want to throw up.

'I have homework to do.' I rush upstairs before either of them can say any more. Marvin is sleeping on my bed, away from the chaos of Mum and Nick. He raises his head sleepily when I enter the room.

My phone buzzes when I get upstairs. It's from Ella.

How's it going?

Not great. I reply. At least I have someone I can be honest with. *Mum's back with Nick.*

Nooo that's awful.

I know tell me about it. How are you?

Usual not wonderful but surviving. Had some police round questioning me about the night of the accident.

Thought you'd been through all that

I have no idea why they keep wanting to go on about it. Its not like it will change anything.

Don't you wonder who did it though?

Of course, but it won't change the fact that I have no legs.

Sorry.

It's not your fault.

Wow, we both sound so depressed.

We should meet up again. It sounds like we both need cheering up, I suggest.

Great idea. Maybe Dad could drive me halfway to meet you or something.

That would be cool.

I'll ask him later.

Despite our previous meetings that haven't gone so well, I am desperate to see Ella again. Eager to find that bond we should have. I'm sure it's there somewhere. It just might take a bit of work discovering it.

CHAPTER FORTY-FIVE
Ella

Before I have a chance to ask Dad about seeing Maddie, adoptive Mum pops over. I can see that Dad is just as surprised to see her as I am. He even drops the forkful of food that he is halfway through stuffing in his mouth.

'Liz.'

'Hi Max. How are you, Ella?' I wave and smile from the other end of the dining table. 'I just came to get some things.'

Suddenly I have a strong urge to tell Dad that Mum knew about his affair way back when it happened. I'm not sure what it all means but I feel he has a right to know. Of course, I don't. I can't form the words to blurt out something so life-changing.

Mum can barely look at me anymore. I know they all feel guilt, but can't she see that I need her more?

'I'll go and get them.' She sidles awkwardly towards the stairs.

'Wait can we talk?' Dad jumps up from the table.

Mum does not look like she wants to talk at all and moves away from me, out of sight.

'It's not a good time,' she says quietly but loud enough for me to hear.

'It's never a good time for you.'

'Max, we've been through this. What else is there to talk about?'

'I'm sorry about the affair but it was sixteen years ago.'

'It wasn't just an affair. You had babies and then deceived me about our adoptive child being yours.'

'I told you I didn't know about that.'

'How am I supposed to believe that?'

Her voice, getting louder, is making me angrier and angrier. Who is she to talk about being truthful? I can't take it anymore. I wheel myself furiously to where they are.

'How can you stand there and talk about Dad lying when you've been lying all this time.' She tries to hide a guilty look but we both know what it means.

'What does she mean?' Dad asks angrily, his eyes ready to wage war on Mum.

'It doesn't matter now.' Mum tries to walk away but Dad grabs her arm.

'What did she mean Liz?' She sighs.

'She knew about your affair with Becky at the time,' I blurt out, unable to keep it in. Mum shoots daggers at me.

Dad scrunches his eyes up in confusion. 'I don't understand. How did you know?'

'It doesn't matter.'

'But if you stayed with me then why are you mad at me now?'

Good question. Something I'd like to know as well.

'I don't need those things now. I'll come back later.' She shakes her arm free and strides towards the front door.

'Liz, you can't leave now. We need to talk.' But Mum doesn't stop and is gone before either of us can stop her. 'I'm so confused,' Dad says turning to me. 'When did you find out that she knew?'

'Only the other day. She let it slip.'

He shakes his head as if shaking it will make everything he's heard fall into place.

If I thought telling Dad would make it clearer then that failed miserably. Now we have two people who don't know what the hell's going on.

'What are you going to do now?'

'I have absolutely no idea. I guess talk to Mum. Maybe when she's calmed down, she'll be in a position to tell me what's going on.'

I wheel myself back to the dining table where our dinner has now gone cold. I push it to one side. 'Do you want me to heat it up?'

'No, I'm not in the mood for it now.'

'How about some ice cream?' I smile.

'That would be great.'

Mum would have gone mad. No dinner equals no dessert in her eyes. Good job she's not here.

'Dad, I'd like to see Maddie again.' He stops eating his ice cream and smiles.

'Of course. What were you thinking?'

'Maybe you could drive me somewhere and meet her halfway.'

He raises an eyebrow. 'It's a bit cold for country park gatherings at this time of the year. Why can't she come here again?'

'Her Mum, I mean our Mum, doesn't drive and besides, she's kind of busy with Nick.'

'Who's Nick?'

'Her boyfriend. He sounds like a right idiot.'

'In what way?'

'He's got her Mum drinking again and even tried to come on to Maddie.' Dad looks horrified and I instantly regret telling him so much. 'You won't tell anyone, will you? She doesn't want to be taken away again.'

'No, I won't. I have a better idea. How about I pay for Maddie and her Mum to come here? I'll pay for a hotel too. It sounds like they could do with a mini break.'

'That's a fab idea Dad. You're the best.' He beams in delight. 'I'll go call her now.'

It occurs to me that maybe Dad still has feelings for real Mum, despite her drunken ways.

When I explain it to Maddie on FaceTime, her smile is almost off her face.

'Your Dad is the best.'

'Your Dad too.'

'Oh yeah. I keep forgetting.'

'Hard to keep track. Do you think our Mum will be up for it?'

'I'm sure she won't want to be parted from Nick but she never can resist a weekend away in a hotel.'

'Three whole days together. I can't wait. Will you tell school what you're doing or call in sick?' I ask trying to contain the excitement I'm already feeling.

'Hmm maybe call in sick. Fewer questions that way.'

My heart is beating fast when we end the call. This weekend is going to be the best and a welcome break from all the tension round here.

I hug Dad tightly when he comes into my room later.

'Thanks Dad.'

CHAPTER FORTY-SIX
Maddie

Persuading Mum to go back to Kent might be harder than I think but I'm up for a challenge. This is something I want, I need. She'll have to go for it.

When I get downstairs, she is staring sadly at the TV.

'What's up?' I ask tentatively.

'Nick and I were supposed to be going away this weekend.' I hold my breath. 'But he's cancelled on me.' Phew.

'Oh no that's so disappointing.' Mum regards me suspiciously. 'I have something that might cheer you up.'

'Not likely but go on.'

'Ella's Dad, I mean our Dad, Max, whatever you want to call him-'

'I know who he is, get on with it.'

'He's paying for us to stay in a hotel this weekend for three nights so I can see Ella again.'

'In Kent?' She looks disgusted with the idea. Her weekend with Nick was probably somewhere more glamorous.

'Yes, but I think it's got a jacuzzi.' Her eyes perk up.

'Really?'

'Yes, and a posh restaurant.'

'Which he's going to pay for?'

'Of course.'

'It's about time he paid me his dues. Let's go.'

I run to hug her. 'Can't wait Mum. Be great to spend time with you.'

I wish Mum felt the same, that she wasn't just going for the jacuzzi and the posh food but one step at a time.

Mum is buzzing for the rest of the week. You would think she's going to stay with the queen. Even the fact that Nick has ditched her for the weekend can't put a dampener on her mood. She has even bought a new dress.

She didn't ask me if I wanted one but never mind. I would have said no way but that's not the point. It's the principle of the thing. She should ask me if I want new dresses.

...

Friday finally comes. Fortunately, Great Aunt Margaret has agreed to Marvin sit.

'Ready Mum?'

She grabs her bag and throws it on her back like we are going on a big adventure or something.

'I'm always ready.'

Thankfully Nick hasn't been round much this week and Mum has barely touched the alcohol. So, things are looking up in lots of ways.

'Wow this train has charging points for your phone,' Mum says excitedly like a little kid at a toy store. I merely smile. Why do I always feel like the more responsible one in our relationship?

Mum is fidgety on the train, not able to sit still for more than five minutes. I long to shout at her to sit down but I bury my head in a book instead to try and escape her.

'Do I have to come to Max's house?' she asks finally when she has been to the toilet for what feels like the hundredth time.

'To start with at least, please.' She sighs dramatically.

'For me?' I beg, in a quiet voice.

'It won't be for me.'

I get up grumpily. I am fed up with her and her moods. When do I get to be the moody teenager?

We pull into the station at about midday, ready for our first meal out with Ella and Max. Mum's nerves are starting to turn into excitement at the thought of a free lunch. I've decided to call him Max from now on. Calling him Dad is too weird. He doesn't feel like my dad. Maybe one day he will.

Mum almost falls out of the train as she tries to step gracefully onto the platform. I close my eyes and look away. I spot them straight away. I only hope they managed to avoid Mum's dramatic entrance. Ella has the biggest smile I've ever seen on her. Max's smile is somewhat cautious. He lifts his arm in an attempted wave.

'Good to see you, Maddie,' he says when we are closer. 'Becky, good to see you.' Mum grunts and glances around.

'There a toilet here?' Her Essex accent makes me want to cringe.

'It's out of order,' comments Ella. 'Again.'

'Great.' I can only imagine what else she wants to add about this being a backwater town which coming from her is pretty rich I have to say. I silently pray she can hold her tongue.

'It's not far to the restaurant,' adds Max, clearly wary of Mum and her ever-changing moods. Was she like this when they went out? When they... No, I don't want to think about that.

It may not be far to the restaurant, but the tension between Max and Mum makes it feel like it takes forever. I sit in the back of the car next to Ella. Occasionally she smiles at me but we don't speak, not like this. I need to break the ice but how?

'I hope you guys like pizza?'

'Love it,' I reply politely, although I would have preferred Chinese. Mum scowls like it isn't posh enough or expensive enough but cheers up when she finds out it is Prezzo's. Not a place we go to often, due to its price.

Max finds us a seat outside looking over the seafront.

'Ooh you can see the sea,' I say excitedly. Ella giggles. 'Sorry, I don't know why I'm getting so excited it's not like I haven't seen the sea before. Only it's exciting.'

Mum gives me a funny look. I shrug. Suddenly I feel like a little kid on holiday, why shouldn't I be happy?

'I guess I take it for granted living so close to it not that I've been able to go down to the beach recently,' Ella says smiling.

I'm about to ask why when it occurs to me exactly why a wheelchair user couldn't. I close my mouth and pretend I wasn't about to embarrass myself.

'Have you got everything you need?' Max asks Ella, touching her gently on the arm.

'Yes, Dad.' She seems frustrated by his attention while I'm thinking how lovely it is that someone cares about her that much.

'Right, I'm going for a pee,' Mum announces before clunkily going inside to find the toilets.

'Sorry about her,' I say, hoping I'm not too red in the face.

'You don't need to apologise,' Max says with the same caring smile he uses on Ella. Maybe I will warm to this guy after all. 'I remember very clearly what she was like.' He rolls his eyes but before I can ask what he means he asks 'How was the journey?'

'Great.' In between all the toilet trips and trying to pretend I wasn't with Mum. 'Quite long, but you know.'

'I do. It's a trip I've done often for business but not so much recently. Ella's really excited to have you here and I'm glad you could come.'

'Me too. Thank you for paying for us.'

'It's no trouble.'

How rich is he exactly and if Ella's parents get divorced does that mean she'll try and screw him for everything? Wait, no, maybe she's nice, not like Mum.

'This place is well posh,' announces Mum appearing behind me suddenly.

I smile awkwardly while trying to avoid Ella and Max's gaze.

CHAPTER FORTY-SEVEN
Ella

I'd forgotten how in your face our real Mum is. No wonder Maddie is embarrassed by her. I feel sorry for Maddie having to live with her all these years. I can't work out why she wouldn't prefer to live with Great Aunt Margaret who seems so much more sensible and together.

They are staying at the posh hotel on the seafront, no expense spared, where Dad's concerned. Hopefully real Mum won't continue spouting out exclamations every time she sees something remotely posh.

When we leave them to settle in, I am desperate for some alone time with Maddie, but can't see how it will happen.

'You could come over later if you want,' I whisper to Maddie as we are about to say goodbye to them. 'Just you.'

'Perfect, Mum'll be in the jacuzzi anyway.'

'Dad is it okay if Maddie pops over later?'

'Sure, do you want me to come and get you?'

'I'm sure I could get a bus.' I look around doubtfully, not sure how often a bus would run in this place.

'You'll be lucky,' he laughs. 'I'll pick you up in a few hours. Six o'clock okay? Becky, are you coming?' Why did he have to say that? Real Mum's expression turns panicky. 'You don't have to. I'm sure the girls would like some time to themselves and you'll want to acclimatise yourself to the hotel.'

'Yes, I do need to do that. I'm pretty tired after the journey. You don't mind, do you?'

'No, of course.'

I'm very relieved but sometimes I want to shake adults for tiptoeing around how they feel. They hate each other, why not come out and say it?

Maddie winks at me. Finally, we can have that chat which I'm longing to have.

'See you then,' she chirps.

Later can't come quick enough. I could have gone in the car with Dad but it takes so long to load me into it. I decided to not feel like a burden for a change. I busy myself with finding some snacks instead.

When Maddie arrives, she looks out of place but I beckon her into my room and signal for her to sit on the bed next to me.

'This is weird,' she says finally.

I laugh. 'I know. It's so strange, but I'm very glad you came. It's been miserable round here lately.'

'Yeah, not much fun at my house either. We sure ended up with messed up parents.'

'Didn't we.'

Silence follows. I wish we were like real sisters, never too shy to know what to say next, shared experiences, but all we share right now is a dramatic mother.

'Tell me about Nick?' Maddie rolls her eyes.

'I hate him. He's so smarmy and letchy. I have no idea what Mum sees in him. Every time they're together she's like a child who's been allowed to stay up late and she starts drinking again. He apparently doesn't see anything wrong in that.'

'He sounds like a right pain. Hopefully one day she'll see sense.'

'I told you about the black eye too?'

'No, what black eye?'

'They were drunk dancing in the lounge. When I went in there, he pulled me into him and accidentally punched me.' I can't very well tell her the truth.

'No way, that's crazy. You should sue him for something.'

'I should.' Another silence. 'So, what did happen the night of the accident?'

I knew this was coming and it seems right that the first person I talk to about it all is my twin sister. I take a deep breath.

'I got persuaded to go to this party, a bit of a dumb party as it was at Georgia's house and I hate her but my friend Kaitlyn persuaded me to go. Mum and Dad didn't want me to as it was Grandad's birthday but Dad is easy to win round when you know how. Dad would have never agreed to it if he'd known Sam had a motorbike.' Maddie's eyes widen. 'I was really scared.' The tears begin to flow, I can't stop them. 'I didn't want to go on it but I was afraid that if I said no, he'd think I was a wuss and now he's dead,' I wail.

'Oh Ella, that's horrible. You didn't know. If I'd been offered a ride on a motorbike with a good-looking boy I would have gone. He was good looking, right?'

I laugh through the tears. 'Very.'

'You can't blame yourself. How did you crash?'

'I don't exactly know. We were going so fast I'd closed my eyes.' Maddie nods. 'Then I saw lights, car lights that blinded me. The next thing I know I'm being flung from the bike into the air. I still remember the thud as I hit the ground. I thought that was it. This is how I'm going to die, but I didn't. I lay trapped under the bike and the car drove off.'

'Like a hit and run?' Maddie has gone pale.

'Exactly like that.'

'Who would do that?'

'Probably a druggie.'

'That's awful. I can't believe they left you there.'

'And Sam had been thrown onto the road next to me. He wasn't moving and I was trapped. I couldn't do a thing about it.'

Relief floods me, it's good to get it out finally.

'I wanted to die when I found out I had no legs but I could never figure out what the best way to do it was.'

Maddie doesn't speak, stunned by what I've told her but she strokes my arm.

'I'm here now,' she says finally.

I hug her and I feel closer to a bond than I've ever felt.

CHAPTER FORTY-EIGHT
Maddie

The next day Max invites us over for dinner, and says he's going to cook up a feast. Mum doesn't look impressed and complains privately to me that she'd been promised posh dinners out. I ignore her sniping, I'm happy that things are going well with Ella. I feel like we broke through a barrier last night, or something like that. Our bond can only grow from now.

Mum is as uncomfortable in the house as she can be, constantly jiggling her leg up and down under the dining room table. I put my hand on it to stop it and give her the look. Her expression is pleading. She clearly doesn't want to be here. I'm beginning to wish I'd come alone.

Max, oblivious to Mum's mood, has cooked an Indian feast, complete with naan bread and bhajis.

'This looks great,' I say as I take my plate enthusiastically. Mum looks less impressed and I hope she is not going to make some racist comment about Indians.

'Yeah lovely,' she smiles with the most fake smile I've ever seen.

'Dad is the best cook,' says Ella beaming. Mum would be doing the gagging motion if they weren't here, I know her too well.

'How's the hotel?' Max asks.

'It's fantastic,' I answer. Last night Mum complained multiple times about different things; the water was too cold, the sheets were not as soft as she'd expected, the minibar didn't have much in it, the whole place felt like a 1950s hotel. The list was endless. In the end, I told her to shut up as we were getting it for free. Some people are not grateful for anything. She doesn't tell Max any of this but smiles in that way that is beginning to infuriate me. I wish I'd left her at home. Remind me next time to do that.

We are happily chatting about Ella's school when I hear

a key in the door.

'Mum,' explains Ella with a big grin on her face. Max rolls his eyes as if to say it's not good timing.

She walks straight into the dining room, already I can see she is a world away from Mum in her high heels and hair neatly tied in a bun. Dressed in a suit, she looks like she means business. When she spots us, her face turns the palest white I have ever seen.

She turns to Max. 'You didn't tell me they were coming?' The words are shaky and in complete contradiction to how she appears.

Mum stops eating, drops her fork, and stares hard at her. 'You don't live here anymore, I don't need to-'

'You,' shouts Mum standing up. Ella and I exchange confused glances. Has Mum gone completely mad? 'You,' she repeats.

Ella's Mum clutches the wall and grabs hold of the mantelpiece to steady herself.

'You two know each other?' says Max, clearly confused as the rest of us.

'What are you doing here?' Mum demands.

'I can explain.' Ella's Mum steps backwards as Mum moves aggressively towards her.

'Explain?' roars Mum. 'No amount of explaining can fix this.'

Before Ella's mum can answer, Max interjects with 'Will someone tell me what's going on?'

'You planned this all along,' Mum continues, ignoring Max.

'It wasn't what you think,' Ella's Mum answers finally.

Mum moves closer, her body language threatening her.

'It is everything I think,' she spits at her. 'You ruined my life.'

Before any of us can stop her, Mum grabs hold of Ella's Mum and shoves her against the wall. The crack of Ella's Mum's head makes me cringe. I jump up.

'Mum, Mum stop. You're going to kill her.'

Mum turns to me. 'Let her die. She deserves it.'

'WHAT'S GOING ON?' shouts Max loudly at both of them, standing in between them both. 'She bribed me to give up my baby.'

'WHAT?' everyone shouts at once.

'She told me to leave it at the public toilets in Greenwick.'

Max's face turns to thunder. 'So when you suggested we adopt Ella, you knew it was my baby?' Liz looks down guiltily.

'That was never part of the plan.' 'LIAR,' Mum screams at her.

Ella appears shell-shocked next to us, turning to Liz with confusion written all over her face. 'You bribed my real Mum to give me up, why?'

'Because I found out she'd had an affair with your dad.'

'I can't believe this,' Max says, leaving his position in between the two women to pace the room. 'Why would you do something like that?'

'Because you cheated on me.'

'How did you even know she was pregnant?'

'It doesn't matter how I knew.'

'I don't understand,' I say looking to Mum. 'Why would you give up your baby because someone random came up to you and gave you money? Did you know she was Max's wife?'

'No, I had no idea. I was so young,' she wails. 'I thought having a baby was going to ruin my life so I took the money but then when I found out I was having twins I thought I could keep one. I know I know it was a stupid idea.' Tears are flowing down her face at great speed as I stare incredulously at her.

'You didn't think to question why this random woman would be offering money?' I shake my head at her.

'You obviously weren't a fit mother,' retorts Liz angrily, suddenly finding her feet.

'You bitch.' Mum lunges for her, only stopped by me

throwing myself in the way.

'Mum, you can't. Violence doesn't solve anything.'

'Liz, just get out,' Max says quietly.

'It's my house.'

'GET OUT,' he repeats, this time a lot louder.

She doesn't move but then seems to realise it's maybe best she does and turns around, leaving without a word.

The minute she is gone, Mum bursts into tears again.

The rest of us can only stand there in shock.

CHAPTER FORTY-NINE
Ella

I have never felt so confused in my life. A mass of emotions are running through me. My adoptive Mum bribed someone to give me up and my real Mum was too weak to tell her where to go. Unbelievable!

'I need to sit down,' Real Mum says falling into the sofa. Maddie throws me a look of disbelief.

Dad stomps off into the kitchen and starts clattering around. Neither Maddie nor I know what to say next.

'I want to go back to the hotel,' Real Mum mutters weakly.

'I'm going to stay here awhile,' says Maddie, smiling at me. Real Mum looks rejected but doesn't argue.

'Can someone call me a taxi?'

I quickly find a taxi number and dial it. When I am finished Maddie is looking at me with a new respect.

'How do you do that?'

'Do what?'

'Phone someone. I hate phoning anyone.' I shrug. 'You don't mind if I stay awhile, do you?' Maddie asks timidly.

'Of course not. It would be good to talk.'

'What about me?' Real Mum suddenly yells. 'Do you not care at all how I feel about all this?'

Before I can say anything, Maddie says 'Of course we do Mum but you said yourself you need some time alone and I want to spend time with Ella.'

She has a lot more patience than I do. I probably would have said something I'd later regretted. She doesn't argue further but grunts quietly to herself. I am relieved when the taxi arrives. Dad doesn't even leave the kitchen to say goodbye.

When she has gone, Dad appears, looking flustered. 'Do you girls mind if I go out for a bit? I need to clear my head.'

'Absolutely Dad. We'll be fine here. If I need anything

Maddie can help me.'

'Yeah. We'll be cool,' adds Maddie.

'Okay, I won't be long. I'll just get some fresh air.' He is out of the door before we can change our minds.

'This has been a weird day,' says Maddie laughing when we are alone.

'It sure has. I can't believe my Mum bribed our real Mum.'

'I don't understand why she stayed with Max after she found out he'd had an affair.' I shake my head as if that will help this all make sense.

'All I know is that Mum was desperate to have children and couldn't. She had this ovary problem as a teenager and was devastated when they told her she'd never have children.'

'That must have been hard for her.'

'I think it was but that doesn't excuse taking someone else's baby.' Maddie is quiet. It's a lot to take in for both of us.

'So, what now?' she says finally.

'I've no idea. I wish I knew.'

It seems like there is much more to talk about, but we are both exhausted. Despite the fantastic feast Dad made still on the table, I order us pizza. Maddie stares at me, eyes wide, when I order it on the app.

'Won't your dad mind?'

'Mind? Why would he?'

'He cooked that.' She waves her hand dramatically towards the table. 'And pizza is expensive.'

'We get it all the time and besides he's used to me rejecting his food,' I laugh. She smiles.

I'm guessing Maddie doesn't order pizza much as she doesn't even know what toppings there are. Whereas the pizza menu is like an old friend to me.

We are halfway through our food when the doorbell rings. Maddie offers to get it. I don't hear what she says but shortly after she is back in the lounge with Mum (adoptive Mum). I didn't expect to see her again so soon. Her face is bright red and her sparkling eyes are unlike I have ever seen before.

'Are you okay?' I ask slowly.

'I'm so...rr...y,' she stutters through tears that seem never-ending. 'I never meant to hurt you.'

'Have you been drinking?' asks Maddie with disdain in her voice. I stare from Maddie to Mum. Of course, Maddie can spot a drunk from a mile off.

Ignoring Maddie, she carries on. 'I didn't know it was you. If I had I would have stopped I promise.'

'Mum, what are you talking about?'

'Never mind,' she answers and stumbles up the stairs, leaving Maddie and me to puzzle over what she meant.

'What was that about?' asks Maddie throwing her arms up in the air.

'No idea. The stress must have got to her. Hopefully, she'll sleep it off, and besides, I don't want to talk to her right now.'

'I don't blame you.'

Dad arrives home just as we have finished our pizzas.

'I should get going,' Maddie says. 'You look tired and Mum will be getting twitchy without me.' As much as I want to object, I am exhausted. The days' events have been too much for me.

'I understand.'

'I'll take you back,' Dad offers. Maddie nods. Sometimes I forget she is his daughter as well. A twinge of jealously flashes over me. I push it away. She is entitled to see her dad too. I watch them go before taking myself to the lounge. I should go to bed, but find I want to watch some TV instead. Moments after I have switched the TV on, and am laid on the sofa, I feel my eyes start to drift.

The next thing I know Dad is rushing into the room.

'We need to call an ambulance.'

'You're back,' I mutter sleepily. He grabs his mobile phone and starts punching buttons. 'What's going on?' I ask but he is too busy concentrating on the task ahead. 'Ambulance...my wife has taken an overdose...I don't know...88 Sapphire Gardens...please hurry.' I stare wide eyed at him, not believing what I am hearing. Just when I thought we had a moment to breathe.

Before I can ask him any more questions, he is running upstairs while I sit helplessly on the sofa unable to follow him. I carefully pull myself into my wheelchair and wheel it over to the bottom of the stairs. I lean forward to listen but all I can hear is Dad shouting at Mum to wake up.

The ambulance takes half an hour to arrive. I am praying that she is not already dead. I open the door the minute I hear the sirens.

'Hello love. We're here about Liz-'

'She's upstairs.' I point them in the right direction. I sit and wait impatiently. I want to be up there doing something to help, anything at all.

Ten minutes later, they carefully walk back down with Mum on a stretcher.

'Is she okay?' I ask.

'She's still breathing,' one of them answers as they zip past me at a speed I can only dream of. Dad follows closely behind.

'Wanna come to the hospital with me?' he asks.

'Yes please.'

...

Despite having been at the hospital several times since my accident, it still sends shivers down my spine. This isn't a place anyone should have to go, especially not in an emergency.

Dad and I have to sit in the waiting room. Is this where Mum and Dad sat when I was brought in? Is this how they felt? Not knowing if I would live or die?

Finally, a nurse calls us over and tells us we can go and see Mum now.

She is awake when we go in, pale-faced and lifeless like she's not slept in weeks. She starts crying when she sees me.

'I'm so sorry,' she wails.

'Mum, don't worry about it now.' I sit down next to her and clutch her hand. Dad sits on the other side and grabs hold of Mum's other hand.

'No, you don't understand. It was me.'

'What was you?'

'The accident. I was the driver.' I let go of her hand and push myself backwards. The room is spinning and I feel like I have been hit by a car all over again.

'What?' Dad exclaims, standing up.

'I didn't know it was you or I would have stopped. I've felt guilty ever since. It was an accident. I'm so, so sorry and I-'

'No.' I hold up my hand. 'No. I can't deal with this.' I wheel out of the door.

Outside I am plunged into a busy corridor. Suddenly I can't breathe. People are rushing past me and I want everything to stop. The world around me starts to go blurry. Then a strong arm from behind me takes hold of my wheelchair.

'Let's go somewhere quieter.' Dad's voice is reassuring amongst the chaos.

I let him wheel me to a room down the corridor, feeling like none of this is real. I must be in some kind of nightmare.

When we are alone in the room, Dad sits down in front of me.

'I don't know what to say,' he starts. 'I never expected that.' I shake my head, unable to get words out. 'I can't believe she did it and kept it from us.' I stare at him, no tears, no emotion, not able to feel anything anymore.

We sit in silence, undecipherable thoughts running through my head.

'I need to talk to her,' Dad says standing up.

'I'm coming too.'

'You sure?'

'Yes.' Though I'm not sure I am.

When we return to Mum's bedside she is staring out of the window like a lost soul. She turns to face me, tears running down her face, eyes drooping.

'I've told the nurse to get the police. I'm going to tell them everything.'

I don't know what she expects me to say to that. *Don't do it. You don't have to confess.* But in reality, she does. She is my Mum and I love her but she needs to pay for what she has done. She has put me in a wheelchair for life.

'Why didn't you tell me?' Dad asks. 'It was an accident. We could have worked through it.' I beg to differ. I don't think I could have worked through this.

We leave as the police arrive. My heavy heart feels like it will break.

CHAPTER FIFTY
Maddie

'Bloody hell Ella.' I exclaim loudly as Ella and Max join us for breakfast the next day. Ella can barely keep her eyes open. Mum is still in bed sleeping off a hangover. 'I can't believe she did that.' Ella nods slowly in agreement.

Before she can stop them, giant sobs escape her, rendering her incapable of rational speech.

'How could she?' she blurts out finally.

'Oh sweetheart.' Max runs over and pulls her to him. 'I had no idea.'

On top of a lying cheating real father and a drunken real mother, Ella now has a murdering adoptive mother. I don't even know where to start in helping her through this. To think she is responsible for Ella ending up in a wheelchair. No wonder Liz was acting so weird.

I watch Max trying to reassure Ella while I feel like an idiot, not knowing what to do.

'I can't believe it,' Ella says.

Max shakes his head. His eyes have a sad tinge to them.

'I'm guessing it was an accident though. She would never deliberately run you over, you have to know that.'

'I know but she's been lying to me all this time, let me think there was some unknown person out there who'd done it.'

'It must have been killing her,' I say, not feeling like my opinion is worth anything. Max smiles encouragingly. Ella glances out of the window, a distant look in her eyes. 'You would feel so guilty.'

'I'm tired.' Ella starts to lean over in her chair.

'Maybe we shouldn't have come. This is too much for you.'

'I'll be fine,' she insists but she clearly isn't.

We finish our breakfast in almost silence before Max announces that Ella needs a nap and takes her home. I know it's not personal but it's hard not to take it that way. We are supposed to be bonding.

Mum is lying flat out on the bed when I return to the room. The mini bar door is open. I can't take any more of this. I shouldn't have to deal with this at my age.

'Get a grip,' I yell at the oblivious mother.

She stirs slightly and opens one eye at the sound of my voice.

'Hey Maddie.' I am suddenly longing for my own home, with my own bedroom, somewhere to escape to. 'What's up?'

'Turns out Ella's Mum was the one who ran her over.'

'Seriously?' Mum sits bolt upright in bed. Her face brightens. 'How do you know?'

'The police arrested her last night.'

'No way!' Full of energy she jumps out of bed and grabs the glass next to her and begins glugging away.

I want to point out that she is no angel. She may be delighted at someone else's downfall but she is in no position to judge.

'What's going to happen now?'

'Who knows! Ella has another screwed-up parent.'

'Fancy going out for breakfast?' She glances at her watch, struggling to focus on it.

'I've had breakfast,' I snap.

'Alright. Alright. How was I to know?'

I stop myself from saying she would have known if she wasn't so drunk last night and hungover this morning.

'I'll go on my own then.' I don't stop her but sit on the bed and switch the TV on. Peace at last.

CHAPTER FIFTY-ONE
Ella

When I wake up the next morning, the full force of what happened the previous day hits me like a ton of bricks. I badly want it to be a dream, that my own mother didn't really run me over and leave me to die, that she didn't kill my boyfriend, that she didn't help me deal with an accident that she had caused. I drag myself into my wheelchair and peer into Blueberry's cage, trying to ground myself in some kind of reality.

'How you doing?' Dad asks when I finally make it to the dining room.

I'm pretty sure my puffy eyes and droopy shoulders will give him all the information he needs on that, but I answer, 'Okay.'

'You don't have to lie to me. This is a lot of crap to deal with.'

'It sure is.' When I think the tears have stopped, another one rolls down my face. I don't want to cry again but I can't help it.

'I need to ring the police station and find out what's going on with Mum and whether she's getting bail. Would you like to talk to her?'

'I honestly don't know. What would I say?'

'We'll leave it a few days then. Why don't you do something fun with Maddie today? You deserve it after all this.'

'Good idea.'

I pull my phone out of my pocket and text her.

Fancy meeting up to do something fun?

She instantly replies with *yes please. I'd really like to go crazy golf. Could you manage that?*

I cringe at her words. I hate that she has to ask me that but am grateful that we are getting on well enough for her not to skirt around the issue.

They have wheelchair access and I can cope with batting a ball into a hole. It's not like I could ever get it in before anyway.

Lol. Do you mind if mum comes?

I do mind but I don't say that.

As long as she's not drunk.

I'll make sure she isn't.

I don't need another messed-up parent to deal with.

'Maddie wants to play crazy golf,' I tell Dad.

'You okay with that?'

'Of course,' I snap. 'Why does everyone think I'm incapable of doing things like that?'

'Sorry, we care about you.'

'I can still do some things.'

'Of course you can. Do you want me to come?'

'No drop me off. You go and deal with Mum and all that.'

He nods. He seems relieved, one less person to worry about for a little while.

...

Real Mum and Maddie are already waiting outside the crazy golf centre when we get there. Maddie waves enthusiastically. Real Mum looks worried. She should be. One step out of line and I'm having her. I am not in the mood for her games today.

'I didn't realise Becky was going,' says Dad as we pull up. 'Are you okay with that?'

'I said it's fine as long as she's not drunk.'

'She doesn't seem to be and I don't think they sell alcohol there, fortunately,' he grins. 'Call me if you get fed up and want picking up.'

'I will.'

'How you doing?' asks Maddie, as though she hadn't witnessed my world fall apart yesterday.

'I'm good,' I answer. I'm not really but I want to be and if I keep saying that maybe it'll come true.

'Great let's go and get our clubs.' She leads the way followed by real Mum who smiles uneasily at me. No doubt she has heard all about Mum's arrest.

'I'll see you later honey,' Dad waves as he leaves me by the gate. 'You be okay?' he mouths.

'I'll be fine,' I whisper back.

Real Mum can barely meet my eye as we get our clubs and start off on the course.

'It's great here. You can even see the sea,' says Maddie beaming, oblivious to real Mum's discomfort.

'I suppose I don't notice it anymore. I've lived here all my life.'

'What was your life like before?'

Ah, the question, not one I want to answer but it had to come sometime.

'Fun, more varied, less stressful. Of course, I didn't know I was adopted then or that my Dad was a cheater or that my Mum was about to run me over.'

Real Mum looks shocked at my outburst, probably dreading I'm going to say something about her not-so excellent parenting skills.

Then she surprises me by saying 'I'm sorry Ella. I was a shit mum. I should never have given you up.' She begins to cry and I wonder if this is the right place to have this conversation. 'I should have kept you and ignored that woman, your mum.'

I know she wants me to tell her it's all okay and that I forgive her, but I can't. It's never going to be acceptable. You don't give up your baby because someone gives you money.

'I think we should talk about something else,' suggests Maddie, sensing the tension in the air.

Real Mum's dejected face says it all but I don't give in to her emotional blackmail. It may work on Maddie but it's not going to on me.

'I bet I can get this one in one shot,' I laugh as I fail to get the ball anywhere near the hole.

'Good try Ella,' Maddie says encouragingly while trying not to laugh.

As we approach the next hole, I hear real Mum whisper

'I was only trying to make things right.' to Maddie.

'Mum, leave it. Not now,' Maddie furiously whispers back.

I'm glad she's got my back. She knows how much I can take. At moment I need a sense of normality in my life or as close to it as I can get.

We manage to make it round the whole way without real Mum freaking out or me having a go at her although I frequently felt like it. I hate her whiny tone. I'm beginning to appreciate how lucky I was in being given away. I had a normal childhood, until now anyway.

'I'm feeling a bit tired. I think I'm going to go back to the hotel room to lie down,' says real Mum when we are outside the golf centre.

'You do that Mum. We're going to grab some lunch. If that's okay Ella?'

'Of course,' I answer, delighted that it will only be the two of us. Real Mum looks hurt but carries on walking.

'See you later then Maddie,' she calls after us.

'Have a good rest, Mum.'

I want to talk honestly about real Mum with Maddie but I get the feeling I would only offend her. I don't think she's ready for my true opinions of our real mum. She has grown up with this woman and however messed up she is she's the only mum she's ever known. At least we have that in common.

'What's your dad up to today?' she asks. 'I mean our dad. Sorry I keep forgetting he's my dad too.'

'It's fine. There have been a lot of changes round here recently.' We both laugh. 'He's gone to the police station to see what's going on with Mum.'

'Oh wow. That must be so weird. Do you think she'll get bailed?'

'Quite honestly, I don't care. She can rot in jail.' Maddie doesn't speak, too shocked by my fury no doubt. 'I know she's my Mum and all but she left me for dead. Yeah, she didn't know it was me but the fact that she'd leave anyone is bad enough and she killed my boyfriend. I can never forgive her for that.'

'It's hard to know how I'd feel if my mum, our mum, did that to me. I get that you're angry.'

We make our way down to a small cafe overlooking the sea, perfect for tourists. They also do amazing milkshakes.

'What was it like growing up in a place like this? It's so beautiful.'

'It was very boring. I hated it as a child. I wanted to get out and see the world but now it's comforting. After everything I've been through, I need something familiar.'

'I can understand that.'

'What was it like where you grew up?'

'Scummy.' She laughs but I can tell there are scars hidden beneath that exterior. 'I always felt like the poor kid at school. Our town is pretty dull, our house is tiny.' She doesn't say unlike your massive house but I know that's what she meant. I can't imagine living in a small house. Our house is perfect. I'm only sorry I have to live on the ground floor now. I miss my old bedroom.

Later after lunch and a walk, Dad arrives to pick me up. I don't want to ask about Mum. I want to not care, but I do.   'What happened?' I ask when he is about to drive off. He stops and turns round.

'She has a bail hearing tomorrow, but they are unlikely to grant it due to the fact that she didn't stop in the first place and the fact that she's very unstable now.'

'Did you speak to her?'

'Briefly. She didn't make much sense. Our lawyer is trying to get her moved to a mental institution. He doesn't think she's fit to stand trial.'

I didn't even realise we had a lawyer let alone one who can be called upon so quickly.

'She wants to see you.'

'I don't want to see her.'

'Maybe when she's settled into the hospital.'

'Maybe.' But the answer will still be no.

CHAPTER FIFTY-TWO
Maddie

Our final day in Broadstairs comes too soon. I don't want to go home and leave Ella. We are just starting to talk about things. Mum seems relieved to get out of here. I will be glad to get out of that hotel room. Being with Mum in such a small space is driving me crazy.

Ella and Max come to take us to the station. I tell Mum before that she should thank Max for paying for the hotel and especially as he's about to get a big mini-bar bill. She is not keen but agrees like a grumpy teenager.

'Thank you, Max for the hotel,' she says so quietly it's a wonder anyone heard.

'You're welcome, Becky,' he answers cheerfully. 'I'm glad the girls got to spend time together. Maybe we'll come and visit you guys, next time.'

Mum looks horrified at this but quickly hides it.

'That would be great,' I reply, grinning at Ella.

Ella promises to FaceTime me that night. I whisper goodbye to the sea. I will miss that view.

If I had thought that we would have a quiet night when we got back, I was wrong. Nick bounds over like an excited puppy pleased to see his owner again. Excuse me while I find a corner to gag in. Thankfully Marvin is safely at Great Aunt Margaret's until tomorrow. He doesn't need to be traumatised by Nick on his first night home.

'How was the seaside, Maddie?' he asks me as though I were a small child. I raise my eyebrows at him and hold back the words I really want to say.

'Lovely.'

'Turns out Ella's adoptive Mum is a criminal.' Nick's face lights up.

'Really?'

'It's not quite that simple,' I interrupt but my protests fall on deaf ears.

'She only went and ran over her own daughter and then drove off.'

'NO!'

'I'm going upstairs.' They don't react as I sneak past them, leaving them to their distasteful revelling in Ella's circumstances. Sometimes I wonder if Mum cares about anyone else but herself.

It's good to be back in my own bed. Despite the hotel looking grand from the outside, the beds were about as comfortable as a table. The best thing is, I now have space and time away from Mum. I think I might have killed her if I'd spent much longer with her.

I plug in my headphones, trying to block out the noises from Mum's room. Our walls are far too thin. I imagine I'm in a place far away. My mind goes back to the question Ella asked me once, *why don't you just live with Great Aunt Margaret?* And it's times like these that I wonder that myself. It would be so peaceful there, so simple. A single tear runs down my face as I think of James and how I've treated him. I wish I had someone right now. I miss Ella and I miss him.

I fall asleep to the sounds of Taylor Swift singing in my ears.

'GET OFF, GET OFF.' When I wake up it's to the sound of Mum shouting. Something about her tone scares me, this is not normal.

I jump up, pulling my headphones out as I go, and rush to her bedroom. Nick is standing over the bed, butt naked, fortunately facing away from me, holding Mum down. Not sure I will ever be able to get that image out of my head.

'Get off. I don't want to,' she is screaming.

'You wanted it before.'

'She said no.'

Nick turns his head at the sound of my voice.

'Who was asking you?'

'She asked you to go. Have you not heard of the word consent?'

'She gave it earlier.'

'That's not how it works.'

Nick stares me in the eyes, probably considering whether it's worth taking me on or not. He decides, wisely, not to.

'Fine, have it your way,' he says, directing his anger at Mum, who has started to sob into the pillow.

I stand with my hands on my hips while Nick pulls on his pants and his t-shirt.

He leaves like a child who didn't get what he wanted but not before having the last word. 'You women are all the same.'

I don't move until I hear the front door slam.

'He wanted to-'

'Mum, I don't need the details.'

This is why I stay. Mum needs me. I am the grown-up in this relationship. The responsible teenager who has to look after her mother.

'I'll go and make us some food.' I don't look at her lying there, half sober, dishevelled, as I make my way down the stairs. I know my duty.

I double lock the front door as I go by, just in case.

Half in a dream state, still tired from my nap, I glance at the clock. It's 2 am. No wonder I'm so tired. I shove some bread in the toaster. It's the best I can do at this time of night. Not sure whether it will satisfy my rumbling stomach but it'll have to do.

'Are you making me some?' a little voice behind me says.

Mum looks as ever bit a child as she sounds.

'Of course. Would I ever forget you?'

'I'm sorry Maddie. I'm a terrible Mum.'

They are words I've heard so many times. Every time I want to protest and tell her that she's wonderful but I can't. 'Do you think Ella likes me?'

I consider telling her the whole truth, that Ella can't stand her and absolutely looks down on her but I suspect she knows that already.

'She just needs time to get used to you. You're unique.' I laugh at my joke.

'And you always were good at being diplomatic. You should go into politics or something.'

'Maybe I will.'

'What happened to that boyfriend of yours, Josh is it?'

'His name is James and we're not together anymore.'

'Aw why not? He was so posh.'

'I don't need a man in my life to make me happy.' How do I tell her that I don't even think I like boys at all?

'Unlike me you mean,' she retorts angrily.

'I didn't say that.'

'You didn't have to.'

'Mum, it's late or early, depending on your perspective, I'm not in the mood for an argument.'

The toast pops. I shove them onto two plates and begin buttering Mum's slice fast. I need to get out of there before I explode. I hand it to Mum.

'Eat your toast and get some sleep.'

'Yes Mum,' she says saluting me. I roll my eyes. I don't need her games right now.

I butter my toast at top speed, barely covering each corner, and rush past Mum upstairs.

'Can't we eat it together?' she pleads.

'I'm tired,' I call after her.

Finally alone, I am torn between wanting to cry and falling asleep before I can even eat a bite. I eat as much as I can before battening down into my cocoon once more.

CHAPTER FIFTY-THREE
Ella

Despite everything, I'm back in school. The only way Dad could persuade me to go was because Kaitlyn was going to be there. I miss her so much. She's not been round as much and has avoided school for a few weeks now but Dad says we all need to move on now.

How I'd love to move on but every time I wake up and remember that I am confined to a wheelchair for the rest of my life I realise that life will never be the same again.

Dad picks Kaitlyn up on the way. I reckon he's got some deal with her Mum. *If I get Ella in, you get Kaitlyn in* kind of thing. It makes sense and it's worked. Her face is pale and her eyes tired, I know she is finding life hard too. The angry part of me doesn't think anyone else has a right to be miserable. She is not going through what I am but the nice part of me begs the other half to understand that the world does not revolve around me. We all need to be kind to each other.

'How's it going?' I ask cheerfully as though we are two normal teenagers going to school.

'I'm here. I'm alive.' 'Same,' I say laughing.

'Sorry about your Mum.'

'Which one?' I chuckle. Kaitlyn looks confused, failing to see the joke. 'Never mind. It's complicated.'

She nods but she doesn't understand, no one does.

Mrs Harper greets us at the door making me feel like I'm in primary school and need someone to take me in. How is this getting back to normal?

'You have a great day, girls,' Dad says as I wheel in past the SENCO.

'Thanks Dad.'

This morning he said he was going to see Mum again. I don't know how he can after what she's done. How is he not more angry at her? I can't even look at a picture of her now.

'It's lovely to see you both again,' Mrs Harper beams at us.

She's probably expecting us to say that we are glad to be back but we don't speak.

'Wow that woman is way too keen,' says Kaitlyn once we are out of earshot. I snigger, trying to hide my expression from the eagle eyes of the SENCO.

We make our way to the quad in the middle of the building, the place where we used to hang out with our friends before school. Everyone is still there as though nothing has changed, except we are missing. A couple of them smile nervously in our direction but none of them say a word. The rest stare at us like we are a circus act, a novelty you don't see every day.

'Ignore them,' whispers Kaitlyn. It hurts. Now I know how the outcasts feel. The smelly boy still stands by the music classroom on his own, the nerdy girl is still sitting by herself on the bench by the PE block. We ignored them, now I wish we hadn't.

'What have we got first?' I ask Kaitlyn, realising that my timetable is in my bag, hung on the back of my chair.

'German, I think.'

Great, the subject I hate most and now feel even more behind in it.

We wait until everyone has gone and the corridors won't be a crush. Not that I have ever wanted to rush to a lesson but turning up late is no fun, especially when you are in a wheelchair.

'Ella, Kaitlyn,' declares Mrs. Frobisher loudly. Way to announce us to the world. 'So good to see you again.'

If I could run in the opposite direction I would. She glances around the room, flustered, searching desperately for a space to put me.

'Daniel, can you move over next to Stacey.' Kaitlyn and I wait awkwardly by the door while the seating plan is rearranged.

Finally, we are able to take our places, regretting the

decision to come back.

'Where were we?' Mrs. Frobisher inquires of the class. Everyone looks down, muttering to themselves while she sorts through her notes. 'Oh that's it, we were about to talk about tenses. Just in time girls.' She smiles in our direction, prompting more people to turn round to stare.

'I hate this,' hisses Kaitlyn at me. I nod, frowning.

After half an hour of Mrs. Frobisher lecturing us, it is time to put into practice our speaking skills, or in my case lack of them.

Of course, none of us speak in German. It's a perfect opportunity to have a chat.

'How are we all doing?' says Holly, eyeing me suspiciously.

'Grand,' I answer sarcastically.

'Anyone been to any parties lately?'

'All the time. I'm out every night,' I reply. Kaitlyn giggles next to me.

'Alright Ella. Just making conversation.'

'Well, it's a stupid thing to ask. It's quite obvious I'm not out at parties.' I take a swig of my water bottle.

'Being in a wheelchair shouldn't stop you living your life.'

I almost choke on my water. 'I can't believe you just said that.'

'I'd love to have a good excuse not to do PE,' she continues. I stare at her but inside I am fuming, debating how I can punch her from my end of the table.

'I think you better shut your mouth,' retorts Kaitlyn.

Holly sends her a dirty look, with eyes that could kill. Fortunately for Holly, Mrs. Frobisher comes over or I might have run over Holly's foot.

'How are we doing here girls?'

None of us answer, still exchanging death stares.

...

'What a bitch,' says Kaitlyn when the lesson is over and we get to leave five minutes early. 'Please let me beat her up.'

'Not if I get there first,' I laugh. 'I can't believe she said that.'

'She doesn't understand.' A voice from behind us makes us both turn around. Natalie, a quiet girl who was also at our table, is there, smiling almost apologetically.

'She absolutely doesn't,' I say. 'She has no bloody idea what it's like. I'd love to be out every night partying but most nights I'm asleep by nine.'

'You don't have to tell me,' says Natalie flippantly, walking ahead, turning back only to smile at us. At least we have one person on our side.

At break time, Dad texts me to tell me that Kaitlyn's Mum is picking us up. Something about Mum having a panic attack.

'I have no idea why he's even helping her after what she's done,' I moan to Kaitlyn when I show her the message.

'She must feel awful.'

'Why are you defending her?'

'Hey don't attack me. I'm only saying it must have been eating her up these past few months.'

I don't care how guilty she's felt, it didn't stop her driving off that night. It didn't stop her lying to me ever since. All those times I wondered who did this to me and all the time it was her.

...

'How was your day girls?' asks Kaitlyn's Mum when she gets out of the car.

I'm beginning to get fed up of being called girls. We are individuals. Just because we've both struggled doesn't mean we can be lumped together.

I am about to give a diplomatic answer when Kaitlyn beats me to it. 'It was hell. Everyone stared at us and made stupid comments.'

'Oh dear, I'm sorry. They are obviously not used to seeing-'

'A disabled person?' I finish. Her face reddens.

'Um... yes... that. I'm sure they'll get used to it.'

Like we all are, I want to add but I don't want to get used to it. I want to get magically healed but that's not going to happen. Somehow, I have to learn to live like this for the rest of my life. A depressing thought that can't be made better by the fact that I now know who the hit-and-run driver is.

Later I relay my horrible day to Maddie via FaceTime. She nods sympathetically at all the right moments. Then I feel guilty, she's going through stuff too, even more so when she hits me with a revelation.

'Ella, would it be a problem if I were gay?'

'No,' I reply straight away, meaning every word. Poor girl that she had to ask, to think that she has probably been holding this in for too long with no support from anyone.

'No problem at all,' I say with a big grin.

CHAPTER FIFTY-FOUR
Maddie

If I was hoping Mum would stop seeing Nick after what went on that night I am mistaken.

'He didn't mean it,' Mum whines at me when I ask why she is going out with him again.

'How could he have not meant it? Consent is consent.' I really don't want to know the details of what was going on.

'You don't understand how it works Maddie, you're only fifteen.'

'Don't do that Mum.'

'What?'

'Say I'm too young to understand. I know more than you think.' I want to add that I'm much more responsible than she ever will be.

'You haven't lived as long as me. When you have then you can fully understand.'

Someone please shoot me if I fail to understand consent when I get to Mum's age.

No amount of arguing with Mum will stop her going out tonight. She has already forgiven him. I only hope I'm around to bail her out the next time he doesn't behave.

'Don't drink too much.' Mum gives me a sulky look.

'And don't be home too late.'

'Yes Maddie,' she mimics like a child.

I ignore her and leave her to get ready in her room, ignoring her pleas of wanting me to help decide what she wants to wear. I have no time for that today.

While she's out, I've decided I'm going to see James. I feel bad about the way I just dumped him. I should at least explain it to him. He was good to me. I think that was always the problem though. I felt like he was too good for me. I'm not good enough. I wonder if I'll ever feel enough for anyone.

'I probably look terrible as you wouldn't help me.' Mum appears in my room, dressed in the tiniest black dress I've ever seen.

'It's a bit on the short side.'

'So?'

'Never mind. It's great.'

'Really?' She is annoying me now. I want her out of the house.

'Yes, wonderful. Just go.'

She throws me a grin and flounces out of the room.

'See you later darling.'

'Whatever.'

I wait until I hear the door go before making a move downstairs and going to James' house. I could walk, get exercise you know but I can't be bothered. I catch the bus instead. It's full of people dressed up ready for a night out. I stand by the door as there are no free seats.

It's not a long walk from the bus stop to James' house but it feels too long when I just want to get there. Great Aunt Margaret's house is lit up with the lounge light on full. I sneak past. I don't want to see her as well. Too many chances for her to ask questions.

James' house is dark. For a horrible moment, I hope he is in, that I haven't come all this way for nothing. I ring the doorbell and see a light go on, probably in the kitchen. An even worse thought occurs to me. What if only his parents are in and they invite me? Suddenly my hands feel clammy and I can't breathe.

To my relief, or not, who knows, James appears at the door.

'Maddie?'

'Hi.' All words have gone out of my head.

'Didn't expect to see you here.'

'Can I come in?' He glances behind him.

'James, are you coming back?' A girl our age pokes her head round the lounge door. 'Oh hi.'

'This is … er … this is Imogen. This is Maddie.' I

wonder if she knows about me. Has he talked about me at all?

'Hi Maddie, great to meet you.'

'Er … you too.' Her hand runs through her beautifully styled highlighted hair. I don't fail to notice her immaculate Corteiz top. Now I wish I'd made more of an effort. 'I'll come back.' I turn away before either of them can notice my ever-reddening face.

'I'll chat to you another time,' James calls after me. I don't turn round. I keep walking until I hear the front door shut.

Relief floods me as I run home, deciding not to wait for the bus. I should be more upset that James has already shacked up with another girl but instead, I feel free. I can be who I want to without fear of upsetting anyone.

As I reach the high street, I spot Lauren coming out of a fast-food restaurant with some other girls. I stand and stare at her. She sees me, she's coming over. My suddenly clammy hands clutch my bag, my legs frozen to the spot.

'Maddie, what are you doing here?' I can't very well tell her the truth.

'I've just been visiting my aunt.'

'Oh wow how cool.' She makes anything sound cool.

'We're going to Tilly's house if you wanna come?'

'Love to.'

My phone buzzes. It's James.

Sorry about that

I ignore it and follow Lauren to where her friends are grouped, giggling and flicking back their gorgeous hair. In contrast, I am massively under dressed and questioning if I even brushed my hair before I came out.

Lauren seems to notice none of that as she takes my hand and we follow the others down the road. I take a deep breath and wonder if I am in a dream.

'I've been wanting to talk to you,' she whispers when we are lagging behind. 'I really like you, Maddie.' I want to cry. I am so happy.

'I like you too.' She stops walking, turns to me, and pecks me on the cheek.

'I've been wanting to do that for a while as well.' Stunned, I stand there like an idiot, a very happy idiot.

. . .

When I finally get home I fall, exhausted, onto the sofa, smiling to myself, unable to stop the grin. Marvin, having been dropped back earlier, snuggles into me and purrs loudly.

When Mum gets home later it's clear she is beyond drunk.

'Hey baby. You still up?' Thankfully Nick isn't with her. 'Yes,' I mutter at her.

'Fancy some food?' For a second I'm hoping she has bought me some food but she thrusts a half-eaten kebab at me. 'I couldn't finish it.'

Beggars can't be choosers. I'm too hungry to refuse.

'Fun night?' I ask.

'So fun. Nick was…' I switch off at the sound of Nick's name. The last thing I need to hear about is him. She flops down next to me.

'Great. I'm off to bed now.'

'Aw wait.' She reaches for me as I try to get up. 'Don't go yet.'

'I'm tired Mum.'

'You're always tired.' I stop myself from reminding her of what she is like most of the time, especially after a night out. Maybe I should remind her of this tomorrow morning.

I scuttle up the stairs before she can call me back.

I lay my head back and dream of Lauren.

CHAPTER FIFTY-FIVE
Ella

I've put it off for as long as I can but today Dad is taking me to see Mum. He thinks it will help. Help who, I don't know. As far as I'm concerned, I don't ever want to see her again, but Dad thinks otherwise.

To distract me before the visit, I FaceTime Maddie. Her smile is the biggest I've ever seen it.

'You look happy?' She grins sheepishly like a little kid at Christmas.

'Are you going to tell me or what?'

'I've got a girlfriend.'

'A girlfriend? That's amazing. What's her name? Tell me all.'

'Her name is Lauren and she's so pretty.'

'Aw, I'm so happy for you. Are you going to tell your mum now?'

Her face falls. 'I don't know.'

'Why don't you introduce her to Lauren? She might surprise you.'

Maddie raises her eyebrows. 'And miracles might happen but you're right. I'm tired of hiding this.'

Dad forces me to end the call as we have to go. I reluctantly drag myself away, cheered by the fact that Maddie has found her way.

...

Mum is imprisoned in the secure unit of the prison until the trial. Dad says she is finding it hard. I have no sympathy, none at all.

It's a short drive to the prison, which I didn't know existed. It's an old building surrounded by barbed wire and high fences. Not exactly welcoming, but I guess that's the point.

Mum is pale and looks like she hasn't slept for days, when we enter the private room we are meeting in. She looks at me like a frightened puppy. It almost makes me want to hug her, tell her it'll all be okay, but I can't do that because it won't.

'Ella, I'm so sorry.' It is barely a whisper that comes out of her mouth. I stare back at her with unforgiving eyes. 'I needed to see you.'

I don't say anything, I don't trust myself to speak.

'You have no idea how hard this has been.' I clutch hold of my chair and grip it tightly. Someone stop me from killing her. 'It has been destroying me ever since I found out it was you on that road. If I had known it was you and Sam I would have stopped.'

I shake my head slowly at her. 'I have no idea?' I spit out. 'You are the one who has no idea. You have ruined my life. I will never walk again.'

'Ella,' Dad's voice barely enters my consciousness.

'You should have stopped whoever it was,' I continue, ignoring him.

'But I didn't know you were out on a motorbike.'

'It was my fault then?'

'I didn't say that.'

'You ran me over, left me for dead, and now you expect me to forgive you because you can't live with yourself. Well guess what, I don't forgive you and I never want to see you again. This was a mistake. Take me home.' I look up at Dad who for once is speechless. Mum starts crying.

'Ella. Please.'

'Now Dad.'

Dad looks from Mum to me, clearly trying to decide where his loyalties lie. He opens the door and pulls me back.

'Sorry Liz,' he says as he wheels me out to the sound of Mum screaming. It kills me to hear her like that and I have to fight hard not to go back in there but I can't.

'Did you need to be that harsh?' Dad asks when we are halfway back to the main entrance.

'She can't just expect forgiveness.'

'Maybe this was too soon.'

'You don't understand Dad. I will never forgive her. I don't ever want to see her again.'

He doesn't answer. When I am safely strapped in, he regards me sternly.

'You may not want to forgive her now but one day you might change your mind.'

'I doubt it.'

That night I can't get Mum's face out of my head as I lay alone in my bed. The thought of her in that cold, heartless place makes me feel panicky. She may be a murderer but she is my mother, not even my real one but I still love her. Her strange behaviour since my accident finally makes sense. I put it down to the stress of dealing with me but now I know the truth. She was living with this horrible thing that she did. I try to imagine how I would feel if I ran someone over but I can't imagine I would drive away. How did she even manage to hit us? Was she driving too fast?

I've never felt so alone as I do now. I have a twin sister miles away, a real Mum who is barely able to look after anyone, and an adoptive mother who killed my boyfriend. Tears run down my face before I can stop them until I am begging for the relief that sleep brings.

CHAPTER FIFTY-SIX
Maddie

I arrive home from school to Nick sitting on the sofa, acting like he owns the place. I've brought Lauren home with me. I'm not sure why, this could be a big mistake, but what we have feels real and I want to include her in every part of my life. Saying that though, I don't want her to see Nick so I tell her to wait upstairs.

'Where's Mum?' I ask him.

'She's popped to the shop.' I don't like the way he is smiling at me leeringly. 'Want to keep me company?' He pats the seat next to him.

'No. I have homework to do.' I rush past him, intent on going upstairs but he grabs my arm. I stop and stare at him.

'Get off me.'

'Come on, we're all alone. We could have a bit of fun.'

Horrified, I tug at my sleeve. 'I don't want to.'

'It won't take long.' He grabs hold of my blazer collar and pulls me to him. 'Don't be a spoilsport,' he whispers in my face, I can smell his foul garlic breath. I feel like I'm going to throw up. I try to break free but he has a tight grip.

'Get off her.' Lauren's voice startles me. She pushes Nick backwards until he lets go.

'Who are you?'

'A friend.'

Nick looks from Lauren to me with a bemused look on his face.

'A friend?' he says slowly. 'Oh, I get it. You're a lesbian.' A big smile fills his face like it's the biggest joke he's ever heard. 'I can't believe you're a lesbian. No wonder you're so frigid.'

Lauren stands rigid on the spot, her eyes narrowing at Nick, her fists clenched tightly.

'Come on Lauren, let's get out of here.' I drag her away

before she hits him and who knows what happens. I knew bringing her home was a mistake.

'You are a homophobic pig,' she yells as we leave.

'Girls, girls, you can both have me.'

The comment is too much for Lauren who launches herself at him.

'YOU BASTARD.' She thumps him on the head but it seems to have little effect on him as he merely laughs.

'Lauren,' I shout, pulling her off him. 'He's not worth it.'

We run out of the house with Nick's laugh still echoing through the walls and straight into Mum who is getting out of her car.

'Oh, hey Maddie.'

'Mum.'

'What's up? You look like something is on fire.'

'Your boyfriend is a homophobic arsehole,' Lauren states matter of factly, while I stand there wishing the ground would swallow me up.

'Who's this?' Mum asks.

'This is my friend Lauren.'

'Friend?'

'Well, girlfriend.'

Mum looks confused. 'Girlfriend? Wait you're-'

'Yes Mum. I'm gay.' I wait for the onslaught, the anti-gay remarks but instead, she says:

'Cool. I knew that.' Lauren's face goes from thunder to a big smile.

'Lovely to meet you Mrs Philips,' while I stand there unable to believe what has just happened.

'Great to meet you too. And Nick he's what?'

'He tried to come on to your daughter and then made a homophobic comment to us.'

This is Mum's chance to redeem herself big time, to show that she won't stand for all that.

'I'll have a word with him.' Lauren raises an eyebrow at me and I shrug. That could have gone a lot worse.

'That was fun,' Lauren jokes when Mum has gone inside.

'Sorry. I told you my family was screwed up.'

'It's cool. I love you for you not them.'

When Ella texts later, I wonder how I will explain it all.

How did the meeting with Lauren and your mum go?

Not good. Nick tried to come on to me.

Lauren saved me.

Nick realised I'm gay and made lots of homophobic comments. I continue, typing the words furiously.

Ouch.

Totally ouch.

Where was your mum.

She was out but she came home as we were leaving. She met Lauren and is cool with me being gay.

That's awesome.

I guess. I didn't expect her to be.

I know you didn't, but she is; that's great. I hope she told Nick where to go.

She said she'd "talk to him".

Oh right so not then.

Nope don't think so.

I'm sorry that sucks.

Tell me about it.

Hopefully one day he'll just die in a hole.

Let's hope so.

CHAPTER FIFTY-SEVEN
Ella

I don't go to Mum's trial. I can't bear to look at that face again. I might be tempted to forgive her if I did and I can't do that yet.

Dad is dressed in a suit, the smartest I've ever seen him in.

'You sure you don't want to come today?'

'Positive. Besides I've got double English today and I wouldn't want to miss that,' I joke.

I've been trying to avoid thinking about it recently but when it's all over the news and everyone at school is giving me funny looks it's hard to avoid.

This morning I woke up considering how I will feel when Mum is sent to prison which I'm assuming she will. Will she cope there? She acts all tough but she's no match for those rough types you see in those prison dramas. She'll be beaten up for sure. Despite what she's done I don't want that for her. I wish I didn't feel sympathy for her. I want to hate her but I can't, not fully.

Dad keeps saying she made a mistake but she could have put it right any time since, partially at least. She could have admitted to what she had done instead of punishing herself with guilt.

Dad drops me off at school on the way to court. Kaitlyn is waiting outside the gates trying to appear cheerful but I know she's putting it on for me.

'You okay?' She asks lightly.

'Great,' I answer. We both know that isn't true.

'Let me know if... you wanna... you know... talk about it.'

'I will.' It's nice that she is trying but it's not what I need. I need to forget about it, immerse myself in English and chemistry and whatever else I've got today.

Miss Marbeck, my form tutor smiles at me suspiciously. She is never that kind normally. She definitely knows. They all do. I hate the way everyone is tip-toeing around me like I'm some kind of fragile, delicate animal. I want to shout and scream at them all to leave me alone.

More than once during the day I regret not going to the trial, trying to keep my mind off it is harder than I thought it would be.

At break time I check my phone secretly for fear of a teacher taking it away but I suspect they would not be so harsh on me at the moment.

There's a message from Dad.

Ring me if you can.

I don't care what the rules say. I tell Kaitlyn I'm phoning away from prying eyes. Kaitlyn says she'll handle any teachers ready to pounce on me.

'Hey Dad,' I mumble into the phone. 'How's it going?'

'I thought you might want to know what the verdict was.'

I'm tempted to say I don't care but I do want to know.

'Yes, I guess.'

'She was sentenced to five years. It would have been less or even suspended if she'd stopped.'

I let out a breath. For some reason I am relieved. It's horrible but it's over at least.

'Ella, you still there?'

'Yeah, sorry just thinking about it. That sounds fair.'

'I think so too. She can sort herself out there.'

'Definitely.' I don't think about the kind of people she will meet or the danger she could get in.

'You gonna be okay at school or do you want to come home?'

'No, it's fine. I need to keep busy.'

'No problem. I'll be here if you need me.'

'Oh and Dad.'

'Yes?'

'Do you know why she was out driving that night and was she speeding?'

'Apparently, she was upset about something and wasn't

concentrating properly. She went out for a drive to calm down.'

'Did you have an argument?'

'No not that I remember. I'm sure I'd remember if we did. Very strange. I suppose it doesn't matter now.'

But it does to me. I want to know what she was upset about.

Mr. Stour, the PE teacher makes me jump, startling me from behind.

'Ella, you know you're not supposed to have your phone out on school property.'

'Sorry sir, it was my dad. It was important.'

'Anything I can help with.'

'No, it's all sorted now.'

According to the rules he should have taken my phone off me but we all know why he hasn't.

A sense of calmness fills me for the rest of the day. Justice has been served. Mum is locked away in a place where she can get help. Maybe one day I'll go and see her but not yet. I need some time. Hopefully one day she can answer those unanswered questions.

CHAPTER FIFTY-NINE
Maddie

It is not unusual to be alone in the house late at night. Mum is often out and I have to fend for myself but tonight it feels eerily quiet. Something doesn't feel right but I can't work out what. Mum went out with Nick a few hours ago, something they do a lot, then why is my stomach flipping out?

As I can't sleep, I take myself downstairs to make some toast. Marvin, seeing that I am up, jumps up hopefully from his position on the sofa.

'You always want food.' I smile at him. He brushes up against me, nudging the back of my leg. 'I never can say no to you.'

I pop some toast in the toaster and pour out some food for Marvin which he happily chomps away at. Anyone would think he doesn't get fed at all.

I stand in the middle of the kitchen, tired and strangely depressed at my life. Before the toast pops, my phone starts to buzz. An unknown number flashes up on the screen. I consider not answering it, probably some nutter, but for some reason, I think of Mum.

'Hello?'

'Maddie, it's Nick. You need to get down here.' I can barely hear him. He sounds like he is in a train station. He also sounds like he is struggling to hold it together, very unlike him.

'Get down where?'

'Your mum... she's... had an accident.'

'What? What kind of accident?'

'She-'

'Never mind where is she?'

'She's at the hospital. Come quick. It's not looking-'

Before he can say another word, I have cut him off and grabbed my shoes from the back door. As I rush to the front of the house, I hear the toast pop but I'm past caring about that now. I run out of the door but don't have a clue how I'm going to get there. Without thinking I dial Great Aunt Margaret's number. She takes a while to answer, I can picture her fast asleep, having gone to bed hours ago.

Finally, she answers.

'Margaret, please help. Mum's in hospital.'

'I'll be there. Where are you?'

'I've just started walking there but it's a long way and I need to get there now and-' I can't finish as I'm crying too much.

'Don't worry Maddie. I'm on my way.'

'Thank you,' I say quietly but she's probably already hung up.

As much as I hate Mum sometimes and am angry at what she puts me through I don't want to lose her and I'm terrified now. There was so much I wanted to say, so much I still want to ask her but haven't found the right time. I pray to a God I'm not sure I believe in. *Please let her live*, I pray. *I need her.*

Great Aunt Margaret is by my side in record time. She must have sped here at top speed. I've never been so relieved to see her.

'Thank you,' I say, getting in.

'No problem. It's not like I was sleeping or anything,' she chuckles.

A little smile creeps on my face. 'You can blame Mum.' 'As usual, she always has to be centre of attention.' 'Totally,' I laugh.

I try to visualise Mum sitting up in the hospital bed demanding she get better hospital food and it makes me laugh. *Where's the alcohol in this place?*

Great Aunt Margaret drops me at the front of A and E while she finds somewhere to park. I want to tell her not to leave me, that I don't know how to find someone in a busy hospital. I'm only fifteen. I can't do this by myself. I've been looking after myself for years but I can't do this.

The first person I see is Nick slouched on one of the

seats. He jumps up when he sees me.

'Oh Maddie. It was awful.'

'Where's Mum?'

'They won't tell me. I'm not-'

I run to the reception desk. Frustratingly there is a queue of three people in front of me. I want to scream that this is a real emergency. Whatever broken leg or falling off finger they are in for is not as important as this. Finally, I make it to the front.

'My Mum was brought in here half an hour ago. Becky…'

The lady types something up on the screen. 'Yes. Yes. If you take a seat, I'll get someone to come and talk to you.'

'Can't I just see her now?'

'If you take a seat,' she repeats and points to the rows of chairs in front of her.

The last thing I want to do is sit down and wait. I pace the room instead. Nick is by my side like an annoying puppy. 'What happened?' I ask.

'She got really drunk.'

'Tell me something I don't know.'

'Then she stepped out in front of this car.'

'And you didn't think about stopping her?'

'I tried but-'

'But what?' I shout at him.

'I didn't see it.'

'You didn't see it? How could you not see the person next to you stumbling out into the road?'

'I was distracted,' he answers like a pathetic two-year old.

'By what? Another woman?' I know I have hit the nail on the head when he doesn't answer. 'Get away from me,' I scream at him. 'I hate you. If she dies it is all your fault.'

I am getting the attention of the room full of waiting people but I don't care. The security guard to my left looks poised to move forward if needed. Nick backs away. I breathe a sigh of relief. I can't deal with him right now.

It seems like hours but is probably only a matter of minutes when a doctor, dressed in green steps out and says my name.

'Yes,' I shout. He moves towards me.

'Are you Madison Philips?'

'Yes,' I answer frustrated that he has to even ask that.

'I'm afraid your Mum is in a bad way.'

'What happened?'

'Shall we go through into the relative's room?'

I want to demand he tells me here and now but he has already walked off. I follow him, shaking all over. The relative's room is sparsely decorated with only a few medical posters to distract you. The doctor points to the armchair by the window. I shake my head, standing by it instead. He doesn't insist on it.

'I'm Doctor Stevens. Your mother was involved in a car accident. When she was hit by the car, it damaged her liver She is on a life support machine. She is not expected to make it through the night.'

I can feel my legs give way beneath me as I reach out for the handsome doctor's arm for support. He holds onto me to stop me falling and guides me towards a chair.

'Can I see her?'

He nods. I jump up. 'Are you ready?' he asks. I nod, tears springing out of my eyes. I'm not sure I'll ever be ready for this.

I hate the clinical feel to hospitals, white, deathly. I wish I could be anywhere but here. The doctor takes me to a room on its own. Mum's face is as white as a ghost and barely recognisable from the bruises. She has a tube stuffed down her throat and one in her nose. She couldn't speak if she wanted to. A machine continuously beeps next to her. I take the seat besides the bed and hold her hand.

'Can she hear me?' I ask the doctor. He shrugs.

'Possibly.'

'Mum,' I whisper turning back to her. 'You can't die. I

need you.' I squeeze her hand tightly, hoping it will suddenly make her spring back into life.

'Do you have any other family we can call for you?'

'My Great aunt is here. She was just finding somewhere to park.'

'I'll get the nurse to go and find her.'

He leaves me alone in the room with my unconscious, drastically changed mother, wondering if this is it for her. The shock of it all suddenly overtakes me and I lean my head into her arm and sob.

After a short while, I feel a hand on my back. As I sit up, Great Aunt Margaret's sympathetic face stares back at me. 'I'm so sorry love.'

I can't form any words to reply but she seems to understand that. She pulls up a chair next to me and we sit in silence.

Minutes turn to hours and I find keeping my eyes open becomes very difficult.

'Why don't you sleep a bit in that chair? I'll wake you if anything happens?' Great Aunt Margaret says. I shake my head violently. There's no way I'm letting go of this hand.

A nurse pops in a few times. She asks if we need anything. Margaret tells her kindly that we don't. I don't think I could be that kind in my response.

My eyes start to droop. I must stay awake. My head falls to one side. Then before I know I am awake again having been unaware that I was even asleep. This repeats for what could be hours. The gentle snoring of Great Aunt Margaret next to me adds to my need to sleep.

A movement, the hand beneath me wiggles. I sit up bolt upright.

'Mum.'

Mum opens her eyes and stares at me. She seems to smile for a moment. I have a moment where I am filled with hope before she crashes, devastatingly, before my eyes and the machine sounds loudly like all hell has broken loose. Margaret wakes up, jumps up, and presses the emergency button.

A group of nurses and a doctor rush in. We are ushered outside the room. We watch helplessly through the window but even I can see their efforts are not going to make a difference.

They stop, one turns to see us, her face falls in sadness.

'Sorry Madison but your Mum is gone,' the doctor says in a kindly voice when he comes to meet us.

'Make her come back,' I shout.

'I'm sorry,' the kind nurse says but her words are like tinklings in the back of my head. They don't make sense. Surely she can't be dead. I turn to Margaret for support, hoping she will tell me this is all a lie but her expression mirrors that of the nurses.

I run into the room and throw myself on Mum, crying, hugging her tightly but none of it makes any difference. She is gone.

CHAPTER FIFTY-NINE
Ella

Seeing Maddie so upset on FaceTime is enough to send me into a spiral of depressive thoughts. After Mum's verdict, I thought we could all finally move on and be happy but now this. I hate seeing her like this. I also feel guilty for feeling nothing. My real Mum is dead and I don't even care. I don't miss her. I'll be honest I couldn't stand the woman and think Maddie will be better off without her but I know she was close to her.

I should feel sorry for our real mum. She had a hard life, partly due to my adoptive mum stealing her child but it's hard to feel sorry for someone who has actively gone out of her way to try and destroy Maddie's life too. It may not have been intentional, I'm sure she cared about Maddie but her childhood was a mess and now she is left picking up the pieces.

'I can't believe she's dead,' Dad says when I tell him after speaking to Maddie. 'Poor Maddie, she must be distraught.'

'She is.'

'We'll have to go to the funeral of course. If only to support Maddie.'

I hadn't thought about going to the funeral but why wouldn't I? She was my mother, Dad's ex-girlfriend, and my twin sister's mum. I have to be there.

I've never been to a funeral before. I would have gone to Sam's if they'd let me or I was able to. I'm glad I didn't though. It's not an event I feel I have been missing out on.

'Do you think she'll need help with the arrangements?'

'What arrangements?' I ask. What could you possibly need to arrange? You buy a coffin, book a date, that's it surely!

'For the funeral.' I shrug. 'I suppose she has her aunt to help her though.' He seems in a fluster like he doesn't know what to do with himself. 'We'll help her in any way we can of course.'

'Of course,' I repeat. Like we wouldn't.

A tear springs to his eye. I didn't expect him to be upset about this.

'Are you okay Dad?'

He swipes it away and turns away. 'Fine. Fine. Don't worry about me. Such a waste of life that's all.'

I wonder if he's talking about the fact that she's just died or the whole of her adult life. She certainly has wasted it. All those years drinking. Last year I spent my weekends partying and drinking but now, I might never touch a drink, not after real Mum. I wouldn't want to end up like her.

'Maybe I should ring her aunt, and see if there's anything I can do.'

'Good idea.' He picks up his phone leaving me to my thoughts. They wander to the problem of where Maddie will live. With her aunt seems an obvious solution but what if there was another one?

Dad swoops back into the room, talking at top speed.

'They're going to try and arrange the funeral for next week. I'll inquire about a hotel and make plans.'

Those plans will inevitably be more difficult with me in a wheelchair. He'll have to ask hundreds of questions about the hotel and whether it is wheelchair friendly.

The church will have to be accommodating as well. I hate that everything has to be overly planned because of me. I hate that I am a burden and always will be.

Maddie is a mess when I speak to her later. She says she's okay but she has a sad distant look in her eyes like she has something missing from her life which I guess she does now.

'It'll be good to see you again,' I say knowing that it isn't good enough to make it all right again.

She smiles weakly. 'I can't wait to see you. I just wish-'

'I know.'

'She wasn't great. We all know that, but I loved her. I don't think anyone else understands that.' I smile, trying to convey some sense of understanding but I fail at it because it's true. No one understands. Maddie had a special bond with her.

'It doesn't matter what anyone else thinks. You loved her, that's all that matters.'

'Thanks Ella. I'm really glad I found you.'

'Me too. To think I didn't even know I had a twin sister until a few months ago.'

'A lot has happened since then.'

. . .

When I return to the lounge, Dad is on the phone, presumably to a hotel, asking lots of invasive questions. From the tone of his voice, he doesn't seem to be getting the answers he wants. Frustrated he hangs up and slams the phone down on the table. He sighs loudly and then turns and spots me, a guilty expression.

'Ella, sorry I was-'

'I understand.'

'I want to make it perfect for you.'

'It doesn't have to be perfect. As long as I can get in and out it's fine. You worry too much.'

A tear seeps out of his eye. 'I wish I could make it all better for you.'

'None of this is your fault,' I say, gesturing at my wheelchair.

'I feel responsible.'

'There's no point in thinking like that. You really think you could have stopped me?' He laughs and shrugs. 'I was going out whatever you said.'

'I know. I wish-'

'We all wish but it doesn't change anything.' He smiles gently.

CHAPTER SIXTY
Maddie

Why does it always rain at funerals? You're bloody miserable already and to make it ten times worse you get soaking wet. Now I'm miserable, wet and cold.

Luckily Max has a large umbrella to shield us as we congregate outside the church. I don't even know why we're having it at a church anyway. Mum hated churches. It was Great Aunt Margaret's idea to have it here, something about tradition and a family plot. *She'd want to be close to her other sister* she said. I'm not sure she would, but I can't be bothered to argue.

As the vicar stands up to begin, a flash of movement behind me makes me turn around. Nick sneaks in and sits at the back. If there wasn't a church full of packed people and it wasn't Mum's funeral, I would go over there and deck him right now. I settle for a deathly stare instead. He offers me an awkward smile. I turn away, shunning him.

The service reminds me of Aunt Jane's funeral and it feels like déjà vu except Mum is not here complaining about it. I almost chuckle when I think of what she would say right now. Great Aunt Margaret stands up at the front and delivers a speech about how great Mum was. I don't know how she managed to find all that material. I learn a lot about her childhood and it makes me wish I could have chatted to Mum about it. Great Aunt Margaret asked me to do a speech but I couldn't. I don't have words to say that express how I truly feel about Mum. It would sound stupid and anyway I want it to be special between me and Mum. I imagine her in heaven now looking down on me, finally having found peace from her troubled life.

Afterwards, the dark clouds begin to circle the church as we all assemble outside. That was it. The last time I would see Mum's body. Gone forever.

'What am I going to do now?' I wail as the sky rumbles

with thunder.

'What do you mean?' asks Ella, staring at me. I love the way she cares about me now.

'Where will I live?'

Max opens his mouth to reply but is interrupted by Nick, who has appeared next to us.

'Darling you're coming to live with me. You've been like a daughter to me. I don't care if you're gay. I will support you whatever.' I screw up my face, trying desperately not to laugh. As if he thought I would jump at the opportunity to live with him. I've never heard of anything so ridiculous.

But before I can reply, Max jumps in angrily.

'She is certainly not living with you.'

'What's it to you?'

'Maddie is my daughter.' I swear my heart has just doubled at the sound of those beautiful words. 'And I know all about your kind.'

'My kind?' He shouts, outraged that anyone would refer to him as anything less than respectable. 'Don't be stupid. I've been caring for Maddie long before you came along.'

I'm about to point out that he only just appeared on the scene before I met Max, and I wouldn't call it caring for me, when Max pushes him violently. Immediately Nick pushes him back.

'Get away from my daughter.' Ella wheels backwards to avoid the crush.

The first fist hits Nick square on the nose sending him stumbling towards the gravestones.

'Dad,' shouts Ella. But you can practically see the steam rising from Max, there's no stopping him now.

Nick gets himself together and punches him back, lunging his whole body at Max.

'Dad.' Ella's voice is lost in the anger of the situation as the pair move in between the graves.

We watch in horror as they push and shove each other like they were school boys. I should stop them but am too gobsmacked. Finally, Great Aunt Margaret appears like the head teacher.

'What is going on here?' she demands. Ella and I both shrug helplessly. 'Seriously two grown men. What has the world come to.'

She strides off towards them, weaving in and out of the gravestones.

'Stop this at once,' she shouts before she reaches them. They both stop, turning to her guiltily. 'This is a sacred place.'

'You're right Margaret. I'm terribly sorry,' Max says. 'I don't know what came over me.' He steps away from Nick who has blood pouring out of his nose and a bruise already forming on his cheek.

Great Aunt Margaret and Max start to walk back but it is too much for Nick who is not liking being defeated. He throws himself onto Max who is taken by surprise and falls to the ground. I am fearing for Max as Nick starts to lay into him but then a booming voice from behind them stops everyone in their track.

'Nicholas, get off him.' Nick stops, his hand frozen in a punch, a terrified look on his face.

'Dad what are you doing here?'

'Stopping you from making a fool of yourself clearly.'

'I can handle it.'

Nick's Dad yanks hold of him and hoists him up to a standing position. 'We are going son.'

Having got over the shock of it, Ella and I start giggling.

'That told him,' whispers Ella through hysterics. We keep laughing until our sides hurt and tears are running down our faces.

Great Aunt Margaret stares at us disapprovingly.

'You know Mum would have been laughing with us,' I shout. Then I see a small smile on Great Aunt Margaret's face as she nods slowly.

Max, having finally picked himself up, stumbles over to

us. He looks shaken but triumphant.

'You girls okay?'

'We're great Dad but you don't look so good.'

'I'll be fine. Sorry I got a bit carried away back there. That man completely rubbed me up the wrong way.'

'He totally deserved it,' I say.

'So back to what we were saying before.' Ella looks at me excitedly.

'What were we saying?' I ask, more confused than ever. 'About where you were going to live.'

'Oh that. I guess it's Great Aunt Margaret's now.' I say it quietly so that she doesn't hear. I don't want to offend her.

'That's not your only option.'

'What do you mean?'

'Dad and I were talking and he said you could come and live with us.'

Something like a spark of excitement runs through me.

Did I hear what I thought I heard?

'In Broadstairs?'

'Yes!' Ella has the biggest grin I've ever seen on her.

'Really?'

'YES.'

I look to Max who nods enthusiastically. 'But what about Great Aunt Margaret? And Marvin?'

'I already spoke to her and she's fine with it. And of course, you can bring Marvin.'

Suddenly without warning, I start to cry. 'I would love that,' I blub through happy tears.

I never thought I could feel so happy at a funeral. For a moment I feel guilty but I think part of Mum would be happy for me, deadly jealous as well but maybe a tiny bit happy.

Finally, I get to have my happy ever after.

CHAPTER SIXTY-ONE
Six months later...
Ella

The day I have been dreading; the visit I would put off forever, if I could, but I want answers, and maybe, I want to forgive.

It's true what they say, that time heals. My heart has been softening over the past few months especially with Maddie having moved in. To begin with, she wanted to sleep in the same room as me but Dad said we needed our own space and he was right. I love spending time with her but I need my time too. Time to think and process everything. Maddie now has my room upstairs. I can't say I'm not a little bit jealous when I see her climb those stairs to my old room. If only I could walk up there again, escape life. Despite that though Maddie is kind and thoughtful, always thinking of me yet joking with me too.

We turned sixteen a few months ago and left school with some exams. Neither of us did very well due to the disruption. We are now at the same college. I'm studying Art. I've found it's hugely therapeutic. Maddie is studying Performing Arts. Apparently, she has a talent for being dramatic. I wonder where she gets that from?

'Ella are you ready to go?' Dad opens my bedroom door as I put the hairbrush through my hair one last time.

'Yep. Ready as I'll ever be.'

Maddie is at the bottom of the stairs, still in her pyjamas, to wave me off. This is something I have to do alone.

'You'll be okay?' she asks.

I nod. 'Don't worry about me.'

The drive to the prison is too long even though it isn't. I just want to be there, to get this over and done with.

It is almost seven months since I saw Mum and the difference in her is striking. She has lost weight and the skin hangs on her face like it doesn't belong there. Her sad eyes make her look like she is a lot older than she is.

'I'm glad you came,' she says taking my hand in hers. This time I let her. I allow myself a little smile, the first step towards acceptance. On the brink of tears, she clutches me tightly.

'It's okay Mum. I'm here to forgive you.'

Any control she had is lost as she breaks down and sobs uncontrollably.

'But I want some answers.'

'Anything,' she whimpers.

'That night you said you went to the shop but you didn't, did you? Why were you out? What were you doing?'

She breathes in deeply to regain her composure. 'A few weeks before that night I received a message from your real Mum. She was angry and demanded to have her child back. I was terrified you would all find out what I had done. I arranged to meet her that night. I sneaked out and drove to our rendezvous point but I was distracted, I wasn't concentrating.'

'You weren't looking where you were going?'

She shakes her head. 'The bike suddenly appeared from nowhere round the corner. I had been in a dreamlike state. I can't remember exactly what happened but the next thing I knew was the car had ploughed into a bush and I could see two bodies on the road. I panicked. I should have stopped. Then when I heard it was you, I was distraught. I should have told you but I couldn't. I'm a terrible person.'

'You've made some terrible mistakes.'

'I will always have to live with the fact that I put you in a wheelchair.'

'I won't condone what you did but I want to move forward.'

'Ella, you have no idea what this means to me.' She looks as though a weight has been lifted off her. 'Thank you.'

As I leave it is not only her heart that is lighter but

mine too. Despite what she has done she is my mother. Maybe I'm more like Maddie than I think.

Maddie

Marvin loves his new home. His first day was spent running from room to room and tormenting Blueberry by sitting opposite his cage and staring at him. I felt the same. I could have happily bounded through all the rooms. I have never lived in such a big house.

Lauren was upset when I said I was moving away. We said we would keep in contact which we did but the texts have got fewer and fewer. I will never forget her, my first love.

Tonight, Dad and Ella are coming to watch my first performance at college. I am so nervous but I finally feel as though I have found something I am good at and that I can be myself in. Dad is the best. You see I call him Dad now. I can't remember when that started but it suddenly felt natural. Not just Max anymore, but Dad. Yeah, he had an affair all those years ago but when you look at Ella's Mum you can understand why. Sorry, I shouldn't say that. Ella is visiting her regularly now and is building a relationship again. I need to support that. I've yet to go and visit. I feel it would be weird, me being there as well. She's nothing to do with me, just my twin sister's Mum.

When anyone at college asks about my family, I don't have the effort to explain it. It's way too complicated for anyone to understand. All that matters is that my twin sister and I are back together.

'Maddie, we're going to be late.' Dad stands in the doorway of Ella's old room. Does he still picture his other daughter in here?

'I'm coming. I have to look perfect.'

He grins. 'You will always look perfect to me.' I make the gagging sound and laugh.

Five minutes later I am downstairs and Ella is excitedly

chattering away about the play.

'I can't wait to see it.'

'I'm so scared. What if I fall over? What if I forget my lines? What if I see the most beautiful girl in the audience and fall in love instantly?' She giggles.

'You'll be wonderful and if you see that girl tell her to wait until afterwards.'

'Okay.'

I hold Ella's hand in the car as I always do now and think of the special bond we have developed. It wasn't instant but now we have the connection. The twin I have been looking for all my life.

The End.

ABOUT THE AUTHOR

After teaching for sixteen years, VICKY decided she needed a new challenge. She now works as a student administrator for the doctorate in clinical psychology course at her local university. She has always loved writing and has been doing it for many years. She has been on numerous writing courses which have allowed her to share her love of writing with others. After the success of her first book, Powerless, she has continued in the genre of thriller and is excited to release her second novel Abandoned. She is also a passionate reader, enjoying a variety of genres, especially thrillers. She lives in North Essex with her husband, two teenage daughters, two cats and two rabbits.

Other Books by Vicky Ball

"A wonderful debut novel, Powerless grabbed me from the first chapter and took me on a journey filled with intrigue and danger."

"Powerless is a thrilling and twisting tale that will take readers on a dramatic and sometimes unexpected ride."

"Dark, raw, gritty and enthralling. The twists and turns mixed in with the intrigue of deceit and danger, pulls you in, to take you on a mysterious journey."

"What a terrifying thriller of exploitation and deceit. Vicky Ball knocked it out the park with her debut novel, Powerless—a dark glimpse into a world that some may want to pretend doesn't exist."

"Contrary to the title, this book is POWERFUL! It is hard-hitting & heart-breaking, but through it all, there is so much love, strength, and a fierce fight to survive."

"Vicky Ball pulls you in and just when you think you've figured it out You Are Wrong! Loved this book."

"Powerless is written in a way that is emotionally sensitive yet real, that raising awareness and empathy. With likeable characters, emotional impact and a clever twist, it's a highly recommended book for young people as well as adults."

"Twists and turns and a fabulous read. I look forward to reading more of Vicky's books."

Milton Keynes UK
Ingram Content Group UK Ltd.
UKHW010627080923
428287UK00005B/121

9 781739 367510